Unmasking the Hero

Pleasure Garden, Book 1

Mary Lancaster

Dragonblade Publishing, Inc. is an imprint of Kathryn Le Veque Novels, Inc.
P.O. Box 7968
La Verne CA 91750
ceo@dragonbladepublishing.com

Produced in the United States of America

First Edition August 2021
Print Edition

ARE YOU SIGNED UP FOR DRAGONBLADE'S BLOG?

You'll get the latest news and information on exclusive giveaways, exclusive excerpts, coming releases, sales, free books, cover reveals and more.

Check out our complete list of authors, too!

No spam, no junk. That's a promise!

Sign Up Here

www.dragonbladepublishing.com

Dearest Reader;

Thank you for your support of a small press. At Dragonblade Publishing, we strive to bring you the highest quality Historical Romance from some of the best authors in the business. Without your support, there is no 'us', so we sincerely hope you adore these stories and find some new favorite authors along the way.

Happy Reading!

CEO, Dragonblade Publishing

The Wicked Husband
The Wicked Marquis
The Wicked Governess
The Wicked Spy
The Wicked Gypsy
The Wicked Wife
Wicked Christmas (A Novella)
The Wicked Waif
The Wicked Heir
The Wicked Captain
The Wicked Sister

Unmarriageable Series
The Deserted Heart
The Sinister Heart
The Vulgar Heart
The Broken Heart
The Weary Heart
The Secret Heart
Christmas Heart

The Lyon's Den Connected World
Fed to the Lyon

Also from Mary Lancaster
Madeleine

PROLOGUE

June 1815

O N HIS WEDDING night, Oliver Harlaw, Earl of Wenning, fought his body's instinct to slumber, just so that he could watch his bride fall asleep in his arms.

Grace. His wife, his countess.

He hadn't expected to give or receive quite so much physical joy on their first night together, but her passion had delighted him. Her every pleasure in his caresses had doubled his own. His whole body sang, his whole being was lost in wonder.

What had he done to deserve this happiness? He had been so right to put this marriage ahead of his career. Offered the chance to be part of a special British embassy to China—a great honor when he was so young—he had reluctantly turned it down because the decreed day of departure was the day after his wedding. Well, he had his reward in his wonderful bride.

She was sound asleep now, her arm around his neck touchingly floppy. Her beauty, her trust, hurt his heart and made him smile.

But having got beyond the first urge to sleep, he could not now be still. He slipped free of her embrace and rose from the bed. He was still smiling as he walked naked across the clothes-strewn floor and into the outer room, where he almost tripped over the baggage before lighting the candles.

Tomorrow, the bags would be stowed on board the yacht that would take them to France to begin their wedding journey. Perhaps, with Napoleon just defeated—again—France might not be at its best, but it was a place to begin their exploration of Europe and each other. Two months alone with Grace, to go wherever they wished, do whatever they wished...

Stumbling into the luggage had knocked one of Grace's personal bags off the trunk beneath. He picked it up to place it more safely, and saw that it was open. A hairbrush and a piece of paper had fallen out of it. He crammed the items into the bag, but the paper was not folded, and words written on it in her hand jumped out at him.

My darling Anthony...

Wenning didn't care for the mode of address, whoever Anthony was, but he had no intention of reading her correspondence. And he wouldn't have, if the phrase *this dreadful marriage* hadn't hit him like a punch in the solar plexus.

He dropped the bag on the floor once more, sat on the trunk, and read the letter from beginning to end.

His world crumbled.

Stunned, paralyzed, for once in his life he did not know what to do.

And then, like a blessed relief, saving him, the anger came.

As though he was someone else entirely, he crumpled the letter between his fingers and threw it in the corner. Then he stood, opened the trunk beneath, and dressed.

He sat down at the desk provided and wrote a short note of his own, to his wife. Then he roused his valet and the stable staff, issuing fresh instructions. And within half an hour, he was riding for Southampton and the ship bound for China with His Majesty's special embassy.

CHAPTER ONE

June 1817

AS USUAL, GRACE, the Countess of Wenning, returned home from the Pantheon Bazaar with a fine haul of treasure. Her footman could barely see above the parcels containing lengths of cloth, pretty ribbons, yards of lace, slippers, stockings, buttons, silk thread, and assorted gifts.

"Have them taken up to my rooms, if you please," she instructed him. "And Lady Arpington and I will take tea in the library."

As she passed, she swiped a pile of letters off the silver tray in the hall. Beside it lay several bouquets, so she took the cards from them, too, before she led her friend upstairs to the library.

Bridget was one of the few people she entertained in the Wenning House library. Oddly, it was where she felt at once most comfortable and most jealous of her solitude. But she was willing to share it with Bridget, who had been her friend since childhood.

As they sat companionably, Bridget picked up *The Morning Post* to allow Grace time to read her correspondence—most of which was invitations. She cast those aside for later, along with a short epistle from her sister-in-law, which left only the cards that had come with the flowers.

"You are not short of admirers for a married lady," Bridget observed.

Grace grimaced. "They circle like amiable and occasionally amusing vultures. They have not yet noticed that they protect me from each other."

"Except Boothe," Bridget observed. "I hear they are taking bets in all the clubs that Sir Nash Boothe will win you by the end of the month."

Grace cast her a crooked smile. "Yes, but the same gossip has linked me to at least five gentlemen in the last year. Equally false. But you are right about Sir Nash. I shall have to find an excuse to cut him before he grows too troublesome. Perhaps I should pay more attention to Sir Ernest for a... Drat it all, one of those bouquets was from Boothe!"

"Definitely time to pay more attention to Sir Ernest," Bridget said, amused, while Grace read the card. "At least you can be safe with him. Seriously, Grace, it is a dangerous game you play and far too easy to lose."

"I know, but what else is there to keep boredom at...? Oh, the *devil!*"

Bridget sighed. "What now?"

"Boothe. He reminds me about attending the masked ball at Maida Gardens tonight."

Bridget stared, but since the tea tray was brought in just then, she waited until the servants departed before hissing, "Seriously, Grace? You made an *assignation* with him? At Maida Pleasure Gardens of all places?"

Grace rubbed her forehead unhappily. "I had forgotten. It was a challenge, which, of course, I accepted. I must have drunk too much champagne. I suppose I had better write at once and plead some previous engagement." She reached for the teapot, then dropped her hand once more. "Oh no."

"What now?"

"I can't cry off. It was a wager. We each chose the other's stake. I chose his sapphire cravat pin. He chose my ruby bracelet. If I don't go, he wins, and I lose the bracelet."

"It's only a bracelet."

"No, it isn't," she said unsteadily. "It was Oliver's wedding gift to me."

"Ah. I see your problem."

Distractedly, Grace poured out the tea and passed one cup to Bridget.

"Well," Bridget murmured. "Sir Nash isn't a monster. Explain and give him some other token instead."

"I can't," Grace said flatly. "I would have to explain, and I won't."

"Then lose it. I'm sure Wenning would rather you lost the bracelet than your reputation."

"I would lose both," Grace pointed out. "If I give him the bracelet or anything else of mine beyond the value of a flower or a handkerchief, that is evidence of intimacy. I would be surprised if that didn't make the rounds of the clubs, too."

Bridget stared. "Why would you have anything to do with a man you believe to be so dishonorable?"

Grace shrugged. "He amuses me. And dash it, Biddy, I am so confoundedly bored! No, I have to go to Maida in order to keep the bracelet." She glanced up decisively. "*You* must come with me, and we will stick to each other like limpets to a rock."

"I can't tonight, Grace," Bridget reminded her. "It's my mother-in-law's birthday dinner party. I couldn't *not* be there."

"No," Grace agreed, deflated. "Of course, you must go. I wonder who else I could trust... Rollo! Of course!"

"Rollo? Trust? Isn't that a little optimistic?"

"Well, of course, he's a terrible loose screw," said Rollo's fond sister, "but I know he often goes to the masquerades at Maida Gardens—well, he would, wouldn't he?—and he wouldn't like me to be in trouble."

"But would he exert himself to prevent it?" Bridget inquired.

"Of course he would," Grace said indignantly. "He isn't really as bad as people believe him to be. But think about it, Biddy, my brother is the perfect chaperone, and he isn't above dueling to sort out his quarrels, so that will be an extra deterrent to Boothe."

"Well, that is true. And he was always a good-natured boy. Perhaps you are right. You'd better send for him now and make sure he is here to escort you on time."

⤜⤜⤜◆⤛⤛⤛

PUNCTUALITY, HOWEVER, PLAYED little part in the Honorable Rollo Darblay's life. He had not answered Grace's summons by half-past eight, and her wager was to meet Sir Nash Boothe at the Gardens before ten. In fact, she finally realized she would have to go to Rollo's rooms in St. James and fetch him. If he wasn't there, presumably his valet at least would know where he was.

And then a knock sounded on the dressing room door. Henley, her maid, opened it and sniffed.

"Yes, it's me," came Rollo's voice, half-amused, half-impatient. "I know she's in there, so you might as well let me in."

"Rollo, thank God!" Grace jumped to her feet and went to him with an enthusiasm that clearly took him by surprise.

He allowed the embrace, even patted her on the shoulder, but extricated himself quickly to scowl down at her. "What have you done now?"

"Henley, leave me for five minutes," Grace instructed, and as soon as the maid had shut herself into the bedchamber beyond, she swung back to her brother. "I've done nothing, except make an extremely stupid wager, which you have to help me win."

"And how do I do that?" Rollo asked amiably enough.

6

He was a tall, very handsome young man with dramatic black eyebrows and glittering eyes. Women seemed to find him irresistible, though Grace thought he should drink less and sleep more. Dissipation was beginning to show around his eyes.

Still, who was she to criticize another's lifestyle?

"You escort me to Maida Gardens for the masquerade ball tonight."

"Can't," Rollo said with a hint of regret. "Not saying it wouldn't be fun, but promised to a party in Cribb's Parlor. Fellows are waiting for me downstairs."

"Bring them, too," Grace said recklessly. "The more, the merrier. And the safer. I need to go to win a wager with Sir Nash Boothe. And I need you with me to remain respectable."

"At Maida Gardens? Don't be daft, Gracie. And I've never done anyone's respectability any good. Take my advice, and don't go."

"I have to, or I'll lose my bracelet to Boothe. *This* bracelet." She snatched it off the dressing table and waved it in front of him.

He glanced at her with a hint of impatience. "What did you wager that for?"

"I didn't. We chose each other's stake."

"Does he know what it is?"

"I don't know. I didn't tell him. But I couldn't refuse it without explaining why, and I can't do that."

His lip curled. "Can't admit you still carry a torch for your own husband? Even after he left you at the altar."

"He did not leave me at the altar," Grace said firmly.

"As good as. If you ask me, a fellow who leaves his wife before the wedding trip to go alone to the other side of the world for two years deserves all he gets. If you like Boothe, have at him. Serve Wenning right."

"*Have at him?*" Grace repeated indignantly.

Rollo grinned. "Don't be mealy-mouthed. Doesn't suit anyone

from our family."

"I don't want, Boothe. I don't want anyone. In fact, I'm going to the country next week to stop all the talk, and there I shall wait for my husband's return."

"You'll only get into more scrapes," Rollo prophesied. He threw himself into the wing chair by the window and drummed his fingers on the arm, a frown tugging his brow as he gazed at her. "Are you saying you need me there to be sure Boothe toes the line?"

"Yes," she said with relief. It was only part of the truth, but she knew it would reach Rollo as losing the bracelet would not.

"Dash it all, I'll come then, but I'll have to bring the others, too. Can we all fit in your carriage?"

"How many of them are there?"

"Just Meade and Montague, but if it makes it too crowded for you, Montague can go up beside the coachman. He likes a turn of driving."

Grace, who had no wish to start the evening by being tipped into a ditch, said hastily that there was plenty of room in the carriage, and Rollo got up and sauntered off downstairs to break the news to his friends.

Grace took one last glance at herself in the glass. She had a little color in her cheeks now that she had recruited Rollo to her cause, which was good. She really didn't want to appear at the ball looking pale and anxious behind her mask. For the rest, her dark hair was elegant but simply styled so as not to draw attention to herself, her jewelry minimal for the same reason. Well, that and she didn't want it stolen by the thieves rumored to haunt the shadows of Maida Gardens.

Her gaze fell to the ruby bracelet, which Oliver had clasped to her wrist in the carriage as they hurtled south after the wedding breakfast. He had given it with a kiss that had turned sweetly sensual.

Before the most wonderful night of her life.

And the worst morning after, when she had wakened to a curt note and the news that he had gone to China after all, and she should journey on alone if she wished, or suit herself as to which of his houses she stayed in.

Everyone had known, of course. She couldn't bring herself to seek refuge at her husband's country seat in Sussex just yet, and so she had bolted to her parents' home in Hertfordshire for two weeks of bewildered tears and utter rage. And then she had gone to London to embrace the notorious reputation she had been left with by her husband's sudden abandonment, and to prove she didn't care.

She was still proving it to everyone but Bridget and, possibly, Rollo.

"Damn you," she whispered to her absent husband. And recklessly clasped his gift to her wrist once more. Perhaps, this time, it would bring her luck.

But mostly, it felt like protection.

MAIDA GARDENS WERE located some distance north of fashionable London, almost in the country beyond the new Regent's Canal, which added a picturesque approach. Like its more famous sisters at Vauxhall and Raneleigh, Maida's heyday had passed, although its location—in the middle of nowhere as Rollo pointed out—had ensured it had never enjoyed quite the same popularity. In the previous century, the park had been called by other names after the people who had owned it. But it had been Maida Gardens for about ten years now.

Squashed into the carriage with Rollo and his friends, bowling north along the Edgeware Road, Grace suddenly remembered going there before, though in broad daylight on a warm, spring day.

"Fennie took us to the reopening," she said. "When it became Maida Gardens. I must have been ten or eleven, for Hope was only little. It was a sunny day, and the gardens seemed like a fairytale place to me…"

"Why Maida?" the ever-curious Grace had inquired of her governess, Miss Fenchurch. "It seems a very odd name to me."

"I suppose because it is a pretty name," Miss Fenchurch had replied, "and also honors the Hero of Maida, Sir John Stuart, who has won a great battle and was made the Count of Maida by our grateful ally, the King of Naples."

Now Rollo let out a snort of derisive laughter. "There's not much of the fairytale about it now!"

"Different during the day, Rolls," Mr. Meade reminded him.

"Never been in daylight," Rollo said without a great deal of interest.

At first glance, the gardens still looked lush and cared for, but even from a distance, the scattering of buildings and follies gave off an air of decidedly faded splendor.

Neither was the clientele drawn any longer from the wealthy aristocracy. The ton was not seen here—at least not beyond a few rakish young bucks on a spree—and to Grace, as soon as she walked through the gates, the place shrieked of vulgarity.

This impression may have been due to the familiar way the girl who sold Rollo the tickets flirted with him at the same time. Or to the distant, somewhat salacious giggles emanating from the undergrowth to her left. Or even to the fact that Sir Nash Boothe, lounging beneath a lantern only yards from the gate, appeared to be besieged by young women in scandalously dampened gowns.

Not that Grace had always been entirely innocent of this trick to make her gown cling alluringly to her figure. But at least she had actually *worn* the gowns in question. These ladies seemed to be half-undressed.

Sir Nash was a handsome, elegant man with cropped fair hair and roguish blue eyes, his good looks marred only by his awareness of them. Grace, walking slightly ahead of the others, rather enjoyed his astonished expression when he caught sight of her.

He sprang up from the bench, shedding the diaphanous maidens like a cloak that was suddenly too warm.

"My lady!" he exclaimed. "I had almost given you up."

"So I see," she drawled, not allowing her gaze to stray anywhere near his disappointed nymphs. "And yet I believe it is not yet ten o'clock."

He took her hand a little too familiarly, although at least he did not try to kiss it. "I misjudged your courage, clearly, in the cold, sober light of day."

"But not my good sense," she said brightly. "Do you know my brother, Mr. Darblay? Also, Mr. Meade and Mr. Montague. Gentlemen, Sir Nash Boothe."

To make her point, she took Rollo's arm. Her brother scowled by way of greeting Sir Nash and strode off up one of the lantern-lit paths with Grace all but trotting beside him. She would have objected to the speed, except she rather liked the idea of Sir Nash relegated to the company of Rollo's youthful and inarticulate friends.

"You shouldn't be here," Rollo said austerely. "Not suitable at all,"

"But it is for you?" she asked wryly.

"Nobody cares what I do. *You* can't hang around a place like this with that man and his floozies."

"To be fair, I doubt he ever meant them to join us."

"No, he didn't think you would turn up at all. Which you shouldn't have. How long do you have to stay to win the dashed wager?"

"Until midnight, I think. Just before the ritual unmasking."

"Oh well, that's not so bad. We'll all stand up with you, bite of supper, and then off. We should brush through—so long as you don't dance with strangers and we don't meet anyone else you know."

By now, they were approaching a pavilion which was, apparently, where the twice-weekly balls took place. The sight of several masked people spilling out of the door reminded Grace to don her mask.

Rollo regarded her critically, adjusted it, and made to go inside.

"Mask, old fellow," Sir Nash reminded him with some amusement.

He was already masked but very clearly himself.

"Never brought one," Rollo said, heedlessly giving away the fact that he had been dragooned into escort duty at the last minute.

"Sell you a mask here, sir," offered a young girl, also masked, standing with a basket to one side of the door. "Only two shillings each."

"Better give me three," Rollo fumed, no doubt seeing his drinking money being frittered away.

While Rollo bought and distributed the masks to his friends, Boothe moved smoothly to Grace's side, offering his arm. She took it but dug in her heels to wait for the others. He seemed both amused and irritated by this, but she pretended not to notice and walked blithely inside with the crowd.

CHAPTER TWO

G RACE WAS USED to attention whenever she entered a ballroom. Ladies looked to her for sartorial hints, and she always had a string of gentlemen admirers, which kept her both safe and fashionable.

At the Maida ballroom, however, attention was much more blatant and much more intense. More than her mask, clearly, made her a stranger here, and therefore all the more interesting.

Sir Nash acted as their host, graciously including Rollo and his friends for whom he ordered wine and brandy. While he was engaged with this process, Grace turned to her brother with another anxiety.

"You are known here. What if people recognize me because I am with you?"

"They won't. Wouldn't bring my sister here."

She laughed and resolved to enjoy her novel masquerade. All the dances appeared to be waltzes, which the orchestra played with considerable verve. Mr. Meade got in his invitation to dance first, which seemed to amuse Boothe, though when Montague stood to ask her as soon as she returned, Sir Nash's amusement clearly turned to irritation.

Rollo smiled at him amiably.

"Your turn next, is it?" Boothe asked with a curl of his lip. "Unless you find it too unfashionable to dance with your own sister."

"Not a fashionable man," Rollo retorted, sitting back and smiling at a girl at the next table.

Beyond that table, Grace noticed a tall man lounging against a pillar. He wore a black and silver-grey mask with a matching domino cloak. And she rather thought he was watching her.

The fact did not trouble her. She had grown used to the stares and the fact that whenever a stranger approached the table, they retreated when Rollo glared at them.

"I'm sorry for spoiling your evening," she told Mr. Montague as she had already told Mr. Meade. "I know you had other plans."

"Not spoiled in the slightest," Mr. Montague assured her. "Very pleasant evening! Always happy to help Rolls's sister."

"You're very kind," Grace assured him with genuine gratitude. "Tell me, sir—I can see this place is perhaps not quite the thing, but what gives it such a *bad* reputation?"

"It's usually not that bad. Though you have to watch out for cut-purses and pickpockets. Most people are just out to enjoy themselves."

"Which isn't so different from more fashionable ballrooms," Grace agreed.

A couple swished past them, and she glanced idly in their direction. Jolted, she blurted, "Oh no! Is that not Sir Ernest Leyton?"

"Shouldn't think so," Mr. Montague said at once.

"You didn't even look," Grace accused.

"Best not to," he said apologetically.

Which intrigued Grace immeasurably. Sir Ernest Leyton was one of her husband's oldest friends, a pillar of propriety who occasionally escorted her to parties, probably keeping an eye on her for Wenning's sake. Did even he have a secret life, a secret mistress whom he met here, far from the unforgiving eyes of the ton?

Or… Her stomach lurched. Had he somehow found out about her wager with Sir Nash? Was he here to watch her? Look after her? Or simply report her transgressions to Wenning? Who would, presumably, seek to divorce her or, more likely, find a reason for separation whenever he came home. Well, they had been separated for two years. His eventual homecoming from China could make no real difference to her life.

In desperation, she thrust the thoughts away, smiled dazzlingly at Mr. Montague, and cast occasional surreptitious glances in Sir Ernest's direction to be sure he was not observing her. She never caught him looking. The lady he danced with was pretty and elegant and smiled up into his eyes. No stranger, she was sure. Sir Ernest had an intrigue, and he was not remotely interested in Grace's presence.

When the dance ended, Mr. Montague conducted her solicitously back to the table, where Sir Nash and Rollo seemed to be playing some kind of drinking game. If it was Boothe's intention to drink her brother under the table, he would have a hard night of it. But perhaps they had simply reached an understanding, for while Grace took her seat once more and sipped some cooling lemonade, Sir Nash asked her to dance. And Rollo made no objection.

Not that she would have listened to him if he had, for she had already decided she would dance with Boothe. Whatever his ultimate intentions, he could hardly carry them out on the dance floor.

The ornate wall clock told her it was nearly eleven o'clock. One hour until they would have to leave, before the unmasking at midnight. It was nearly over. And then she could go to the country and find something else to interest her, something that did not involve juggling entitled and lecherous men for the incomprehensible sake of fashion.

"I have to concede victory," Sir Nash said as he took her in his arms for the dance. "I am outplayed, and my sapphire pin is yours."

She nodded gracefully. "Thank you."

"I confess I thought I would win whatever happened. Either you would not come, and I would win your bracelet as a token. Or you *would* come, and I would win *you*. I never thought of you bringing your rakehell brother and his amusing friends as chaperones."

"I aim to surprise and astonish," she said flippantly.

"And having achieved that, and even put me in my place..." He lowered his voice. "How long do you mean to keep me at arm's length?"

She raised her eyebrows. "Forever."

He blinked, then laughed. "Overambitious, my dear."

"Not in the slightest."

A frown flickered and smoothed again on his brow. "But you would surely be a *little* hurt if I turned instead to another lady?"

"I suspect you already have."

Understanding dawned in his eyes. "Then that is why you play me this trick? Because you imagine I look at Mrs. Fitzwalter?"

"You have a very odd idea of my imagination." She allowed genuine boredom to creep into her voice, and something very like anxiety flickered across his face.

"Grace, you must know I adore you. Only you. No more tricks, now. Come, walk with me in the gardens, away from prying eyes."

She stared at him. "No."

"Why not?" he urged.

"Because at this moment, it is tedious even to be dancing with you."

His eyelids dropped down, veiling his eyes, which she guessed would show mostly anger. She felt it in the rigidity of his arms. And then, as though forcing himself, he relaxed. "You are cruel. But since you insist, I will make small talk instead. Do you go to Lady Trewthorpe's soiree on Friday?"

Grace almost shuddered. Since she was Lady Trewthorpe's sister-in-law, she was always invited and needed a good excuse not to attend. "Probably," she said, and for the rest of the dance made slightly strained small talk, which neither of them pretended to enjoy.

However, if she hoped she had thus lost an admirer, she was

doomed to disappointment, for as the dance ended, he said urgently, "Please, Grace, let's talk. Just five minutes where we cannot be overheard or interrupted by your dratted brother."

"But then I would miss the start of the next dance." Suddenly, she just wanted to be away from him and all his ilk, from herself even, or at least what she had made herself into. And the nearby passage to the ladies' cloakroom provided a brief respite. But before she could take even a step toward it, a man paused just in front of it, scanning the floor as if he had lost someone.

Sir Ernest Leyton. Was he looking for *her*? If she walked right past him to the cloakroom, he would surely see and recognize her as easily as she had seen through his mask.

"Lesser of two evils, Grace?" Sir Nash drawled. "Or is it least of three? Bring yourself to Leyton's attention? Dance with your own brother? No, on the whole, I think you know you had better come with me."

He was smiling, and there was certainly a hint of lechery in his eyes that she did not like. But it was the gleam of triumph that compelled her to act. If he thought she could be intimidated into leaving this room just to be mauled behind a tree, he could think again.

There were any number of men standing and milling about, searching out their next dance partner. Many of them were eagerly watching her, as though waiting only for her to separate from her current partner. She could take her pick.

But because she had noticed him already—and he was again observing her from a different pillar this time—she chose the lounging stranger in the black and silver domino. Spinning away from Boothe, she took one step toward him and smiled her most dazzling smile.

"There you are. This is our dance, is it not?"

The stranger straightened, and, too late, she saw that his eyes were hard as agates and that he was, probably, the one man in the ballroom she could not manipulate or bend to her will. Those eyes bored into hers, then shifted, briefly, to Sir Nash.

His lips curved below the line of the mask, though the smile did not reach his eyes. "Far be it from me to argue with a lady." His voice was low, a little husky, his accent very subtly foreign. He bowed and offered his arm. "It will be my pleasure."

"Your brother won't like it," Sir Nash warned, clearly chagrined that she had chosen a stranger over him.

Grace only laughed and walked away on the stranger's arm. The orchestra began the introduction to yet another waltz, and the stranger took her hand, placing his other at her back. Although he was tall and indefinably imposing, his hold was light, and, to her relief, his gaze did not *ogle*, merely regarded her with impersonal curiosity.

Perhaps she had chosen well after all.

"Lovers' tiff?" the stranger asked sardonically.

"Lord, no. Merely an exchange of views."

"Won't he take his congé like a gentleman?"

"There is no congé, merely a lost wager. But I thank you for your... I shan't call it protection...for your *shade*."

A glimmer of amusement might have broken through the hard eyes. "Am I shading you from ruin?"

"Hardly. Merely recognition. One should never make wagers after three glasses of champagne."

"A universal truth to be taught to all one's children."

She laughed. "Well, there are worse things one could teach them. Do you have children, sir?"

"Mercifully not."

"Why mercifully?"

"I don't believe I care to answer on such short acquaintance."

"It is certainly none of my business," she agreed. "Then allow me to ask a less personal question. What goes on in the gardens outside the ballroom?"

Although she couldn't read his expression, she was sure she had surprised him. Certainly, he took a moment to answer. "You wish to know what fate you escaped by dancing with me rather than walking with him?"

"Exactly," she replied.

"Not knowing the gentleman in question, I could not say." His glance flickered to the bracelet which graced her forearm. "But I suppose you could have had your jewelry stolen or your person ravished. Or both."

She sighed. "Decidedly no more wagers. Sir, I thank you again for your shade, but if we could just dance a few feet toward the left, I shall impose upon you no further."

"You will not stay until the end of the dance and the unmasking?"

"No, alas, I must leave before midnight."

"Why? Is there some enchantment upon you?"

"More like a curse," she said ruefully. "My own nature."

"Alternately bold and fearful?"

"Not fearful," she said at once, although she *had* been fearful of being recognized by Sir Ernest, and it would have been madness to go anywhere alone with Nash Boothe. "Let us say *sensible*, as a sop to my pride, if nothing else."

"By all means," he agreed. She appeared to have amused him. "So boldness propelled you here—"

"And champagne," she pointed out.

"Boldness, champagne, and an unspecified wager propelled you here. And sense will propel you home before the unmasking. Was it worth the trouble?"

"I doubt I will come back, if that is what you mean."

"That is a pity. *I* would ask *you* to dance the next time. On Saturday, for example."

"Sadly, I have a quite different engagement on Saturday." And before then, Lady Trewthorpe's soiree to get through on Friday, God help her.

"My pride clings to the *sadly*. I hope it will be an entertaining evening."

"Not a chance."

"Then Maida is an attractive alternative, surely? I'll throw in a wager. And three glasses of champagne."

She laughed. "I would be offended, except you don't mean a word of it."

Behind the mask, he blinked, and she had the impression she had finally surprised him.

"What makes you think that?"

"You didn't want to dance with me," she said frankly. "Only curiosity and, perhaps, the chivalry of your upbringing, compelled you to *shade* me in my self-made trouble. Don't misunderstand me. I am grateful. But I don't flatter myself that my conversation is anywhere near scintillating enough to have captured your genuine interest. And even if it had, I will not be returning to Maida on Saturday or any other evening."

They had come to the edge of the dance floor, only a few yards from her own table, and she brought herself to a graceful halt. She smiled. "Thank you for the dance, sir. You may now release me and feel free to glower from another pillar of your choosing."

A breath of laughter escaped him, but he released her at once. "You are, it seems, the mistress of the congé. But you are wrong about one thing. I did want to dance with you, and I have enjoyed it immensely. Thank you" He bowed and sauntered away to the nearest pillar, where he leaned, arms folded, and smiled in her direction.

She laughed and directed a mocking curtsey at him before turning to face the glower of her brother.

"Who the devil was that?" he demanded.

"I have absolutely no idea. But it is coming up to unmasking time, so I suggest we leave."

"Wait," Sir Nash said. He and the others had risen to their feet when she approached. He took the pin from his cravat and presented it to her with a bow. "It seems you won our wager hands down."

She took it from him and turned it between her fingers. "Thank you. Why on earth did I ask for a cravat pin? Here, Rollo," She tossed the pin to her brother, who caught it in some surprise. "It's more use to you. Shall we go? Goodbye, Sir Nash. Thank you for the evening."

⸎⸎⸎

FROM HIS PILLAR, the stranger in the black and silver mask watched her depart with her hand on another man's arm. A slight, straight figure, graceful, fashionable, extraordinarily lovely.

A faint smile lurked on the stranger's lips. He hadn't expected her to be quite so…elusive. Or so charming.

The man she had avoided by dancing with him reached for the brandy bottle and sprawled back in his chair, discontented and alone. And without the pin he had given her—presumably his stake in the wager she regretted. Would he feel better or worse if he knew she had just lost her stake, too?

The stranger shoved one hand in his pocket, stroking the bracelet he had concealed there.

The man alone at the table caught his eye and glared at him.

The stranger strolled up to him and sat down. "Allow me to join you in a glass of brandy."

"Why?" came the rude response.

He allowed himself to consider. "Because we are bereft of the same lady? Because I am curious, and you obviously know her better."

"Do I?" the man asked morosely and poured himself a glass of brandy. "Much good it does me."

"She came to be with you, did she not?"

"She came to win a wager and brought half her damned family to play propriety."

"Ah. Those young men are her brothers?"

"One of 'em is, rot him."

"Then she is a very proper lady?"

"Damned if I know," the other man muttered, rising to his feet and walking away.

The stranger sat deep in thought for some time, then he rose also and approached a waiter. "Direct me, if you please, to the proprietor."

The proprietor, one Mr. Renwick, found him in the end as he strolled up one of the side paths that led to a locked gate. Behind the gate appeared to be a cottage.

"Help you?" came a peremptory voice behind him.

"I hope so," replied the stranger. "I'm looking for a place to stay, just for a few days."

"I don't run a doss house!"

"My dear sir, if you did, I would not approach you. Do you have any available accommodation, or know someone nearby who has?"

"There's the old barn," a younger man said, emerging from the gate. "If you don't mind the pony."

"If the pony does not mind me, that will be acceptable," the stranger said.

CHAPTER THREE

G RACE AWOKE WITH an inexplicable sense of relief she was at a loss to account for, until she remembered she had won the wager. And even if she had been recognized, even if it ever came out that she had attended a ball at Maida Gardens, she had done so under the escort of her brother.

And she still had the bracelet.

Today, she would decide whether to go immediately to the country or to brave her sister-in-law's soiree first.

Henley appeared with her coffee and *The Morning Post*, and Grace stretched luxuriously before sitting up against the pillows. "Good morning, Henley."

"Good morning, my lady." The maid set the tray across her knees and began the business of preparing Grace's dress for the day.

Grace frowned suddenly. She *did* still have the bracelet, didn't she? Of course, she did. She just couldn't remember taking it off.

"Henley, where is the bracelet I wore last night?"

"The ruby, my lady? I suppose it is back in its case in the drawer."

"Bring it to me, will you?"

Obligingly, Henley went to the top drawer of the dressing table and took out the familiar case. She paused before she opened it as though sensing from the weight that something was wrong.

"It isn't there, my lady." The maid turned, showing her the empty box.

"But it must be! Didn't you take it off my wrist?"

"No, my lady. You had already removed it before I joined you in here."

Grace's hand crept to her throat, a childish gesture of alarm. "But I don't remember taking it off…"

"You'll have thrown it a drawer without bothering about the case," Henley said comfortingly. "Or it's been knocked into a drawer by accident. We'll find it in a moment."

Of course they would.

Forcing herself to relax—the wretched bracelet had become too associated with trouble in her mind—she sipped her coffee and unfolded the newspaper.

And almost sprayed hot liquid over it. A small headline halfway down the front of the paper leapt out at her. *Special envoys return from China.*

Her heart thundering, she read the small paragraph twice. It stated that the special and highly successful diplomatic mission—led by Sir Geoffrey Spalding and including Mr. Matheson, Mr. Campbell, and Lord Wenning—was expected to land in Southampton this Thursday or shortly thereafter. Which meant they could be in London as soon as Friday.

She let the paper fall from her shaking hands. For two years, she had longed for this moment, for his return, so that she could at least receive some answers. Why had he changed his mind and gone to China when his place had already been filled by Mr. Campbell? Had their wedding night really been so awful, or just so dull, that he had fled the country?

Of course, with answers, no doubt, would come the formal separation she had been expecting. For she had always known in her heart that the only reason for his behavior was hatred. In which case, he should never have married her and ruined both their lives.

The reason he *had* married her still eluded her. She had come with a very modest dowry since her father had more debt than wealth. Wenning hadn't needed to do it. He hadn't needed to pretend love. She would never have…

She blinked away the emotion and the tired, old arguments that made no sense.

He was coming home, and she would need all her strength to withstand the pain. And to make him pay.

*Or maybe…*an insidious, voice began.

Maybe nothing, she retorted firmly. She had spent months praying for him to be sorry, to come back, even to write to her, forgiving her for whatever she had done. And during the months that followed, she finally admitted to herself she had done nothing to inspire his hatred. She was innocent, and his behavior was inexcusable. Even her father acknowledged that.

He could acknowledge it, too, or stay away from her. She didn't much care which.

"My lady, the bracelet isn't here," Henley interrupted her.

Grace stared at her. *Oh, no. Not now. Oh, not now when he is almost home!*

AN HOUR LATER, with every inch of the bedchamber and dressing room searched, Henley was sent to scour the stairs and passages, ask discreetly among the servants, and search the carriage. Even here in Wenning House, such discretion was necessary, for apart from Henley, all the servants were the earl's. They could easily blab to him as soon as he came home, and Grace certainly did not want to put herself at such an immediate disadvantage in their future dealings.

In her heart, Grace knew that if the bracelet had dropped off her wrist in the house or the carriage, it would already have been found and returned. So by the time Henley came back shaking her head, Grace was seated at her desk while she tried to think.

"I must have lost it at Maida Gardens," she said flatly. "It the ballroom, or perhaps the cloakroom."

"When did you last notice it for certain, my lady?"

"When I was dancing." With the man in the black and silver mask. She frowned. "After that, I don't recall... It *might* have fallen off somewhere in the pavilion or on the path leading to the front gates." And it was more than likely that if it had, it had been stolen rather than kept aside for her. All the same, it was her last chance. "I didn't even notice that it wasn't there when I undressed. I was so full of relief at winning the wager. It would be funny if it weren't so maddening!"

She jumped up. "Have one of the footmen fetch me a hackney, Henley." The staff might speculate why she was not using her own carriage, but at least they wouldn't know where she was going or why.

"If you're going to Maida Gardens, I'd better come with you," Henley pronounced.

"No," Grace said regretfully. "I think a lady with such a superior maid would draw too much attention. What happens in the Gardens during the day?"

"The ballroom is closed—apart from tea dances on Monday and Thursday, but even they are later in the day. People walk in the gardens, have picnics, or eat at tables set outside. Sometimes there are concerts or tumblers. And there are pretty fountains and a waterfall. And ices for sale. But it shouldn't be too busy so early."

"So, if I go straight to the ballroom, I am unlikely to be seen? I'll wear the hat with the net veil, just to be safe."

AN HOUR LATER, the hackney dropped her at the open, wrought-iron gates of Maida Gardens, and, after instructing the driver to wait for her, she hurried inside. A pretty young girl sold her a ticket for a shilling.

"You can stay all day," she assured her.

"Tell me, do you have a store of things people have lost?" Grace asked hopefully.

"You could ask Mr. Chaplin in the ballroom," the girl said, "but I doubt you'd find anything of yours there."

Meaning anything she might have lost would already have been sold? Grace didn't wait to ask but hurried on up the path to the ballroom. In daylight, it all looked very different, green and pleasant, with borders of flowers that had barely been visible in the lantern light. No ruby and gold bracelet glittered from the sides of the path or among the flowers and unlit lanterns.

In the sunshine, even the pavilion showed its age and its peeling paint. The doors were all wide open to air it, but as Grace stepped in, the reek of last night's wine and too many dancing bodies still hit her. A man was sweeping up. Two women were cleaning tables.

Since no one paid her any attention, Grace walked straight over to the table she had sat at last night, inspecting the chairs and looking on the floor beneath. Finding nothing, she walked up to the nearest woman.

"Where would I find Mr. Chaplin?"

The woman jerked her thumb to the man with the broom.

"Thank you."

The man stopped sweeping, eying her approach with some suspicion.

"I believe I lost a bracelet here last night. I was wondering if you had found it?"

"No."

"It was a pretty thing with r—" She only just stopped herself saying rubies, and instead said, "red-colored stones."

"No, haven't found anything like that."

"If you do," Grace said a little desperately, "would you please keep it aside for me? I will pay you well for its return."

At last, some interest sparked in his eyes. "Got a card?" he asked. "Or I can take you to the office to write down your direction."

"That won't be necessary," she said at once. "I'll call again tomorrow. Thank you for your time."

She walked out the nearest door and found herself on a different path. Rather than face the stench of the pavilion again, she walked a little farther along the path she was on. She was about to cut across a narrower path toward the one she wanted, when a patch of grass and a garden swing caught her attention in the other direction.

On impulse, she walked across the grass to the swing and sat down to think. Sighing, she pushed up the veil to the top of her hat.

She didn't think she was any closer to recovering the bracelet, although the offer of money was clearly inspired. If it had been found on the premises, presumably Mr. Chaplin would wrest it from the finder and sell it back to her. She would just have to hope its true value would escape him.

She kicked out with her feet to make the chair swing. It creaked a bit but seemed strong enough. Birds sang in the nearby trees, soothing her. Even the distant voices and the occasional laughter of children sounded pleasant. She could hear the splashing of water, too— presumably, one of the fountains Henley had mentioned.

Why was she so worried about finding the wretched bracelet in any case? To her, it should have no more value than the marriage did to her husband. He had no right to complain if she had lost it during the two years he had been away. In fact, it was probably insured. He would not care.

No, she admitted to herself at last; it was *she* who cared. Because he had given it. Because, somewhere, she still clung to the foolishness that it had been a token of his love.

"Stupid, *stupid* little girl," she murmured.

"Surely you don't mean yourself?" another voice asked behind her, at the same time as the swing moved with a little more force. A low, soft voice with a hint of a foreign accent. Surely, the man with the black and silver mask? But when she tried to turn, he said, "No, don't look. Unless you want me to see your face, too."

That was a fair point. She stilled, letting him push the swing, and pleasant little flutters formed in her stomach at the motion, almost like being a child again.

"Why are you here?" he asked.

"I lost something and came back to find it. Why are you here?"

"Waiting for someone. What did you lose?"

"My bracelet. I was wearing it when I danced with you, but I believe I lost it between then and when I left."

"But you didn't come out here during the evening, did you?"

"No," she replied, almost turning in surprise that he had noticed. She stopped herself in time, and the swing moved higher. But then, she remembered, she had found him watching her at least twice. *Why?* "Did you notice it?" she blurted.

"I noticed it on your wrist when we danced. I didn't see you drop it. Is it valuable?"

"I don't know. I expect so. It was a gift."

"Sentimental value then."

She couldn't help it. She laughed. "Something like that."

"Perhaps you should ask the men you were with."

The accusation was clear, if understated, making her scoff. *"They would not..."* She broke off. Rollo and his friends would not take anything of hers or even stay silent if she dropped something. But Boothe was another matter. Why had he been so determined to win their stupid wager? At best, the wager was ungentlemanly. "Perhaps I should," she said bleakly.

"Or Anthony."

"Who is Anthony?" she asked, bewildered. "Does he work here?"

"I expect I got the name wrong. You puzzle me, madame. Why does a lady of birth and wealth come to a place like this? To a masquerade, and leave before the unmasking? To the garden and sit alone on a beautiful day, sighing in sadness? Have you no family to look after you? No husband?"

"I prefer to look after myself." She laughed, "Though as you see, that is not going so well."

"Talk to your husband," he urged.

Another hiss of laughter escaped her. "Wouldn't that be an event to behold? Are you married, sir?"

"Yes."

"And do you cherish your wife?"

He was silent, and for want of pushing, the swing began to still.

"Sir?"

Receiving no answer, she pulled down her veil and turned her head. And saw no one at all.

She smiled unhappily. "No, then. It seems to be common among husbands."

She wriggled off the swing and walked on toward the gate, hoping her hackney was still waiting.

As she went, she thought about the stranger, wondering who he was and what his life was like. She rather liked his odd humor and the contradictions in his nature. Last night, he had noticed her, and yet, unlike most men, he had not jumped at the chance to dance with her. It had even entered her head he would refuse her bold invitation, though in the end, he hadn't. And today, he had appeared out of nowhere, apparently interested in her problems but not exactly thrusting himself forward to help.

Perhaps the wife he did not cherish would object.

For some reason, he intrigued her. She felt a strange thread of intimacy between them, quite at odds with the nature and number of their encounters. Dancing with him, too, had caused a little flutter, a tug of attraction. But he seemed to be a gentleman for, unlike Sir Nash, he had made no effort to take advantage of her. He had merely asked her to stay until midnight. What would have happened then? Would he have tried to kiss her?

That was a vexing question. She had to confess that she would have quite liked to allow that kiss. And yet, she would have been disappointed if he had tried, and she certainly wouldn't have let him.

In any case, this was a quite inappropriate direction for her thoughts when she was trying to recover her husband's wedding gift, and he was due to return on Friday. Her stomach twisted. The day after tomorrow.

To the devil with it, she told herself crossly as she climbed into the hackney, which was indeed still waiting for her. The misguided sentimentality she had attached to it did not matter in the slightest. If she found the bracelet before he came, good. If she did not, he would just have to live with its loss, as she had lived with the loss of him.

CHAPTER FOUR

MR. PHINEAS HARLAW was the only member of her husband's family who Grace found remotely congenial. She was glad to accept his escort to the theatre that evening. In fact, it promised to be a pleasant outing since Bridget, Lady Arpington, was also to accompany them.

In her first Season, before she had even met the Earl of Wenning, Grace had been stunned by the sheer racket in the theatre that had prevented her from concentrating on the stage. It hadn't taken her long to learn to filter out the noise of the audience and enjoy the play rather than the gossip. And if she occasionally missed remarks made to her, well, they were usually spoken by admirers who had to be kept in their place anyway.

Naturally, she maintained her own box, from where she had an excellent view. She looked forward to the play, which boasted the talents of Frances Caldwell, an actress she had noted and admired before, although Mrs. Caldwell rarely played the leading roles.

Phineas fussed about the box, making sure everyone's chairs were placed correctly, and pronounced himself the happiest of men to be escort to such beautiful and charming ladies.

"Oh, what tosh, Phineas," Grace said with only half-amused impatience. "You know you are the perfect escort, so there is no need to flatter."

"I'm just grateful not to see Nash Boothe here," Phineas said, frowning with mock severity. "I have to tell you, cousin, your name is linked too often with his, and certain other family members are noticing. It might be politic to—er...keep him at a distance. For a while, at least."

"Indeed, I will," Grace agreed cordially.

Bridget had leaned to the other side of the box, exchanging bows with friends as she spotted them.

Phineas shifted closer to Grace and murmured, "Have you heard his lordship is expected home on Friday?"

"Indeed, yes," she said neutrally.

"Did he write to you?" Phineas asked in tones of surprised pleasure.

"Lord, no. I read it in the newspaper like everyone else." It no longer even hurt that this was the only way she received news of him, so she could speak with quite genuine carelessness.

"What will you do?" he asked.

She shrugged. "What can I do but welcome him home?"

"Would you, perhaps, be more comfortable in the country for the next few weeks?" he suggested hesitantly. "Rather than conducting a difficult reunion under the glare of the ton's gossip machine."

"I think *reunion* is somewhat optimistic. I was planning to go to the country, though. Perhaps I shall, next week. But I will not run from him like a guilty wife."

He looked appalled. "Oh, my goodness, no! But there are those who misunderstand your liveliness, who misconstrue your string of admirers and might bring such nasty suspicion to his lordship. It strikes me that until he better understands, a little distance might be...helpful."

She regarded him with affectionate gratitude. "You are kind. And I know you mean to help him understand. But the truth is, if he wants to make a cake of himself, I see no reason why I should care."

Phineas subsided, although she had the impression he was not happy with her answers. Poor Phineas walked a fine line of family loyalty and doing what was right.

Despite her determination not to care for either Wenning's return or the loss of his wedding gift, she found it annoyingly difficult to concentrate on the play, the talents of Frances Caldwell notwithstanding.

At last, she gave in and whispered, "Has he written to you?"

"I received a letter last week," Phineas admitted.

She didn't want to ask, didn't want to know. And yet she blurted, "Did he mention me? Has he said anything about me or his feelings for me now?"

Phineas shifted uncomfortably. "He would not. Not to me."

"You are his cousin, his heir, his friend. Who else would he talk to?"

"Oliver is a very private man. As usual, he says very little about personal matters."

Very little. Which meant he had said something and that Phineas didn't want to tell her what. Which meant it had been bad.

It doesn't matter. I don't care.

She returned to the play, but already the curtain was coming down for an interval, and the audience had begun its true purpose of visiting each other's boxes, of seeing and being seen. Among Grace's guests at the first interval was Sir Ernest Leyton, always so proper and polite. And yet, she had seen him waltzing with an unknown lady at a Maida Gardens masquerade.

Which meant, of course, that he might have seen her.

Over the two years her husband had been away, she had appreciated Sir Ernest's friendship. He never criticized or advised and rarely spoke of Oliver. And yet he had been there more than once when situations among her admirers had grown heated, castigating them for daring to bandy a lady's name about. And so, the trouble had always been nipped in the bud.

Tonight, he broke his habit by saying, "I suppose you will have seen the news of Wenning's return."

"If I hadn't, I would still know. Everyone has been desperate to tell me."

To her annoyance, Sir Nash entered the box. She ignored him.

So did Sir Ernest. "I'm sure. I look forward to seeing what changes travel has wrought in Wenning, as must you." His gaze flickered to Sir Nash, who was conversing with Bridget.

"Feel free to let me know."

His attention snapped back to her. "You don't expect to see him?" he murmured, frowning.

"I don't expect anything at all," she said frankly.

For an instant, and quite unusually, she caught a glimpse of pity in his eyes and a spurt of anger that did not appear to be directed at her, for he pressed her hand and reluctantly made way for Sir Nash Boothe to speak to her.

"Am I forgiven?" Boothe asked lightly.

"For what? Losing a wager? I hold nothing against you. Lady Mary! How delightful to see you. I did not know you were back in London. Come, sit by me."

There was nothing for Boothe to do but give up his chair to Lady Mary. Sir Ernest, she noted, stayed until after Sir Nash had departed.

ALTHOUGH IT WAS tempting to continue her social butterfly existence and go on from the theatre to Mrs. Wortley's ball, she felt too exhausted. Phineas seemed disappointed.

"Take the carriage," Grace offered as compensation.

"Thank you. I hope this is not simply to please Oliver? He has never been one to object to anyone's innocent pleasures."

"Of course not. I believe I am simply finding town life dull." She smiled. "Present company excepted, of course!"

"Well, one mustn't burn the candle at both ends, I suppose. Ah, this is your home, Lady Arpington. Allow me to see you inside."

He alighted, ready to help Bridget from the carriage. Hastily, Bridget embraced Grace. "It will be well, truly. And remember, I am always here. Arpington will be delighted to receive you, too. Good night, Grace."

Grace smiled a little bleakly after her. Even her best friend seemed to think she should run before Wenning returned.

It is he who should run from me. He has insulted and neglected me. He should expect a little revenge.

⋙✕⋘

BEHIND HER UNCLE'S cottage on the boundary of Maida Gardens, shading the sun from the side of her face, Kitty Renwick peeped cautiously through the half-open barn door. Discovering their mysterious guest to be absent, she walked in, patted Betsy, the old pony, gave her a piece of carrot, and edged into the stall their guest used to sleep in.

On her uncle's instruction, Kitty had made up a comfortable straw mattress, covered with decent sheets and blankets. Presumably, the man was paying well. It was her duty to tidy up for him and launder his clothes when asked.

There was not much tidying to do, for he seemed to be clean by nature. She spread up the makeshift bed, then turned to his two coats hanging from a hook in the wall. His morning coat was looking a little tired, so she took the clothes brush from her pocket and gave it a good brush down.

Something, however, was preventing the brush's smooth passage. Frowning, she felt the lumpy spot with her hand and realized the coat must have an inside pocket. She delved inside and came out with something cold and metallic.

Something that shone, even in the barn's dim light. Her breath caught at the beauty of the thing. Real gold and rubies and diamonds, if she was not much mistaken. And definitely a lady's bracelet.

A shadow fell over her, and she spun around to face the barn's temporary occupant. He had paused at sight of her, and his gaze fell at once to the bracelet dangling from her awed fingers.

Tall and darkly distinguished, with even features and compelling eyes, he was undeniably handsome. In fact, their guest had always struck her and the rest of the family as a gentleman. But he was no fop. His skin was too browned by the sun, and his body was too muscular, which was particularly obvious when, as now, he stood in his shirt sleeves. His eyes were too hard and too perceptive. If Kitty owned the truth—and she tried to—she was a little afraid of him. For after all, what was a gentleman doing lodging in a barn at Maida Gardens? He had to be in hiding, which made him dangerous. And now he had discovered her holding the feminine bracelet he had kept in his coat's inside pocket.

Was the bracelet the reason he was hiding?

She felt a growl rise in her throat, which could easily become a yell for help, and Rob and Uncle would come running. But being no coward, she turned it into a cough and swallowed back her fear.

Since he made no move toward her, merely captured her gaze and raised his black eyebrows, she held out the bracelet to him. "It spoils the hang of your coat."

He strolled toward her and took possession of the bracelet without touching her fingers. "Do you think so? I had scarcely noticed."

She turned back to the coat, her neck prickling as she finished its brushing. Her heart thudded, but she wasn't foolish. She kept the brush in her hand and made sure she was nearer the door before she blurted, "There is a lady looking for a bracelet just like that one. She lost it here the evening you came."

He smiled faintly, clearly unconcerned. "I know."

"Will you give it to Chaplin for her?" she asked boldly.

His hand closed, and he reached for his coat with the other hand. "No. I will give it to her myself."

She had no reason to believe him, yet she found herself smiling at him. "Good," she said and turned for the door, though not before she saw she had finally surprised him.

She went rather thoughtfully back to the cottage, where her uncle was enjoying his breakfast. He grunted by way of greeting. Since he was up late every night, mornings never found him at his best.

"Do you know who he is?" Kitty asked. "Our barn guest?"

"Don't ask questions, and you stay out of trouble."

"Is that what he's doing here? Staying out of trouble?"

"I don't know, and I don't care. And if you know what's good for you, you won't pry."

Kitty's eyes widened. "Are *you* afraid of him?"

"No," Uncle scoffed. His eyebrows twitched. "Not that I'd care to get on the wrong side of him."

"Because he might take his money elsewhere?"

"No," came the unexpected answer. "Because in spite of his being a nob, I quite like him."

ONCE MORE VEILED and traveling by hackney through the morning sunshine, Grace returned to Maida Gardens. She almost didn't bother since she was sure she would not find the bracelet. But she had said she would, and in any case, the journey would fill up her day and prevent her thinking about her husband's return. About his sister's soiree tomorrow evening.

She hoped a storm at sea held him up. Not that she wished him to die—the very thought induced a sense of panic she was at a loss to account for. But she wouldn't mind if he was vilely seasick. And if it put off his return for another day or so, she would be very glad.

Or would she? Shouldn't she just get it over with and begin the rest of her life, whatever that would entail?

A wave of desolation swept over her. Was that the best she could hope for? Imprisoned in a name-only marriage with the trappings of a countess...

I will not care. I will not. Perhaps I will meet my stranger here and flirt for an hour before I go home.

Accordingly, she walked up the path to the pavilion. The doors were open once more, although no cleaning appeared to be in progress. However, in a tiny office on the left of the door, she found Mr. Chaplin.

"Good morning," she said pleasantly.

He scowled up at her before his face cleared. "Oh, it's you. I ain't found your bracelet nor anything else. I even asked around in the right quarters, if you know what I mean, but if anyone took it, they ain't telling me, even for the readies."

She hadn't expected to hear any different. She took the gold coins from her purse and laid them on his desk. "Thank you for your time. Good morning."

"Wait, ma'am!" Chaplin jumped to his feet. "I have a message for you."

"A message?" She swung quickly back to him. "From whom?"

"Don't know his name. But he—"

"Then who did he leave the message for?" she interrupted.

He frowned. "The veiled lady what was here yesterday. That *is* you, isn't it?"

"Yes," she agreed, relaxing. "What is the message?"

"For you to meet him at the same place. Says he has something for you."

"Thank you," Grace said civilly and walked back out into the fresh air.

She hesitated, for the message, presumably from her stranger, bore a distinct resemblance to a trick once played on her shortly after her marriage. Foolishly hoping for even a word from her husband, she had gone alone to a private room during a ball to find a well-known rake waiting for her.

Only Sir Ernest had got her out of that one. He shouldn't have followed her, of course, but she couldn't help being glad he had. He had explained many things to her after that, truths that had ended what was left of her naivety, but which had made the social battlefield of the Season easier to navigate. There was safety, she had learned, as well as prestige, in numbers. At least where admirers were concerned.

Was her stranger setting some kind of trap for her? Did he want a tryst by the swing, away from prying eyes? Or did she have an unknown enemy? An unknown admirer?

Eventually, she resolved not to come upon the swing from the same direction as yesterday, where she would be seen approaching. Instead, she took the path he must have used then in order to have come upon her from behind.

And there he was. Of course, she could only see his tall beaver hat, the back of his head, and the considerable breadth of his shoulders. But she was sure it was him, idly swinging in a blink of sunshine, the breeze catching a lock of his unfashionably long hair.

The clouds were ominous this morning, so she had brought her umbrella. Clutching it before her like a soldier marching into battle, she stepped forward.

She meant to approach him quietly, perhaps even see his face, for whether he was good or evil, she was, suddenly, insatiably curious about him. However, she had only crept forward three paces before he rose from the swing and sauntered off toward the other path.

Devil take him! "Sir!" she called, walking faster. "You asked to see me."

To her surprise, he spun around, sweeping off his hat and bowing. By the time he straightened, he was already completing his spin and returning to his path. He had revealed no more than a blur and a shock of black hair, which she had already seen at the ball.

What on earth is all this about? She walked on more slowly, in no hurry to catch him up in case it was some kind of ambush. How could she suspect him of so much ill, while remaining so curious?

Because she did not trust anyone. Except perhaps her brother and Bridget. And Henley, up to a point.

Meaning to sit in the swing for a few minutes, she approached it, her eyes sweeping the lawn and the path ahead for a sign of him or anyone else. She found none and so spread her skirts to sit.

Only then did she see something on the cushion of the swing. It glittered red and gold.

She all but fell onto the swing, snatching up the bracelet. Oh yes, it was hers, without doubt. And with it came a folded note, held in the bracelet's clasp.

Involuntarily, she pressed the bracelet to her cheek. Her sight was blurry, and there was a lump in her throat. *I don't care. I don't. But it is as well to have it back.*

Blinking back the foolish tears, she released the note and dropped the bracelet into her reticule. Then, after glancing behind her once more for any unwelcome company, she unfolded the paper.

> *Yours, I believe.*
> *There is something else you should know. If you are curious, come to the next masked ball this Saturday.*
> *Now if thou wouldst, when all have given him over,*
> *From death to life, thou mightst him yet recover.*

She frowned. It was not signed. She could not even be sure it came from the stranger. He could have been simply the messenger. Either way, he had found the bracelet and returned it to her.

She rose, rereading the note as she followed his trail to the path. He had not used the bracelet to entice her. But still, he asked. Did he, too, feel that tug of forbidden attraction? Or was there really something important he wanted her to know? About what? Was someone dying? The lines at the end seemed to suggest so, and yet they read like poetry and made no other kind of sense.

Was he deep in some melancholy and needed her help? There was no doubt she owed him a debt for the return of the bracelet, and she would not willingly see another human being so low. He had not *seemed* blue-devilled, just very much in control, which could have hidden anything.

Well, she didn't have to make any such decision right now. Though she doubted her chances of persuading Rollo to escort her a second time.

She had the waiting hackney drop her at Bridget's house in Brook Street, since they had planned to spend the morning together at a newly fashionable modiste. And as soon as she was alone with Bridget, she showed her the bracelet.

Bridget exclaimed with gratifying delight. "Where did you find it? Was it in the house all along?"

"No, at Maida Gardens. Someone found it there."

"And did not steal it? Either they didn't recognize its worth, or the place is not as bad as its reputation."

Grace eyed her speculatively. "Would you consider going on Saturday night? For the masquerade ball? Incognito, of course. Would Arpington escort us?"

"He might," Bridget replied, shifting uneasily in her chair. "But Grace, Lord Wenning will be home by then, and you really should not put his back up with any of your mad starts."

"I have no interest whatever in the position of his back. I shall not let his return make one whit of difference to my plans."

"But I thought you were going to the country?"

"I still might. But I refuse to look as if I'm running away from Wenning. And I have a notion to go to Maida again when I can be relaxed enough to enjoy it, without worrying about silly wagers and avoiding people like Nash Boothe."

"I should think the masked balls are full of people considerably less manageable than Nash Boothe."

"Which is why it would be more comfortable to have Lord Arpington with us. But in truth, although the affair was a lot less formal than we are used to, I saw nothing exceptionable there. Not *inside* the ballroom, at any rate. And, of course, we would leave before the unmasking. Unless…we could get up a *large* party for the occasion. With lots of our friends. A daring expedition! And there is always safety in numbers."

Bridget laughed. "You are mad! Let us leave aside the large party for now! But I'll agree to the smaller if Arpington does. Providing Wenning does not put the hems on it, of course."

"Wenning is in no position to control anything I do."

"He is your husband, Grace."

"If he does not remember that, I see no reason why I should."

Bridget bit her lip as though unsure whether to laugh or try to talk sense into her. In the end, she changed the subject, though only slightly.

"Do you go to Lady Trewthorpe's soiree tomorrow evening? Do you suppose Wenning will be there?"

"I have no idea."

"Then he is not home yet?"

Grace shrugged. "I don't know. I believe they are only expected in Southampton today, and I left early for Maida Gardens."

"Perhaps you should go home and see."

"I would rather go to the dressmaker's. If I like her, I might order a new riding habit in that adorable green velvet I bought at the Pantheon Bazaar."

Bridget nodded and stood up. "Very well, let us go. But Grace?"

Grace glanced at her, brows raised.

"Be careful what games you play," Bridget begged. "He may deserve a metaphorical smack, but never forget that he holds the power."

GRACE HAD NEVER forgotten where the power lay, not once in the two years they had been apart.

Perhaps that was why, on Friday afternoon, her heart seemed to be jammed in her throat as she returned to her Mount Street home. She had just attended a Venetian breakfast in Lady Mary's garden, which had been pleasantly distracting. But now, *un*pleasant reality, in the shape of her returning husband, intruded with a vengeance.

She didn't expect him to show any interest in her, but if he did, she had a thousand and one ways of keeping him at arm's length—learned from managing her occasionally turbulent and rakish court.

It was an effort, as she stepped down from the carriage and ascended the steps to the front door, to retain her attitude of careless calm, but she tried her best.

Of course, the footmen did not declare, "He's home!" Or "We're still waiting for him!" She wished they would, just so that she would know. Even breathing was painful as she entered the house.

And saw at once that he *was* home.

Trunks and bags were piled in the front hall. Some of them she even recognized from their abandoned wedding journey, which hadn't got further than Worthing. She paused, eyeing the baggage without favor.

"Has someone come to stay?" she inquired of Herries, the butler, who was making his stately way across the hall.

"His lordship has returned, my lady," he said, beaming.

"Then be so good as to have his bags taken at once to his rooms. It cannot be a happy return to find his servants have grown lax in his absence."

"His lordship—"

"Now, Herries, if you please," she said pleasantly. It was possible he was leaving again immediately or was unsure of his welcome until he had spoken to her. Or wondered which room to have them taken to. "I cannot be falling over these all day. I'm assuming you remember where his lordship's rooms are?"

"Yes, my lady," Herries said warily as she stepped delicately between trunks and made for the stairs.

"Er… Where is his lordship?" she inquired casually.

"He has gone out, my lady."

Of course he had. She didn't know if she felt more relieved or furious. Having worked herself up to meet him, he had put off the inevitable, and she must suffer more hours of purgatory.

There was only one thing to do in the circumstances. Invite herself to dine with her parents.

CHAPTER FIVE

"SO, WENNING IS home," her father, Viscount Darblay, said, frowning over his wine glass at her. It was as close as he came to looking disapproving.

"Well, his bags are home," Grace said, "I can only assume he is somewhere close by."

Her little sister, Hope, all of fifteen years old, giggled, and Grace allowed herself a quick, subtle wink in her direction.

"But Grace, don't you feel you should dine at home on his first day back?" her mother said anxiously.

Grace picked up her fork. "Why? I doubt he does. I'm sure we shall meet in the fullness of time."

"*I* will meet with him," her father promised. "Very soon. Dashed insulting way to behave. I was very angry at the time." He took a sip of wine and made a discovery. "Still angry."

"Feel free to call tomorrow," Grace invited. "Talk vaguely about annulments and lawsuits."

"I *could* only talk vaguely," her father assured her. "The settlements were all on his side, and I can't give most of 'em back. But we're not no one. The Darblay family is older than his, and he has no business scampering off to enjoy himself when he should have been escorting you on your wedding trip. Downright offensive."

"Well, it was a very flattering position he had been offered," her

46

mother put in, always anxious to keep the peace. "And so young. I'm sure he thought it was for the best, for both of them. And you do *like* being the Countess of Wenning, don't you, my dear?"

"The title has a certain cachet and opens many doors," Grace said lazily.

"And offers certain protections for behaving badly," her father put in unexpectedly.

"I never behave badly," Grace said. "I am merely on the fast side of fashionable."

"Hmm," her father said, eyeing her with unusual fatherly interest. "See much of your brother?"

"Lord, no. Though he did oblige me with an escort the other evening."

"Wouldn't let him too often. Going to the devil, is Rollo."

"Only according to some," Grace soothed. According to others, he was merely following in his father's hedonistic footsteps. "What have you been doing since you came to town, Hope?"

"Shopping," Hope said gloomily.

"She keeps growing," their mother sighed. "But she has no interest in clothing."

"There are excellent book shops," Grace offered. "I'll take you to a coupletomorrow if you wish."

Hope's face lit up. "Really? What about the British Museum?"

"Maybe the day after. I have a social flibbertigibbet reputation to keep up, you know. I can't have the word spread that I am a secret bluestocking."

Hope snorted, and their mother beamed. "Especially not now your husband is home to enjoy the social whirl with you."

ON LEAVING HER parents, Grace knew a cowardly urge to slope back home and hide from her husband until she felt stronger. But since she had no guarantees that he would not be there expecting to see her, and she had already promised herself and anyone else who would listen that she would not change her plans for him...

She took a deep breath and directed her coachman to Lady Trewthorpe's residence in Barclay Square.

Lady Trewthorpe was Wenning's eldest sister, so Grace felt quite justified in dispensing with the conventional male escort and arrived alone. Such boldness tended to draw all eyes, and for once, this suited her perfectly.

She had dressed for the evening with a care she would admit to no one. Her glossy black locks shone, highlighted by the diamonds winking in her hair. She wore an evening gown of sheer, deep-red muslin net over a cream silk underdress. The decolletage was not as low as some, but she liked the way the bodice clung to her shape. A necklace of tiny rubies was wound around her throat, with matching drops in her ears. But she did not wear the recently retrieved bracelet, though it actually went very well with the whole ensemble.

With her head held high and a faint smile on her lips, she walked unhurriedly upstairs to the salons. Here, she found Lord and Lady Trewthorpe welcoming their guests. And if her ladyship's smile slipped very slightly when she caught sight of Grace—well, that could easily have been Grace's unkind imagination.

"Grace, how delightful! I was not sure you would come."

"Honoria," Grace returned, not even bothering to kiss the air above her sister-in-law's cheek, as Honoria did to hers. "How could I not?" She turned to her host. "My lord, you look well."

"And you are ravishing as always," Trewthorpe assured her, causing his wife an instant of clear irritation.

Grace smiled beatifically and passed into the first salon, where, it seemed, all eyes were avidly awaiting her. Under normal circumstances, she would be quickly surrounded by male admirers, and tonight, several men, including Sir Nash Boothe, did smile and bow to her. But came no closer.

Then he is here.

She was glad of the moment's warning. From the first salon, doors at either end of the room led to others. Since she had already turned left to receive a glass of wine from the liveried footman, she kept walking in that direction. She meant to pause and talk to friends who were beckoning to her, but without warning, a gentleman appeared in the doorway, and her breath stopped.

Oliver Harlaw, fifth Earl of Wenning, was everything she remembered and more. Tall, handsome in an angular kind of way, his black hair cropped fashionably short. She knew formidable intelligence and sharp observation lurked behind the deceptively amiable dark eyes. There had never been anything soft about Lord Wenning, except, she had once foolishly imagined his feelings for her.

All of that, she remembered as if he had never been away. But she couldn't recall him being quite such a powerful presence. Surely, his shoulders had filled out further, and something had changed in his posture. A casual yet commanding poise that suddenly made nonsense of all her petty revenge plans.

But the world was watching. Even the chatter in the room had stilled to little above a murmur as all avid eyes turned toward this meeting, which would, she knew, be gossiped about and analyzed for days.

And so, she only smiled and nodded at her friends and passed on toward the door. For his part, her husband—*husband, dear God!*—strolled into the room. They were on a collision course, and she had no hope of avoiding him.

She had never intended to. As they drew nearer each other, she almost heard the room's collective intake of breath. His gaze locked with hers, and it felt like a blow to the chest. She could read nothing in his expression. Neither pleasure nor regret, let alone annoyance or even recognition. But he *had* seen her, *had* recognized her. Somehow, she knew that much.

About two yards away, he came to a halt and bowed. His face was darker, bronzed by foreign sun and weeks spent at sea.

She halted, too, and curtseyed. "My lord. Welcome home," she said amiably and passed on to the door without another word or backward glance.

SHE WAS, THE Earl of Wenning had to admit, magnificent. She had put him in his place firmly and publicly and with perfect courtesy. Part of him might have wished she had whitened, dropped her glass, and crumpled into his arms in grateful joy. But by now, he knew that would not happen. He had been sure she would keep her dignity, but he hadn't expected her to outplay him at his own game.

He might have deserved it, but he didn't have to like it. He was left looking, he suspected, like a callow boy who had just had the impertinence to accost, without introduction, an accredited beauty who also happened to be a lady of the first rank and importance.

He allowed himself to watch her graceful back only for an instant before he turned and walked on. The noise started up again, since the show, for now, was over. He hoped Honoria appreciated how much he and Grace had done for her attendance numbers.

His gaze fell on a familiar and much missed figure just entering the room, and he swerved toward him, smiling. "Ern!" He thrust out his hand to his old friend, Sir Ernest Leyton, and they shook warmly. "I hoped I would see you here."

"Likewise, although after such a journey, I half-expected you to sleep for a week."

"Nothing to do on journeys *but* sleep! Thank you for your letters. They kept me sane."

"Thank you for yours. At least I could tell your wife you were not dead."

"Not here, Leyton," Wenning murmured, keeping the smile fixed to his face.

"Nor anywhere, I suppose. I'm sure you don't need me to tell you how ill you behaved."

"You already have," Wenning pointed out. "Without hearing all my reasons."

"Tell them to your wife first."

"Stop it," Wenning said. "Or I'll change my mind and tell Honoria I *shall* sing this evening."

Leyton gave one of his reluctant laughs. "God preserve us all from that fate. What's happening through there?"

"Some sprig declaiming bad verse. But I believe we are about to begin the main event. Honoria claims to have found a tenor to die for."

As word got around, even before Honoria's announcement, guests began to drift in from the other two salons to hear the promised singer. Wenning was greeted by lots of other people, all apparently delighted to see him back and promising themselves to hear all his stories about the east in the very near future.

As the tenor approached the pianoforte, Wenning had reached the outskirts of the avid audience and saw a carelessly dressed young man amble in from the left-hand door. He had to look twice before he recognized Rollo Darblay, who had still been at Oxford when Wenning had married his sister. He now looked to be a very rakish young man about town. Until the tenor began to sing, and an expression of outrage crossed Rollo's face as he made a quick escape into the passage.

Wenning moved on his leisurely way, reflecting that the tenor did indeed have a wonderful voice. On any other evening, he might have sat down to enjoy it to the full. On this evening, he had a more pressing desire.

At the door of the left-hand salon, he saw that the room was quiet. Two ladies and a young man talked quietly near the fireplace. At the middle of three tall window, his wife stood perfectly still, gazing out at the night. In profile, she was elegant, poised, breathtaking.

God, she was beautiful. He remembered her slender, elegant neck, the way her naked body had arched when he had kissed her nape. The memory fed his sudden, flaring desire and the old, familiar ache in his heart.

But he had run away long enough. He walked into the room.

"GOOD GOD," GRACE had murmured, coming across Rollo in the second salon, where a poet was holding forth with great drama. "You look very like my brother."

"I knew I shouldn't have come," Rollo said, casting a look of disgust at the poet. "Thing is, I heard Wenning would be here, and thought I should warn you. In case you didn't know already."

"Why, Rollo, that was kind," Grace said, impressed and touched.

"I thought so, but this is devilish, Grace. I don't know how you can stand such stuff. I was keeping my eye on Wenning, but I don't see him now."

"He's in the other room," Grace said calmly, although the fingers holding her untouched glass of wine had a tendency to shake. "We said good evening."

Rollo cast her a searching glance. "Did you, by God? Can I push his teeth down his throat yet?"

"Why, no, his return can make no difference to any of us."

After a moment, Rollo's lips twisted into a crooked smile. "That's the way you want to play it? Fair enough. Should I stay?"

Even more touched by this offer of sacrifice, she patted his arm.

"No, you have already suffered more than any brother should. Thank you for being here, but you had better escape before the tenor begins."

Rollo grinned and made for the door to the main salon behind everyone else.

"Lady Wenning," young Mr. Curtis greeted her eagerly, as though he couldn't believe his luck to find her unattached to any other arm. "Are you coming to hear the tenor? May I escort you?"

"Thank you." She laid her hand on his arm, and they walked together toward the door.

But on the other side lurked her husband, and she wasn't quite ready to meet him yet.

"Save me a place, Mr. Curtis," she said lightly, dropping her arm and turning back. "I will join you in a moment."

He bowed without demur and carried on. But he would, she knew, keep a seat beside him free for her, and she fully intended to take it. A little young, a little serious, but very good looking, he was an excellent companion for the evening. And she needed one, if only to keep Wenning guessing.

She swerved to the window and stood looking out into the darkness. With the bright candlelight inside, she could see nothing outside, but the blackness was curiously soothing.

This was what she had been waiting for. She would not be intimidated or afraid just because he, too, had grown up and become a stranger. He had always been a stranger. The man who had left her on their wedding night with nothing but a curt note was not the man she had imagined only hours before.

The tenor had begun without her noticing. His voice was as fine as she remembered, and Honoria would receive almost equal adulation for finding him. She doubted her sister-in-law would reveal it was Grace who had actually done the finding. She had thrown his name to her in order to deflect a long and annoying scold about something that was none of Lady Trewthorpe's business. It had worked, too, for a couple of days.

A shift in the air gave her a moment's warning. An achingly re-membered masculine scent of woodland and citrus mingled with something fainter, spicier like cinnamon, yet also elusively familiar. A man leaned in the window embrasure. She didn't need to look to know who it was.

"You don't care for Honoria's tenor?" he murmured.

Not the opening she had expected, but she didn't let it throw her. "I have heard him before. And I can hear him from here. Or at least I could."

Somehow, she knew his lips twitched at this implied criticism. "I hope you will excuse my blundering interruption. I had not meant our reunion to be so public."

At that, a genuine breath of laughter escaped her, but at least she kept the bitterness from her eyes and her smile as she looked at him at last.

Oh yes, he could take one's breath away by his very presence. So unfamiliarly solid, so physical. And his intense, steady eyes offer-ing…what? Peace? Truce? A new beginning?

It didn't matter. This was not a battle that would be fought on his terms.

"Reunion, my lord?" she mocked. "For that, there would have had to be some kind of union in the first place."

She turned from the window, inclining her head as if to a stranger—which he was. "You will excuse me while I renew my appreciation of Honoria's tenor."

"I remember a union," he said softly as she began to walk away. "It was very sweet."

There was no doubt what union he meant, the very physical one that had been their last encounter two years ago. She was annoyed that it stayed her step, if only for an instant before she walked on.

"You are mistaken. That was not a union. Not in any sense that matters." She kept her voice light, amused, and didn't turn back. She didn't really expect him to follow her after such a sally, yet she could not help a spurt of disappointment. The old Oliver would not have left it there.

She slipped into the main salon, smiling and nodding in response to those acquaintances she encountered in her search for Mr. Curtis. Somehow, he had found two chairs for them to the side and a little behind the tenor, who was now singing his heart out in an operatic aria.

Mr. Curtis's eyes lit up with flattering and half-surprised pleasure as she took the place beside him.

For several minutes after that, she ignored her sense of being watched. But it was not Wenning's gaze that bored into her. It was Honoria's. And that of her sister, Lady Barnton. They were gazing at her with the avidity of scientists examining a specimen for signs of reaction. She ignored them, and exchanged smiles with Mr. Curtis.

She did not see her husband reenter the main salon. But when the tenor had finished his performance, she caught sight of him near the passage door with Sir Ernest and Lord Barnton.

"I believe there is a buffet supper served through here," Mr. Curtis said, indicating the third salon she had not yet investigated. "May I help you to a morsel?"

"Why not?" Grace said with a smile. Sir Nash Boothe was approaching, and she had no desire to speak to him.

Mr. Curtis was most attentive, choosing for her from the array of elegant dishes, but it was Grace who chose their seats by sitting down beside Bridget on one of two facing sofas. Mr. Curtis took the other beside Bridget's escort.

"Well?" Bridget murmured. "How has it been? Have you spoken?"

"Barely. I did not see him until I came here."

"You can't avoid it, Grace," Bridget warned.

"Well, that's the thing, Biddy," Grace said. "I am in the best possible position to do exactly as I like."

"And if he claps you up in the country like an errant wife?"

"I like the country," she drawled.

Although she never let herself look for him, she was aware more than once during the evening of his gaze upon her. Once as she listened to the recitation of a Shakespearean sonnet, that for some reason reminded her of the note clasped into the returned bracelet. Once when she was the center of an admiring group that included Mr. Curtis, Sir Nash Boothe, and Phineas Harlaw, who had appeared halfway through the evening. And once when she made her thanks and farewells to Honoria.

"Thank you, Honoria," she said civilly. "Such a lovely evening, with beautiful music and fine poetry."

"You are leaving so soon?" Honoria said, clearly affronted, with a darting glance at her brother, who lounged over the back of a sofa talking with a group of old friends. His gaze drifted up toward them, then back to his companions.

"Well, it is nearly midnight," Grace pointed out, "and I promised Lady Brocklehurst I would look in on her ball."

"Perhaps Wenning will escort you," Honoria suggested.

"I would not disturb his pleasant reunion. And I have two escorts." She did, for Bridget and her husband and Mr. Curtis left with her.

⟫⟫⟫⟪⟪⟪

IT WAS AFTER three o'clock in the morning before she reentered Wenning House and sent the sleepy porter to bed. In many ways, the ball had been as much torture as Honoria's soiree. For she hadn't truly wanted to be there, despite throwing herself into the event with almost hectic good spirits. She had danced every dance left, including a waltz with the faithful Mr. Curtis. And a more reckless one with Sir Nash Boothe, who had appeared just at the end.

"So, your husband is home," he had said intensely, staring down at her. "That is why you made such a fuss about the wretched bracelet, why you now try to hold me at arm's length."

She had held his gaze but said nothing. He could make of that what he wished.

But an eager warmth had entered his eyes. "My dear," he had said softly, "have you not yet realized that eluding the husband is half the charm?"

At the time, it had seemed exquisitely funny, largely because eluding her husband had not been exactly challenging over the last two years.

Sir Nash had looked encouraged. But it was Bridget's carriage that had brought her home.

And now, exhausted, she wanted to sleep for a week. She took a candle from the table at the foot of the stairs, lit it from the covered wall sconce, and made her weary way upstairs.

On the first-floor landing, she almost dropped her candle when the flame flickered over a man standing in the drawing room doorway.

Oliver, without his coat and cravat, his waistcoat unbuttoned. He held a brandy glass in one hand. A picture of handsome, elegant decadence that made her mouth dry and her stomach tingle.

"I disagree," he said.

"About what?" she managed.

"Union. As I recall, we both enjoyed it very much."

She laughed, being too tired for subtlety. "Oh, *that?* There is a very different word for *that.*"

He moved aside, waving her into the almost dark drawing room. "Come in, explain it to me over a nightcap."

A surge of panic took her by surprise. Even worse was the insidious temptation. *Thank God for anger.*

"I should not have to explain it," she snapped. "Not to my husband, though you have never been that. Ask a friend or someone else who might care. Good night, my lord." She carried on up the stairs, trying to enjoy her fierce satisfaction in his silence.

To be on the safe side, she locked the bedchamber door after Henley departed. Not that she expected an assault, but men could behave badly when their pride was attacked. And by law, she was still his wife.

CHAPTER SIX

"PHINEAS," WENNING GREETED his cousin who strolled into the breakfast parlor the following morning. "You're abroad early."

"Always, dear boy. I'm a martyr to insomnia."

"Well, help yourself." Wenning waved his fork toward the dishes on the sideboard. "There's a mountain here for a mere two people."

"Oh, her ladyship won't come down to breakfast," Phineas informed him. "She always has a tray in her room."

Wenning paused, then carried on eating. "How odd that you know my wife's habits better than I."

"Not so odd since you never lingered to find them out."

"Touché. I have to thank you for keeping an eye on her."

Phineas brought a heaped plate to the table and sat down. Wenning poured him a cup of coffee.

"I have always been available to escort her to parties or advise on the latest fashions, to warn about the more dangerous rakes and cover for her would-be scandals. She is, as you'll have gathered, something of a dazzling social butterfly, but there is no vice in her. It is all a hectic, if an innocent pursuit of entertainment. And she has, of course, a huge circle of admirers who outdo each other in their efforts to escort her, amuse her, and win her favor. Honoria and Patience will have it she is not so innocent, but I have seen no evidence of guilt."

"Nor has Leyton."

"Ah. Well, Leyton is pretty much at her feet, too, if you must know. Nothing remotely improper, of course. It is Leyton, after all! But she is quite enchanting, and he is only human."

"You misunderstand. I asked Leyton to look out for her, too."

"What, even to Maida Gardens?"

Wenning's gaze flew to his face. "Maida?"

Phineas sighed. "She was seen there on Tuesday evening. Nothing to worry you. She went with Rollo Darblay's escort and returned with him, too. Not who I'd choose to protect a lady's honor under most circumstances, but there, he is her brother! *But*, curiously enough, Leyton was also there."

Wenning searched his face. "Were you?"

"Well, no, but I heard from a friend. She is not quite as discreet as she imagines." Phineas smiled tolerantly. "I doubt she is quite as sophisticated as she thinks, either. The Maida fling is a one-off, I'm sure."

Phineas drank his coffee, then returned to his ham and sausages. "Incidentally," he added. "Young Curtis's Christian name is Anthony."

Anthony. The name still had the power to fill Wenning with rage. But last night's serious young sprig with the devoted eyes did not fit his image of the mysterious first love who had seduced his wife and retained her affections. For one thing, Curtis could not be more than four and twenty summers now, which would have made him a mere two and twenty when Grace married.

Two and twenty. Three years older than Grace at the time.

Wenning himself had been only six and twenty. And behaved as though he had been ten years younger. Sheer hurt had driven him from her. And perhaps, the sop to his pride of ambition. But no matter that he had been allowed to accompany the embassy to China, after all, no matter what success had been attributed to him, he had not done right by his wife.

Leaving her as he had was an all but public insult. Perhaps justified by her dishonesty and infidelity. But he could not be proud that he had left a girl of nineteen years old to fend for herself amongst the avid gossip, the hostility of his family, and the unfamiliarity of her position as Countess of Wenning.

He had read his steward's reports, as well as the letters of his friend and his cousin. He knew she had found her feet and run his estate with good sense and hard work—all the more remarkable considering her father's poor example in this regard. She had Wenning's people *and* the ton at her feet, and she had done it all without him.

Because he had behaved like a spoilt little boy rather than the earl, the husband he was supposed to be.

I could at least have talked to her. That so-often-repeated knowledge had been with him since before he had been two days out at sea. But by then, he could not turn back. He could not disembark and scamper home to her. He did not deserve to be taken seriously by either the government or his wife unless he proved himself now. And so he had, and imagined that when he came home, they could talk about everything, including *Anthony.*

But as he had grown up, so had she. She wasn't even displeased to see him, except in so far, apparently, as he might interfere with the life she had made without him. He had become…irrelevant.

As both his sisters had been at pains to tell him yesterday before the ball. *"She is positively fast, Oliver, as hedonistic as her father and even her unspeakable brother. She drags our family name through the dirt and is perfectly blatant about her lovers, even if Phineas insists they are mere admirers…"*

Success in China had come at the expense of his marriage, and he had no one but himself to blame.

"So, what will you be doing with your day?" Phineas inquired genially. "Official business? Or relaxing with your countess, perhaps?"

"The beauty of my extended leave of absence," Wenning said, "is that I need make no plans at all. What of you, Phin?"

"Oh, a long appointment with my tailor and perhaps an afternoon nap at my club. I am, you perceive, as busy as ever."

Wenning regarded him with affectionate amusement. "You make a very good pretense of the idle man-about-town."

"What makes you think it is pretense?"

"You have gone out of your way to help me," Wenning said quietly. "To do what was my duty, not yours. I shall not forget that."

Phineas smiled. "Then I'll send you my tailor's bill."

"Please, no! Even I am not that wealthy."

Phineas laughed and rose from the table. "You are right, as always. A man's account with his tailor should remain sacred. I hope I will see you tonight at the Plumfields'? I believe Grace is going."

"I have no plans as yet."

"Well, I imagine it will be a dull affair. Enjoy your peace, Ollie! My tailor calls."

Only his tailor, Wenning reflected with some amusement, could have got Phineas out of bed before midday, despite his claims of insomnia.

Thoughtfully, Wenning finished his coffee, then rose and strolled upstairs to his wife's sitting room.

He was her husband. He owed her no warning knock. But he gave her one anyway before entering immediately.

Yes, this was the Grace he remembered. While the rest of Wenning House was kept immaculately tidy, with everything more or less as it had been when he left—apart from a little tasteful redecoration—she had made this room her own. Comfortable old furniture. Bookshelves. An elegant vase of roses, another of lowlier flowers. A book lay open on the chair by the fireplace. A clutter of miniature portraits on the table beneath one window. A harp stood by the other, with sheets of music littered around it.

He had forgotten she played the harp. And yet, that was what she had been doing when he had first laid eyes on her. It hadn't been so much her beauty that had captivated him in that initial moment. It had been the intense focus she had brought to bear on the music, not on her surroundings, her audience, or the potential for catching a husband on the marriage mart.

A swishing sound from the inner door to the bedchamber drew him from his reverie to the present. His wife, dressed to go out in a very fetching walking gown and matching spencer, with a pretty hat whose feather curled over her face, swept into the room and stopped dead at the sight of him.

At last, it seemed, he had taken her by surprise. Startlement and then wariness flickered across her once so expressive face before the veils came down.

"My lord," she drawled. "What a pleasant surprise. To what do I owe the honor?"

"You are going out," he observed. "I shall escort you and explain at the same time."

She was not even tempted. "That will not suit. My sister awaits me downstairs. We are browsing bookshops and museums." She bit her lip as though she resented telling him even where she was going.

"And I should be de trop," he said gravely. "I understand. In that case, allow me to ask now, have you planned to hold any parties here for the rest of the Season?"

"I had sent out invitations to a ball next week, but I mean to cancel it."

"Why?"

She shrugged. "I thought I might go down to Harcourt instead. And then I thought you would probably prefer the peace."

"How thoughtful. But on the contrary, I believe a ball would be quite appropriate. Do you have a theme in mind?"

"No. As I told you, I lost interest in the scheme."

"Then might I suggest a masked ball? Perhaps that will revive your flagging enthusiasm. Masquerades were, I'm told, all the rage at the Congress of Vienna. Give my regards to Hope." He bowed and left her without waiting for her opinion.

He spent the next couple of hours catching up with estate business, then rewarded himself with a walk to White's, where he had engaged to meet Leyton and a few other friends for a light luncheon.

To his surprise, the first person he met in the coffee room was Lord Darblay. Grace's father was an amiable hedonist. One knew all his faults but couldn't help liking him. So when he encountered Darblay's glare from the wing chair by the door, he smiled involuntarily, changed direction, and thrust out his hand.

Darblay did not smile back. At least he reached up and took Wenning's hand for the briefest of instants before he said. "Sit, if you can spare me a moment."

"Always." Wenning took the chair nearest the viscount's. The only other members present were on the other side of the room, and it crossed his mind that his supposedly irresponsible father-in-law had arranged it that way. Wenning was, he saw, in for a verbal battering.

"Do I have to explain how you disappointed me?" Darblay asked abruptly.

"No, sir. I behaved ill."

The quick admission seemed to disconcert Darblay, who blinked and scowled. "You did. You insulted my daughter, and therefore her family, to pursue the glory of your career. I never thought you dishonest, Wenning, but you proved me wrong."

Wenning felt a flush rise to his face, but he had always known how his actions would appear. "I never intended dishonesty. I married in good faith. The decision to go to China after all was a sudden one."

"With no thought for the consequences to anyone else. Do you know what your abandonment did to my daughter?"

"No. That is my shame and our business to resolve. But I am glad to find her thriving."

"No thanks to you. Do you have any idea of the courage it must have taken to walk into Society when she should have been on her wedding trip? But she would not skulk in the country with us beyond two weeks because *you* had made her look like a guilty wife. She braved it all with a smile and a joke, made herself the rage, and then set about keeping your estates running smoothly."

She was *a guilty wife!* He would never speak the words to anyone, least of all to her father. In any case, they were an excuse, not a justification. Whatever she had done, what *he* had done was unforgivable. If he had not been so deeply in love, in pain, he would have been able to think more clearly and found a way to give the gossips less fodder.

"I owe her a great deal," he said steadily.

"You do." Darblay sat forward. "And if you ever hurt my daughter like that again, I promise I will come and thrash you myself. Tears of temper or hurt pride or even grief, I can deal with—ignore, if I'm honest, for they're natural. But tears of such *anguish*? No, never again. I will not tolerate that. Do we understand each other, Wenning?"

Wenning found his fingers dug into the arm of his chair and forced them to relax. His face felt suddenly cold, as though the blood had drained away to his feet.

"No," he said slowly. "I'm not sure we do. You are telling me I hurt more than her pride?"

Darblay stared at him as though he were an imbecile. "What do you think? She *loved* you. Foolish chit imagined you loved her. Apparently, you told her so. Do you know what, Wenning? I think it would be best if you stayed away from her. You have an heir. You don't need another."

Wenning's heart beat hard against his ribs. Guilt and hope and loss swirled around him, disorienting him, pulling him from his last anchor.

With an effort, he tried to hold himself in place. "Sir, are you aware of any friend of Grace's called Anthony?"

Darblay blinked. "Anthony? No, I don't know any Anthony, except my cousin's son, who's twelve. Who do you mean?"

Wenning shook his head slowly. "I don't know. I've never known."

Grace's father gave a grunt of disgust, then rose and stalked away, leaving Wenning gazing into the empty fireplace.

It was there Leyton found him five minutes later. "Wenning? What are you doing in here? We're all waiting in the dining room."

Almost surprised to see him, Wenning shook his head and stood. "Sorry. I was miles away."

"Is everything well?" Leyton asked uneasily.

"No, I don't know that it is," Wenning replied. "I think I might have made an even bigger mistake than I was aware." He smiled quickly and slapped his friend on the back. "But who knows? Maybe I can sort that out, too."

⊱⊰

AFTER AN ENTERTAINING few hours with her sister—hours blessedly free of anyone associated with the fashionable world—Grace allowed herself to be inveigled into Gunther's for an ice.

Only then did Hope ask the awkward question. "Are you glad he is home?"

Hope had been there when she had flown from the south coast to Darblay Hall two years ago. Grace could not deny she had ever cared. So she said lightly, "I scarcely know. I have hardly seen him."

"Do you want to?"

Grace shrugged. "No, not really." *I want him to see me.* "To be honest, I don't even want to talk about him." She dipped her spoon into Hope's ice, and her sister did the same to hers, thus averting any further difficult talk.

After that, she returned Hope to their parents and went home to Wenning House to change in time for the fashionable promenade in the park.

She drove herself, as she liked to, in her smart phaeton, pulled by matching chestnuts. She wanted to be seen not changing her habits in the slightest, by her husband as well as by the ton. Since she had honored Mr. Curtis with her favor yesterday evening, she merely smiled at him, pausing for the briefest instant to exchange a few words before letting the chestnuts move on. She chose the slightly more rakish Lord Effers to climb up beside her for a circuit. Since he was a friend of Rollo's, and she had known him forever, she trusted him to keep the line of what was pleasing. He was, besides, an amusing gossip.

She was rewarded five minutes later when, laughing quite naturally at one of Effers's sallies, she caught sight of her husband sauntering along the grass beside her.

"My lord," she greeted him carelessly, pausing the horses once more.

He took off his hat and bowed. His movements were always graceful, and she was glad he had to look up at her for once. He did not appear to mind. "What a very smart equipage. And such skilled driving."

"Oh, the chestnuts know their own way," she said modestly. "I'd offer you a turn about the park, but I have only just taken up Lord Effers here. Sir, my husband, the Earl of Wenning."

Effers looked somewhat uneasy, although Wenning stretched up a lazy hand to shake.

"How do you do?" Wenning said affably before turning back to his wife. "Phineas tells me you are promised to Lady Plumfield tonight."

Drat Phineas and his big mouth. She had quite other plans for tonight, and she didn't want Wenning turning up at Lady Plumfield's and seeing she wasn't there. Not that she had any intention of altering her social calendar to please him, but a Maida Gardens masked ball might well be grounds for even the most casual husband to put his foot down.

More than that, she wondered again if his mention this morning of holding a masked ball had any reference to her previous visit to Maida. Leyton could easily have recognized her and told him. Or either of Rollo's friends could have blabbed.

She managed to keep the polite smile on her lips. "Do you go to Lady Plumfield's also?"

"Alas, I have made other plans."

Thank God. "Then enjoy your evening, my lord. Forgive me if I move on. The horses are restive."

He smiled but was already turning away to greet another lady. In fact, as Grace glanced over her shoulder, she saw him take this woman's hand and kiss her cheek. She even recognized her.

Mrs. Fitzwalter. Once, more than two years ago, she had been the beautiful Miss Irwin, and the betting money had been on her marrying the Earl of Wenning before the end of the Season. She hadn't. Wenning had married Grace instead.

Why? she wondered for the millionth time. Miss Irwin had been more beautiful and bettered dowered. She would have made an excellent countess, a much more conventional and yet sophisticated one than Grace. But he had chosen the next-to-penniless daughter of an expensive and almost bankrupt viscount. Only to abandon her before they had been married a full day.

It made no sense. Her original view of the earl made no sense. She had a more accurate opinion, now, and the fickle, faithless being that he truly was would pay for the anguish he had inflicted.

The trouble was, none of her cavaliers seemed to worry him. She needed someone more...substantial. More constant.

CHAPTER SEVEN

"So," BRIDGET'S HUSBAND said on the journey, "we're going to Maida Gardens, dressed up like figures of fun in domino cloaks and masks, so that Lady Wenning can say thank you to a stranger who found and returned a bracelet, which she managed to lose on her previous visit to the gardens?"

"More or less," Grace answered. She tried a winning smile. "And I'm very grateful to you and Bridget for coming with me."

"You are welcome," Lord Arpington said politely. Although not a particularly handsome man, he was both kind and humorous, and Grace liked him a great deal. "Providing you don't lose anything else that compels me to wear such garments again."

"I'm afraid I must ask you to do worse," Grace said. "Wenning has taken it into his head that our party must be a masked ball, so I thought it would be much more fun if we also dress up as historical figures."

Bridget giggled.

Her husband said, "You are torturing me."

"Nonsense. You would make a splendid Sir Walter Raleigh, would he not, Grace?"

"And you could be Queen Elizabeth," Grace told her friend with enthusiasm.

"Then who would you be?"

"I had this idea of being Mary, Queen of Scots, with a cloak buttoned right over my head and carrying a head-shaped object under my arm."

It won an involuntary laugh from Lord Arpington, who said, "I am almost resigned to coming if I can see that."

"Good man," Grace said encouragingly. "And this is Maida Gardens. Masks, my friends!"

Lord Arpington instructed the carriage to return at a quarter before midnight, and, with a lady on either arm, walked up the lantern-lit path that had become familiar to Grace. She was glad, for the sake of her companions, not to hear too many giggling noises coming from the undergrowth tonight, although a vulgarly loud party led by a matron in puce with a squealing laugh, did cause Lord Arpington's aristocratic lip to curl.

"I begin to wish I told the coachman just to wait," he murmured. "Half an hour is more than time to thank your friend."

"But not time enough for you to dance with us both," Bridget pointed out.

"I can't dance with either of you," Arpington said grimly, bowing them into the pavilion. "If I did, it would leave the other unprotected."

Bridget frowned. "Drat, I never thought of that. We should have brought another gentleman. Perhaps your brother will be here, Grace."

"If he is, I doubt he'll be glad to see me," Grace said. "I'm sure I cramped his style enough the last time. Where shall we sit?"

Lord Arpington led them to a discreet table in the corner, and while they settled and he ordered wine, Grace scoured the ballroom for a figure lounging against a pillar. Her own eagerness surprised her, as did the realization of butterflies in her stomach. He intrigued her too much, this foreign stranger who had somehow found her lost bracelet and promised to show her something. *And* quoted mysterious poetry.

Most of her cavaliers quoted poetry to her. One even penned it himself and delivered it in a scroll tied with a rose. Such admiration had once been balm to her wounded pride. Now, it was an accessory to fashion, like a matching reticule or a head dress. And at least some of those admirers regarded her the same way. It was fashionable to be at the Countess of Wenning's feet, and so they were.

No wonder Wenning did not take them seriously. She needed a lover of standing, a man different enough and handsome enough to intrigue her. A man with just a hint of danger, of risk, distant, perhaps, from the world of the ton, who would not care about creating scandal. A genuine threat to her heart and Wenning's complacency. A believable lover that might easily sweep her off her feet.

Her gaze stopped at a pillar opposite the main door. A tall man in an unusual black and silver domino with matching mask stood there, not quite dallying with a daringly dressed lady in yellow.

Her heart gave a funny little lurch.

He would be perfect.

Only how could Wenning get to know about him? Her breath caught, and she laughed aloud.

"You're right, of course," Bridget agreed, clearly following the direction of her gaze. "That jonquil is hideous."

"But the man with her is the one who found my bracelet."

"It seems he will be finding someone else's this evening," Bridget observed, just as the stranger smiled, stepped back, and bowed to the lady in yellow before walking away. Straight toward Grace's table.

So he had seen her entrance. He must have been waiting for her. Exciting thought...

Nonsense. He had asked her to come, after all, and he could not have known she would not be alone. Did that bother him?

It didn't seem to. He bowed to Grace, the fascinating half-smile she remembered playing on his lips beneath the line of the mask. "Madam."

She inclined her head. "Sir." She turned to her friends. "This is the kind gentleman who retrieved my bracelet. Sir, these are my good friends."

He bowed again, and it struck her that there was something different about him tonight. In fact, her stomach clenched with the sudden suspicion that it was not even the same man, and she had just blurted out that she had lost her bracelet here. Did it matter? Hadn't she just decided that she wanted news of her visits to Maida to reach her husband?

But, no, even here in one of the dimmer corners of the ballroom, she could see he was the same height and build she remembered. He had the same smile, and when he murmured greetings to the Arpingtons, he had the same soft, low voice with its slightly foreign inflection.

It was his hair, she realized with relief. He had cut his hair into a fashionably short style.

"Join us in a glass of wine," Arpington invited, in something of the same tones a father might use toward a suitor he doubted was an acceptable son-in-law.

"Gladly, at another time." His eyes strayed back to Grace. "I was hoping Madame would dance with me."

Grace blinked. "It is the middle of a dance."

He smiled. "Are there rules governing such in your world? There are none here."

"Except manners," Arpington muttered below his breath.

Hastily, Grace stood. It was why she had come here, after all. "Take the opportunity," she advised her friends. "Dance. I won't tell."

"Why would they care?" the stranger asked, leading her onto the dance floor.

"Because it is not fashionable to dance with a mere husband."

His smile flickered, and he turned, taking her gracefully into his hold. Butterflies gamboled in her stomach. She supposed he would not be such a perfect solution if there was not some danger to her heart.

"Is that your wife?" she asked hurriedly. "The lady in yellow?"

"No. Let us not talk of wives or husbands, just of you."

"That will be dull, but what do you want to know?"

He danced with more...*verve* than the English, spinning her among the other dancers with skill, elegance, and a sheer enjoyment that was catching.

"Everything," he replied. "Your favorite color, your first memory, your ambition."

"It depends on my mood, but often red. Waddling about with a large, hairy dog in a field and him licking my nose when I fell over. And I don't think I'm going to tell you my ambition just yet. What are yours?"

"Black and silver, clearly. Being thrashed for something I didn't do. And I won't tell you mine yet, either. Your turn."

"Where did you learn to waltz?"

"In a room full of other boys all laughing and falling over each other. And dancing with each other."

She laughed, enjoying the comical image.

"And you?" he prompted.

"Merely in my own home with a dancing master. I told you my life was dull. What is your name?"

His eyes searched hers, unblinking. "Rudolf. What is yours?"

She hesitated, but it was a common enough name, and in any case, he would need to know if she carried out her plan. "Grace."

He smiled. "It suits you perfectly. My turn. Who do you love most in the world?"

Her answering smile died on her lips.

"It was not meant to be a sad question," he said gently.

"Oh, it isn't," she assured him. From the corner of her eye, she saw that Bridget and her husband were indeed dancing. "Once there would have been an easy answer. Now I can only say I love my family.

Perhaps my little sister the most since she, at least, needs me a little. What of you?"

He shrugged without losing his grace or the rhythm of the waltz. "Like you, I no longer have a simple answer. Once, it was my wife. Perhaps it still is."

"And yet here you are dancing—and flirting—with me. To say nothing of the lady in yellow."

"I neither danced nor flirted with the lady in yellow. Though she might have flirted with me."

"Do you have children?"

"No, but you have asked me that before, and it isn't your turn."

"I made it so because your questions are too difficult. Would you do something for me?"

"Anything."

Startled by the promptness of his answer, she didn't know whether or not to take him seriously. The ballroom was not so well lit as those she was used to, and his eyes seemed an odd amber color, at once seductive and wicked.

"Would *you* do something for *me*?" he asked softly.

For no good reason, her heart plunged into her stomach, causing chaos inside her. She swallowed. "If I can. I owe you a debt."

"No debts between us," he said swiftly, as, maddeningly, the music came to an end. He released her and bowed. "Walk with me."

She curtseyed. "Now?"

"It's as good a time as any while everyone is milling about."

"My friends will miss me."

"You won't be long. I promise not to ravish you in the moonlight. Unless you would like me to."

She ignored that, although she took his offered arm somewhat warily. "Are you going to show me what you talked of in your note?"

His lips—well-shaped, firm lips, as mysterious and as attractive as the rest of him—quirked. "Yes."

"Five minutes?"

"Less if you wish."

Reassured, she allowed him to lead her through the throng and out one of the side doors into a sweet-smelling garden. Honeysuckle and something light that might have been hyacinth. Another couple was coming toward them, and he steered Grace around a quieter path beneath a chestnut tree.

"I never thanked you for the bracelet," she said abruptly.

"There is no need."

"Why not? Because you took it in the first place?"

She caught the white flash of his teeth in the darkness. "Yes."

"Why did you take it?" she asked curiously.

"So that I could see you again."

"Hmm." She didn't know whether or not to believe him, let alone trust him. All her trust was limited these days, in any case. "I ask because I could pay you for what I would like you to do. If you are short—"

"Let there be nothing as sordid as money between us. What is it you need of me?"

"Something a little like this." She waved her hand toward the masked couple and the pavilion. "I would like you to attend a masked ball."

"With you?"

"No, though I will be there. And I'm afraid I cannot invite your wife because I would like you to be as mysterious and charming there as you are here. I would like you to flirt with me and perhaps be discovered alone with me, if I can arrange it correctly."

His face turned toward her, but they had paused under the tree, and the branches blocked the lantern light. She could not see his expression.

"Why?" he asked. "Am I to make someone jealous?"

Her smile was lopsided, though he probably could not see that either. "Sadly, such an outcome is doomed to failure. But a little humiliation, a little rumor of cuckolding would suit me well enough."

"Then we are going after your husband? He humiliated *you* once, perhaps?"

Humiliation was only the beginning of what he had done to her, but she would not admit that to a stranger, let alone one she wished to use against him.

"Does he deserve it?" Rudolf asked lightly.

"Oh, and more," she said cordially. "Will you do it?"

He appeared to think about it. "Very well. I'll do it on one condition."

"What?"

He smiled. "A kiss."

She had certainly walked into that one. They stood alone beneath the tree, and as he leaned closer, a breeze disturbed the leaves, and light flickered over his masked face.

A kiss. Where would be the harm in a kiss? With a stranger who looked and moved and spoke as he did, reminding her she was a woman, a wife who had known only a taste of passion.

How does he kiss? How would it feel?

His head dipped, and her breath caught. She moved back the way they had come. "No. I do not bargain with kisses."

"Of course, you do not, and I am a scoundrel to ask." He walked beside her, his stride easy and unhurried as before. "Now you know the worst of me, and I'll do your bidding without the kiss and hope only for a smile."

"You are teasing me," she said severely.

"I am. And my five minutes is up. But I still mean it. Dance with me again?"

"Now?"

"Why not? Your friends will see you on the dance floor."

That was true enough and would give Bridget another dance with her husband, whom she loved.

"What is your favorite fruit?" he asked as they reentered the pavil-ion, and she laughed at the resumption of the silly game.

"Raspberries. What is yours?"

"Peaches. Where were you born?"

"Here in London. Where were you?"

"I don't actually know. No one ever told me."

"Then where were you educated?"

He swept her into the dance once more, and the warm tingles in her stomach intensified and spread. She had done the right thing, but somehow, she regretted the loss of his kiss. Now, she would always wonder.

"In the best and most expensive school in my country," he replied. "Where were *you* educated?"

"At home, of course, with a governess."

"Was she old and fierce and disapproving?"

"No, she was fluttery and kind and well-read and worth ten of the wealthy people who abused her before she came to us. She teaches my sister still." Which was too much information. "What is your favorite animal?"

"My horse. Yours?"

"The dog who licked my nose as a child."

The questions went on with the dance, increasingly light and amusing. She had a feeling the answers he gave were honest, because occasionally, like her, he refused to answer, presumably because he would not lie. It didn't seem to matter. He intrigued her and made her laugh, and the dance flew past too quickly. Though he never held her too close, she had never been so aware of a waltz partner, every casual brush of his fingers on her hand, her waist, every movement of his body, guiding hers, so close and yet never touching.

"And now," he said reluctantly, "I return you to your friends. Or will you join me for supper?"

"I shall return to my friends," she said firmly, placing her finger in the crook of his arm. A thought struck. "Drat, what was it you meant to show me?"

"My haircut," he said in apparent surprise.

"I'm not sure I believe that."

He only smiled, bowed to Bridget, and wandered off.

CHAPTER EIGHT

"**H**OW LONG IS it until midnight?" Lord Arpington grumbled. "I'm starving."

"I believe supper is included in the price of the ticket," Grace said. "We can go and look for it if you like?"

"Why not?" Bridget said. "That fellow in blue keeps looking at me. I'm sure he means to ask me to dance."

"Then I'll punch him in the nose," her husband said staunchly.

"Definitely supper time," Grace murmured.

In the end, they found a buffet supper in a large room upstairs. It had probably been quite magnificent at the beginning of the evening, but a plague of locusts had clearly visited since then, and the remaining choices were not wide. Nevertheless, the three of them helped themselves and each other to a few morsels, the ladies piling things willy-nilly onto Arpington's plate while he courteously searched for the tastiest bites for them.

They found an empty table by the window, and Arpington went off to find wine to drink with it.

"What are you up to, Grace?" Bridget murmured as soon as he was out of earshot. "I know you went off alone with the bracelet man."

"Nothing happened," Grace assured her. And God help her, she was still sorry. It might have been her last chance of a kiss. A proper lover's kiss such as she had only known with Oliver a long, long time ago. Besotted and naive, she had imagined these kisses betokened his love as well as hers. And though she had swiftly learned better, the memory of those kisses could still melt her bones. *Physical reaction, physical desire...*

There was a special cruelty in one night, one taste, and then total celibacy.

"But you would have liked it to," Bridget said shrewdly. "Oh, Grace, why now? Why wait until *he* is home? You have had two years to succumb to the charms of handsome men."

"I shan't succumb," Grace said, amused. "It isn't what you think."

"I'm not sure yet *what* I think. Who is he?"

"I don't know. His name is Rudolf, and he is not English. But I believe he is a gentleman." *A gentleman who steals jewelry? And gives it back...*

"Does he know who you are?"

"Of course not." *Not yet.* But when she told him where to come for her masquerade ball, he would guess. And when he was there, he would know. And then she would send him back to his wife. And he, being a gentleman, would go.

But stupidly, dangerously, she already felt the loss of excitement he had brought her. Bridget was right. In the two years of Oliver's absence, she could have pursued any number of discreet affairs. She had never been tempted. She wouldn't be tempted now if she didn't have a plan of petty revenge.

Wouldn't I?

There was something about Rudolf, her masked stranger. The way he looked, the way he moved. An honest thief, an opportunist, a manipulator. But one who had let her go when he could have easily have stolen the kiss he wanted. And more. And yet, she had felt in no danger. Not from him. From her own weakness, yes. From the loneliness of her own future.

What would she do after she had punished her husband? Live with his wrath? Apart from his wrath, more likely. He did not need an heir.

Phineas was his heir, and Phineas had brothers if there were no heirs of *his* body.

Bridget's fingers closed over her wrist. "Come back to me, Grace. You've been odd and tense and different ever since we knew he was on his way home. In fact, ever since you came here the last time. Don't fall in love with this man or whoever you imagine him to be."

"I am no longer that foolish," Grace assured her. "But what a pity we can't all have a husband like yours."

"I second that," Lord Arpington said, sitting down with the wine. "You see, wife of my bosom? You are indeed a lucky woman."

If Grace had hoped to see Rudolf in the supper room, she was doomed to disappointment. She did glimpse him through the window in the garden, with a group of people to whom he appeared to be listening rather than talking.

It came to her gradually that she needed to speak to him again, to establish some means of easy communication, for she could not keep coming to Maida Gardens. For one thing, she had probably run out of tolerant friends to accompany her. Although the thought of coming alone, with no one to answer to, hide from, or look after—apart from Rudolf—was suddenly alluring.

Bridget was right. This man did present a danger. She had to draw back from that. An address to write to was what she needed. And then some distance from him and greater focus on her purpose. And then...

She would not think beyond that. She could not.

But as the huge wall clock crawled beyond half-past eleven, and they walked toward the ballroom exit, Grace glanced over her shoulder and saw the unmistakable figure of Rudolf moving toward the other door, the one that led into the scented garden.

He glanced back, and their eyes met, and then he walked on, vanishing through the door. Grace's breath caught. She made a decision.

"Go on ahead," she said to Bridget. "I'll either catch up with you on the path or by the gate."

"Grace—"

Ignoring her friend's inevitable warning, Grace darted back through the courting couples and prowling groups of masked males. She avoided two outstretched hands and pretended not to see several lascivious smiles. And then she was in the blessed fresh air of the garden.

Which was busier now. A couple flirted loudly on an ornate bench. A group of young women competed to be noticed in their perambulation while an opposing group of predatory men watched them. It was all rather unsavory, she thought with distaste. Although, perhaps, it was merely a more blatant version of what went on in society's ballrooms. There were marriage marts and intrigues everywhere.

A figure waited beneath the chestnut tree. She was sure it was Rudolf, and her heart thudded foolishly. She made haste toward him, praying that it *was* him, for she did not fancy her chances of fighting off amorous men in this place—not without violence, at any rate.

But as she drew closer, he moved, letting the lantern light find his masked face for an instant before he stepped back under the branches. It was enough. She quickened her step farther, and a moment later, his hands drew her into the welcoming darkness, close to him. He smelled of some exotic eastern soap that was almost familiar: lemon and cinnamon.

A taste of passion. She had known only a taste, and he was tall and strong and intriguing. His closeness aroused her unbearably. The darkness was her friend...

"Where can I reach you?" she demanded, hating the breathlessness of her voice. "To tell you about the service we discussed?"

"There is no need. Tell me where and when to come, and I will."

Then I will not see you again, not before and not after. The thought filled her mind, even as she murmured her address and the date of the ball. No love for her, no possibility of it. Only loneliness stretched in front of her. And she *yearned*.

"Grace," he whispered, his breath warm against her cheek. A hint of wine on his breath. And coffee. She could smell his skin, too— strong spices, a hint of earthiness and warm male. It did not seem so dark now, for she could see the glinting silver of his mask and the steady intensity of his eyes as he gazed down at her.

End this now. Walk away. But it seemed she didn't have the strength to do it twice in one evening. When his head lowered, she made no attempt to run. Her body seemed to be melting into a heap of desire, communicating only with his.

At the first touch of his lips, she gasped. At the first touch of his body against hers, his arms closing around her to hold her there, heat flamed through her.

But it was a gentle, tender kiss, caressing, achingly sensual. She had wanted it so much yet meant it to last only a moment. But everything in her leapt toward him. Her mouth parted for his, and for one glorious moment, she kissed him back, as sweet, hot desire seemed to fuse their bodies. He held her close with one hand at her back, the other at her nape. And she loved it all.

It was a moment. And it was wrong. It had always been wrong.

With a sob, she tore her mouth and her body free and fled.

⫸⫷

SHE WOKE THE following morning, her head buzzing with a very peculiar mixture of shame and happiness. She had known a very special kiss with a stranger, and she felt bold and desirable. And when all was said and done, it was only a kiss. Nothing to the infidelities of her husband. She told herself she had nothing to reproach herself with, and yet there was a lingering guilt. Because she had known it was coming and had let him. Had even kissed him back.

It was only flirting, only a kiss. But it was not truly fair on Rudolf, for she had no intention of beginning an affair with him. She liked him, and he deserved more than a woman's vengeance. He deserved his wife's love.

She had long ago given up dreaming of her husband's. But she had some pride, some personal standards, and she would keep to them.

No more Maida Gardens, she told herself severely as she reached for the coffee on her tray. Today, she would send amended invitations to her party, requesting all her guests to masquerade as historical figures, with an unmasking at midnight and a costume competition.

And then Oliver walked into her bedchamber. Her own sense of guilt made her angry as did his careless, handsome appearance. He had not even troubled to dress properly, sauntering in without coat or necktie, or even waistcoat.

"It's a little early, is it not?" she said waspishly. "Neither of us is dressed."

"I believe we are married. Even the highest sticklers for propriety could not complain. Besides, it's the only time I can be sure of finding you at home." He rubbed the back of his neck. "I got a crick talking to you yesterday in that impressive phaeton."

"I shall bear that in mind the next time we meet in the park."

"I'm sure you will." He lounged on the edge of her bed, and she wanted to swipe him off.

It was easier not to look at him, so she sipped her coffee instead.

"I came to ask for your company this evening," he said unexpectedly.

"I'm afraid I have engagements all week."

"I was sure you did, which is why I came especially to ask you to cry off or at least go late to whatever event you are promised to. We are invited to dinner at Fife House."

Grace set down her cup in its saucer. "The prime minister invited you?"

"Invited *us*."

"Then I suppose I must go. Is it something to do with your recent trip?"

"Lord Liverpool is pleased with the outcome."

"Then all must rejoice," she said flippantly.

"Except you?"

"I see no reason why you should think so."

"You have asked me nothing about it."

"You have asked me nothing about my admittedly much more trivial life, looking after your estates and your houses."

"That is true." He picked up her coffee cup and took a sip before offering it back. "Since my return, we have not exactly spent enough time in each other's company to ask anything."

She took the cup from him and placed it firmly in the saucer. Spoiling her gesture, Henley topped it up from the coffee pot and withdrew.

"We could do better, Grace," he said gently. "Spend the day with me, or at least a few hours. We can exchange news, big and small."

Once, she had dreamed of him returning and speaking such words, a precursor to his abject apology, perhaps some important reason for leaving her that she had never thought of. But she had long ago recognized that she could not trust such words. She could not be the devoted little wife, picked up and dropped at his careless whim.

"What a charming idea," she said, sipping the fresh coffee. "But I cannot alter my day plans as well." It was a Sunday, and her plans were few, but he could not know that, although he might guess.

"Of course, you cannot," he murmured. "Perhaps another day."

"Perhaps," she said carelessly. "Oh, I have decided on a historical masquerade for our party, just to make it more amusing."

"What an excellent idea. How will you decorate the ballroom?"

"I have not yet decided. As a medieval garden, perhaps, with a large mural of a castle on one wall. If Lord Tamar is still in town, I might engage his help with that."

"You must do as you see fit. I leave the matter in your capable hands."

"I shall endeavor not to disappoint. And I shall be ready to join you for dinner. For now, take yourself off, my lord. I need to dress."

He met her gaze as though wondering whether or not to resist her blatant dismissal. A faint smile curved his lips. Then, with perfect grace, he rose and strolled away. "Until this evening."

It came as something of a shock to realize he smiled a little like Rudolf, that from behind, he moved a little like him, too. Lowering to think that she was probably attracted to the stranger simply because of his physical similarities to her faithless husband.

※

WITH LITTLE EXPECTATION of being received by her parents at this hour, when she arrived at their somewhat crumbling townhouse, she took herself to the schoolroom, where both Hope and Miss Fenchurch, the governess, greeted her with enthusiasm. Since it was Sunday, they were not at lessons but indulging in separate pastimes in each other's company. Miss Fenchurch was reading. Hope was daubing discontentedly at an easel.

Hope was lonely. Her face lit up as Grace walked in, no doubt in partial relief to be distracted from the not-terribly-inspired watercolor she was working on. It was a view from the schoolroom but seemed largely gray, like the day's weather.

"Perhaps a splash of color?" Grace suggested. "There are flowers down there, after all."

Hope giggled and prepared to add the flowers.

Grace walked with Miss Fenchurch to her chair by the empty fireplace. "I have been meaning to pick your brains over a poem. I only have a couple of lines, and I can't think where they come from."

"I might know them, unless the poem is very new. Tell me."

From memory, Grace quoted the lines from Rudolf's note. Something else she had failed to ask him about.

"*Now if thou wouldst, when all have given him over,*
From death to life, thou mightst him yet recover."

Miss Fenchurch blinked rapidly. "Michael Drayton. *Since there's no help, come let us kiss and part.* A sad little poem about lost love. Drayton was a contemporary of Shakespeare, which might explain why he is so overlooked."

"Ah, thank you. I shall look it up at home."

In fact, since she was roped into attending church with her mother, partaking of luncheon afterward, and then taking a walk in the park with Hope, she had no time to read poetry until after she had dressed for dinner with the prime minister. She then went down to the library and raked among the poetry books until, in an old volume of Elizabethan sonnets, she found the poem she was looking for.

She read it through several times, trying to relate it to what she knew about Rudolf and about her relationship with him, which, when he had given her the note, had amounted to even less than it did now. A dance, a harmless flirtation, an attraction strong enough for him to engineer another meeting by stealing her bracelet. If she could believe him on that score. But there had been no time for such regrets as described in the poem. Or perhaps he meant her to be curious and discover the earlier lines, which showed only carelessness and bravado—kiss and part with no regrets.

But that made no sense either.

How could she prevent the death of love for a man she had only just met?

The answer, more worryingly, was that she *did* know him. That the first ball at Maida Gardens was not their first encounter. Had she simply failed to recognize him?

Could he be an admirer she had barely noticed? She was acquainted with a few foreign diplomats, some young or young-ish, and all very personable. And there were always informally visiting dignitaries, noblemen, and princes from overseas. Could one of them be her mysterious Rudolf? And could he have known all along that she was the Countess of Wenning?

"There you are."

At the sound of her husband's voice, she shut the book with a snap. At least she managed not to jump visibly.

"Are we ready to depart?" she asked, replacing the book on the shelf.

"If you are."

"Of course." She rose and looked at him for the first time since he had entered.

He had always been a handsome man, had always sent her heart and stomach into summersaults. She didn't know if he still did because she was too agitated about Rudolf's identity—and perhaps by her own guilt.

How odd, she thought irrelevantly, *that I should feel guilty about allowing another man to kiss me, while I don't feel the slightest guilt about pretending a much more intimate love affair with him.*

As her gaze flickered over her husband's perfect evening dress, from his cropped hair to his black silk knee-breeches, and back to the plain diamond pin winking in his elegantly arranged cravat, she realized he was doing much the same to her.

"Will I do?" she inquired, spreading her skirts in a mocking curtsey.

"Rather more than that. You will make me the envy of every gentleman present."

"Of course, that was my intention."

A frown flickered on his brow and vanished. "You are right. That was a stupid and even demeaning thing to say. I am supposed to be a seasoned diplomat, and yet before you, I am reduced to a babbling schoolboy. What I mean is, you are particularly beautiful in a distinctive and charming way, and your gown is perfect for the occasion."

"Much better," she approved, walking toward the door. "What is a wife for but to practice on?"

He held it for her politely. "You don't believe in my sincerity?"

"Don't worry. I shan't tell anyone."

That reduced him to silence as she sailed past him, downstairs and across the entrance hall, where a footman opened the front door and bowed them down the steps to the waiting carriage. Wenning handed her in and climbed after her.

Annoyingly, he did not sit beside her but opposite, which made looking at each other more necessary. Deliberately, she turned her gaze toward the window.

"I have much ground to make up, do I not?" he said. "May I begin with an apology?"

"Begin what?" she asked flatly.

"Understanding. Reconciliation."

Carefully, she drew her gaze away from the passing Mount Street houses and met his. "My lord, that ship sailed. To China, I believe. There is no more to say."

"And if I think there is?"

She yawned delicately behind her gloved hand. "I make no promises to stay awake."

He sat forward on his seat, a spark of *something*—annoyance or desperation?—in his otherwise carefully veiled expression. "The Grace I married would never refuse to listen, to discuss."

"The Grace you married had a lot of lessons to learn. Fortunately, I am a quick learner. There is no need to coddle me or make a pet of me. Let us merely acknowledge that we both made a horrendous mistake. And let us not add the indignity of shallow pretense with each other. I shall do my duty as I always have."

He sat back, the metaphorical veil well in place once more. "You would make a very cold marriage."

She smiled. "My lord, *you* made the marriage cold. Let us move on. Who will I see at this dinner?"

A moment's silence warned her he would not necessarily play her game. But the timing was on her side, and he replied, "Beyond Lord and Lady Liverpool, and the other members of our embassy and their wives, I cannot say."

"I like Lady Liverpool," Grace murmured. "Although she is a little serious for my tastes, she is very intelligent and compassionate."

"Indeed," Wenning agreed. If there was a shade of mockery in his response, she chose not to heed it.

CHAPTER NINE

T HE PRIME MINISTER and his wife resided in Fife House, a large, opulent dwelling in Whitehall, where the river smells were stronger, but didn't penetrate, fortunately to her ladyship's drawing room or dining room.

The dinner turned out to be a larger affair than Grace expected. Lord and Lady Castlereagh, the foreign secretary and his wife, were also present, along with Prince and Princess Esterhazy and several other foreign ambassadors and diplomats. Among the British guests, Grace was glad to see again the wives of the other special embassy members. Lady Spalding and Mrs. Campbell had been very kind to her when she had first come to London. Aware that in the first instance, they acted from pity for the abandoned bride, she had refused to live in their pockets thereafter. But she nevertheless counted each lady a friend.

A couple of other rising stars of the foreign office were also present. So, if nothing else, the size of the party prevented her from having to deal with her husband's disturbing presence. She could lose him easily and focus surreptitiously on the foreigners, searching for any who regarded her with more than civil interest, straining for the sound of a similar voice and accent to Rudolf's.

Of course, her masked stranger could be a much more minor functionary and not worthy of invitation to dinner with the prime minister, although he had not struck her as minor in any way. By the time she went into dinner on the arm of an Austrian diplomat, Count Grattenburg, she had realized she could not even place Rudolf's accent. His name sounded German or Austrian, though he did not speak like Count Grattenburg. He could have anglified it from Italian or Spanish, or Portuguese. But nobody she heard sounded quite like him.

She did try to pick Count Grattenburg's brains by saying, "I met someone from your embassy in the park the other day. Charming man. Now, what was his name? Rudolf something?"

"I cannot think of a Rudolf," Grattenburg said without interest.

Sadly, it was not a question she could ask again of anyone else, in case she was overheard. Instead, she turned to Mr. Campbell on her other side, who was clearly waiting for a moment to speak to her.

Campbell was not a handsome man, but he was attractive. Short and slight in build, he had laughing eyes, a quick smile, and a sort of restless charm. Grace warmed to him from the beginning, mostly because, unlike everyone else, he did not start the conversation by informing her how much she had missed her husband and how delighted she was to have him back.

"You cannot know how happy I am to meet you at last," he said.

"That is true," she replied, amused. "Nor can I imagine why."

"Because I just spent two years living in your husband's pocket and have been overwhelmed with curiosity to meet the lady who puts up with him."

She smiled serenely. "I've never had to. You have my sympathies, sir."

He grinned. "There were times when we all but came to blows, though fortunately before we had progressed beyond the shoving stage, we recalled that we were gentlemen and representatives of His Majesty. But—and you must not tell him this—I have been ever so slightly in awe of him since he dealt with those bandits."

Grace stilled, then covered the moment by reaching for her wine glass. "Bandits?"

The story Campbell told then, and the ones he entertained her with during dessert, were undoubtedly a distraction. A tangled knot of confusion formed in her stomach, insistent, disturbing. And she had no time to devote to this conundrum, beset as she was by the more urgent need to discover Rudolf's identity. And to that, she was no closer.

However, she thought, as she rose with the other ladies to follow Lady Liverpool from the room and leave the gentlemen to their wine and brandy, the evening was not yet over.

Once suitably refreshed and fortified by a short gossip with Mrs. Campbell and Lady Spalding, she left them discreetly as they began comparing marital reunions, and made her way with some relief to the drawing room.

She chose an empty sofa, which left a place for her next foreign victim. She had already discarded the middle-aged, the short, the plump, and the fair. Of course, there was likely to be a long wait before the gentlemen joined them—they would get into long political discussions...

"Why, Miss Darblay!" a female voice exclaimed jocularly. "I had quite forgotten you were the Countess of Wenning now!"

Mrs. Fitzwalter, formerly Miss Irwin, who had once fancied herself as Countess of Wenning, and was now married instead to a rising politician, a junior minister in the foreign office. And who had won a public kiss on the cheek from Wenning in the park yesterday. Which was more than Grace had achieved. Or wanted, she assured herself hastily.

"I suppose our paths have not much crossed recently," she said pleasantly.

"No indeed, your circles are much more fashionable than mine, which you would no doubt find merely worthy."

"I would hardly presume to judge your friends," Grace said.

"Funnily enough, my path crossed your husband's more frequently. He will have told you I shared his outward voyage as far as Lisbon when I went on my wedding trip. And then, what a coincidence to run into him in Paris on his return journey!"

"Coincidence indeed," Grace agreed, although she doubted it. The stab of hurt was angrier now. Phineas had told her, obliquely, of a woman Oliver had encountered early in the voyage who had, he said, provided a comforting ear. Loath as she was to imagine Mrs. Fitzwalter playing her husband false on their wedding trip, she also knew the woman was making some kind of point. Perhaps simply, *You got the peer, but at least I got a wedding trip.* Or perhaps, *I got your husband, too.*

She didn't care anymore. Really, she didn't. But he would know at least a taste of humiliation before she was done with him.

⇒⇒⇒⋘⋘⋘

MY GOD, SHE is lovely. The recognition hit the Earl of Wenning like a fresh blow as soon as he walked into the drawing room with Lord Castlereagh. Although she sat beside Maria Fitzwalter—a curious choice—her attention was on Spalding and on the Italian Prince di Ripoli.

She was naturally friendly, gave anyone who addressed her—apart from Wenning—her full attention. And she could hold her own in any conversation, as he had overheard at dinner, from bantering to politics and foreign affairs. She would make a perfect ambassador's wife.

Of course, he could not walk over and claim his own wife. He could not even stare at her all evening, or it would set tongues wagging afresh, and she deserved better. She had always deserved better.

He knew he was responsible for the hard shell she had grown. But he knew, too, that the open, passionate girl who had first enchanted him was still in there, beneath that surface charm and the thin veneer of sophistication.

No, he didn't deserve her. But he would still do his utmost to win her back. And those puppies, Grattenburg and di Ripoli, who seemed to fascinate her that evening, would not get near her.

"Thank you," he said sincerely in the carriage going home, "for making the evening so pleasant."

"It's what I do," she said lightly. "And why people invite me. *We'd better have Lady Wenning*, they say, realizing too late that they have invited a horrendous mix of people who will never get on. *She might not make the party a raging success, but at least she will make it bearable.*"

"I think you underestimate your talents. You would make a wonderful diplomat."

"Like Princess Esterhazy? I am not so forceful."

He smiled. "I think you are, in your own way. Do you want the carriage and my escort to go on to whatever party you missed to oblige me?"

"No, I believe I have had enough for one night. And Lord Tamar is coming early tomorrow morning to look at the ballroom—with a view to painting a medieval castle all along one wall."

He inclined his head, as though happy either way. He could not—would not—browbeat her into his company. His deepest desire had become that she would want that company.

And certainly, she regarded him now with a hint of curiosity rather than the desperate wish to be free of him that had been paramount in earlier encounters. It emboldened him when they had stepped down from the carriage and entered Wenning House to suggest brandy in the library.

Rather to his surprise, she agreed and turned her feet at once in that direction.

"You have made the other rooms brighter, more comfortable, and perfect for guests," he observed, picking up the decanter from the small side table between bookshelves. "But I find this one the most homely."

She had just taken a seat in one of the armchairs and cast him a quick look he was at a loss to understand.

Walking over, he presented her with a glass of brandy and sat in the sofa opposite her. He raised his glass. "To home."

She drank without comment, then abruptly rose. For a moment, he thought she was about to flee again and knew a moment of despair, but she merely walked between the tables to the window, glass in hand, and tuned back to face him.

"Mr. Campbell told me what you did," she said abruptly. "Keeping everyone's spirits high and bodies safe on your difficult land journey in the east."

"Brigands are a problem everywhere," he replied. "But none of them wish to be shot."

"And yet you were. Mr. Campbell said the injury was serious."

"Devil a bit. I was better in days."

"And risked your life," she added.

"More thoughtlessness than bravery, I assure you."

"But why take that risk?" she demanded impatiently. "You had the world at your feet, still."

"But I did not have you."

Her eyes widened. The brandy slopped up the side of her glass, and she hastily took a sip as if she had meant to make the movement all along.

He expected a sharp response. *The remedy was always in your own hands*, perhaps. Or just, *You did not ask.*

Would she have come with him? In reality, he could not have taken her on such a dangerous journey, but still, he could not help wondering. She had been adventurous, eager to travel the well-worn, if war-damaged roads of Europe. And instead, he had trapped her alone in a tiny world of gossip and humiliation. And more and more, it seemed, for no reason. Shame did not really cover that...

She did not answer at all, but she was still pacing.

"Mr. Campbell also said it was you who finally won the last of the special concessions, the one you truly went there for."

"They were all important. And Campbell was being over generous."

She looked at him, actually *looked,* in a searching, perceptive kind of way. Then she set down the glass and began walking again. "If you preferred to go to China, you should have said."

"I didn't."

She shook her head as if none of it made sense, but she kept walking. She was escaping him again. He moved from instinct to block her exit but at least recovered enough to pretend he always meant to open the door for her. But he let his hand linger on the doorknob without turning it as he gazed down at her.

Her expression was serene. Only the pulse beating rapidly at the base of her throat gave away her agitation. That, and the fact that she seemed to prefer to look at the door handle than at him, until, carefully, she raised her eyes to his face.

With equal care, he held out his hand, palm upward. Her gaze flickered, her chin lifted as though she would blister him with verbal contempt. She didn't. But somehow, he knew it took more courage for her to lift her own hand and place it in his. He felt his heart break over what he had done to her, and his fingers curled quickly around hers, just firmly enough to discourage instant withdrawal.

"Grace," he said softly.

The pulse beat still in her throat. And at her wrist as he brushed his thumb across it. Yet, she managed to keep her voice calm and light. "My lord, good night."

She smelled of orange blossom and vanilla and, when he raised her unresisting hand to his lips, of something else uniquely Grace that blasted him with sensual memory. Grace's kisses, Grace's luscious, passionate body. She let him brush his mouth across her fingers.

The pulse in her wrist was galloping now, her breathing quickened, though, God knew, no more than his. In the candlelight, she looked attractively flushed, as though his own rampaging heat had spread to her.

But still, she held herself stiffly, desperate to escape him for whatever reason. He wanted to press his lips to that deliciously agitated pulse at her throat, to taste her skin more intimately. But that would be to scare her off, truly frighten her, for behind the deliberate calm in her eyes, he glimpsed a flash of desperation that was very close to fear. His wife was afraid of him.

Dear God, have I done that to her, too?

"One day," he said gently, "when you are ready, we will talk." Deliberately, he did not release her hand, for he wanted to show her nothing bad would come of it. He even curved his lips into a crooked smile. "My lady, good night."

Slowly, reluctantly, he opened the door. She swallowed. As if she had barely noticed his hold, she casually drew her hand free and walked away.

It was, he told himself, a start. At least she had entered a room with him voluntarily. And stayed to exchange a short conversation that had felt, at times, more like an exchange of rifle fire.

She was aloof. She was stiff, hostile beneath her indifference. And that hint of fear disturbed him more than anything. But at least he was aware now of something else, and that alone gave him hope.

She was not indifferent.

GRACE'S LEGS TREMBLED so much they barely carried her upstairs and along the passage to her apartments.

Dear God, what is the matter with me? Glad to find Henley was not waiting for her, she sank onto the bed and stared at the ceiling.

Only yesterday, she had let Rudolf kiss her because the desire had been too powerful to resist. Was she so depraved that she could desire any handsome man with such power? For Oliver's lips on her skin, his very nearness had aroused her without warning or mercy. It had to be memory, because he was, in fact, the only lover she had ever known. Perhaps it was merely that Rudolf had reminded her of bodily desires, given them focus.

But God knew, she could not focus them on Oliver. In many ways, that was worse than Rudolf. And yet...he confused her still. The hero of the China embassy, the young husband who had once made love to her so sweetly, who now kissed her hand, without threat or command, and told her they would talk when *she* was ready.

I have been ready for two years! And yet now, mere talking would not do. She would not let him get around her again. She would never, *could* never, leave herself so vulnerable. The revenge plan had to stand. It had to.

⫸⫷

OF COURSE, HE barely saw her the following day. He shook hands with the eccentric Lord Tamar, marquess and painter, on his early visit, then departed to enjoy a ride in the park.

However, he had left it too late to enjoy peace. A fashionable crowd on horseback had already come together, his cousin Phineas among them, and so he allowed himself to be beckoned across to join them. As he grew closer, he recognized several other acquaintances, including Prince di Ripoli and Mrs. Fitzwalter from last night's guests, Grace's friend Bridget Arpington, and her admirers—lovers, according to some—Sir Nash Boothe and Anthony Curtis.

"Well met, Cousin!" Phineas greeted him. "The ladies are trying to get up a party to see the fireworks at Maida Gardens tomorrow night. What do you think?"

"I think I'm surprised anyone still goes to Maida Gardens," Wenning replied with lazy amusement.

"Yes, but *fireworks*, my lord!" Mrs. Fitzwalter said gaily. "I am convinced it will be quite the spectacle. And it is to be part of a masked ball."

"The masked balls at Maida," pronounced a disapproving lady Wenning did not know, "are ramshackle affairs, like those at the other pleasure gardens."

"Yes, but that is to do with the clientele," Sir Nash Boothe argued. "If we make it a large enough party, then the majority of the clientele is us, and we can make the event into what we wish. With enough gentlemen to protect the ladies from any annoyance."

"I would come," said Lady Arpington. "If we had enough *respectable* people to prevent my husband objecting! You and Lady Wenning would come, too, my lord, would you not?"

Wenning regarded her thoughtfully. Bridget Arpington was Grace's oldest friend and, he suspected, confidante, to some degree at least, for although she smiled, her eyes were not friendly. He could hardly blame her for that.

"Oh, do, Wenning," Mrs. Fitzwalter urged with a dazzling smile, although he could not recall being on such terms with her that she should be comfortable dropping his title.

Nor were they on cheek-kissing terms, and yet in the park on Saturday, she had leaned into him and made anything else impossible. Interesting.

"It will be such fun to have you there," she urged now, "and I know Grace will adore it, too. Remember how you enjoyed the fireworks in Paris?"

He had *endured* the fireworks in Paris in order to deliver the message he had been tasked with. His main focus had been on getting home as fast as humanly possible.

"It sounds delightful," he said politely, "but I cannot speak for my wife's plans. If you will excuse me..."

"Going for a gallop, Ollie?" Phineas guessed. "I'll come with you."

Tipping their hats, they extricated themselves from the group and cantered away from the main public paths.

"I hope you don't mind Grace's name being associated with this Maida expedition," Phineas said as they slowed. "I only joined the plan because she was already being mentioned by the time I came along. Somehow, she seems to be known as familiar with the Maida masquerades."

"How come? Boothe?"

Phineas shrugged. "He was there the night Grace attended with Rollo Darblay and his friends. It could have come from any of them and spread. And there is no doubting that Grace is an asset to any party. Will you be there, Ollie?"

"It depends on Grace," Wenning said thoughtfully. "But if I am there, I may not come in your party. Tell me, Phin, have you any credible evidence that either Curtis or Boothe or any other of my wife's myriad admirers have ever been in my house unchaperoned?"

"Of course not," Phineas said at once. "Because they never have. Beyond the at-home afternoons and parties, where she was always careful to have her father or uncle present as host. Although..." He tailed off with a shrug. "And that is it."

"And that is not what you were going to say."

He sighed. "It is perfectly innocent. I just remembered calling early one morning to take Grace riding in the park—I often indulge in an early ride, as today—and found that fellow Boothe there already. And wasn't best pleased to see me either."

Wenning kept his expression neutral. "And which of you did Grace choose?"

"Me, of course.

"And that is the only evidence of her supposed adultery?"

"It is no evidence at all," Phineas said seriously. "It was perfectly innocent. She likes the admiration—who would not?—but if she has more than flirted, I shall eat *all* my hats."

"Heaven forfend such a waste of hattery."

"As you say. I'll tell you what, though, Ollie. If you want to set your mind at rest, you should come incognito to the ball and the firework display and see for yourself. There is ample opportunity for dalliance at Maida, no matter how many respectable people are present, but I guarantee Grace will not take advantage, even though several of her swains are present."

"You want me to spy on my wife?"

"If her supposed infidelity bothers you, then yes," Phineas said frankly. "If you trust her, as I've told you constantly you should, then don't bother."

"Such sound advice as always," Wenning remarked. "I'm for a gallop…"

»»»«««

HAVING RETURNED FROM his ride to discover Grace had already left the house, Wenning changed into morning dress and walked round to visit his sister Honoria, whom he found partaking of a solitary breakfast.

He accepted a cup of coffee, bade her dismiss the hovering footman, and sat down beside her.

"The truth, Honoria. How much have you actually seen of my wife's supposed misbehavior?"

Honoria shuddered. "All over town, my dear. One runs across her everywhere."

He raised one mocking eyebrow. "*In flagrante delicto?*"

"Hardly," Honoria said, reddening. "But all the same, she flaunts her lovers everywhere."

"And how do you know they are her lovers?"

"I saw young Curtis enter your house after dark. And another day, that fellow Boothe was there, quite at home at a ridiculously early hour when I called on her. Some story about escorting her for a ride in the park."

"And he was...where? In Grace's private sitting room?"

Honoria frowned. "I don't remember, to be honest."

"You don't remember, I suspect," Wenning said with careful lightness, "because you were not there. You heard the story from Phineas, who *was* there and who did, in the end, take Grace riding."

Honoria waved her hand impatiently to the imminent danger of her teacup. "What difference does it make? The point is, Sir Nash Boothe was there when he shouldn't have been."

"And who was it who saw Curtis enter Wenning House after dark?"

"I did," she said with certainty.

"And where were you going at such an hour? Home?"

"No, I was on my way to a party at Lady Sefton's—"

"I see. And was Wenning House in darkness?"

Honoria frowned. "No. All the first-floor windows were ablaze with light."

"The first floor," Wenning said gently. "The public rooms. Is it not possible that Grace was merely hosting a party to which you were not invited?"

Honoria's chin shot up in an old, childhood gesture of defiance. "If you choose to believe that your wife is innocent, I will say not a word against her."

"Good," Wenning replied. He drank half his coffee and set down the cup. "Because the truth is, that even if she were guilty, the fault would be mine for leaving her in such an insulting way, and then failing to be there as her companion and guide. Who could blame her if she did seek a little solace elsewhere?"

He sat back in his chair, gazing in the direction of the window and the light streaming through it. "The thing is, Honoria, I don't think she ever did."

CHAPTER TEN

G RACE SPENT ONE afternoon a week at home and was surprised by what happened. First of all, Bridget arrived early and proposed yet another visit to Maida Gardens.

"The ball will include a fireworks display in the gardens," she said enthusiastically, "and *everyone* will be going."

"Everyone?" Grace repeated skeptically. "Have you and I made the gardens fashionable after all? Even though we took such pains to go incognito?"

"Who knows? To be honest, I have no idea who first came up with this idea, but I rode into a large huddle in the park this morning, and it was already being discussed. Sir Nash Boothe was among them, and Phineas Harlaw, Maria Fitzwalter...oh and that deliciously handsome Italian prince—di Ripoli?"

The last name made her prick up her ears. "Was he, indeed? I met him last night, and it crossed my mind he might be Rudolf, the man who found my bracelet."

Bridget's eyes widened. "Really? Do you still think so?"

Grace shrugged. "He gave me no sign of it, and I could not be sure. His height and build and coloring match, but his voice was different, and I could not quite envision him in a mask."

"Well, you will have the opportunity to see him in one if you come tomorrow night."

"Is Arpington going?"

Bridget looked demure. "I haven't told him yet. He didn't exactly enjoy it the first time, did he? Though he might relax with more congenial people."

"Or he might breathe a huge sigh of relief not to have to bother," Grace said wryly.

"Wenning appeared while we were discussing it," Bridget recalled. "He committed himself to nothing but certainly did not sound as though he would forbid you."

"I wouldn't pay attention if he did," Grace retorted. "As I'm sure he knows. Bridget...Bridget, did you ever think Wenning was a *bad* person?"

"No. Not until he abandoned you on your wedding night. For two years. Why?"

Grace shook her head. "Something does not make sense. He was always clever, quick witted, charming. Certainly, he was ambitious, but ambition seemed tempered by duty and affection. I always thought I split that duty, drove him to behave as he did. He should never have pretended... But everything I ever liked in him is still there. How can that be when he...?"

She broke off as more callers were announced and forced the smile back to her lips to receive the second surprise of the afternoon. Mrs. Fitzwalter, in company with Sir Nash Boothe. Grace wished them well of each other, although she suspected the lady had come merely in the hope of catching a few words with the earl.

She was, it seemed, doomed to disappointment. Grace's at-home afternoons were always well-attended, and today's was particularly so. No doubt everyone wanted to see the long-parted Wennings in domestic surroundings, eager for a glimpse of strife or harmony. Either, she supposed, would feed the gossips. Especially with Maria Fitzwalter in the same room.

Prince di Ripoli was another welcome guest, as was Mr. Curtis.

And inevitably, the scheme to attend Maida Gardens for the masquerade ball and firework display came up, and she was once more pressed to join the expedition. Surreptitiously, she watched Prince di Ripoli and found him smiling directly at her. She wondered if his first name was Rudolfo.

Of course, the staider of her guests were against it, and her sister-in-law Lady Barnton positively flared her nostrils with disgust.

"I doubt my brother would sanction such a ramshackle scheme," she opined.

"Why, here he is," Mrs. Fitzwalter exclaimed with some delight. "Let us ask him."

Grace's gaze flew to the door, and there indeed was her husband strolling into the drawing room, every inch, she thought resentfully, master of the house he had not even visited for two years.

Something seemed to mesh inside her brain, something to do with his arrival, familiarity, and the discussion of Maida, but it eluded her before she could grasp it. She had to concentrate on calmly pouring another cup of tea for Wenning and passing it to him with civility.

"An unexpected pleasure, my lord. I believe you are acquainted with everyone?"

"Indeed I am. And with your Maida Garden scheme, which I heard all about this morning." He walked over to the extra chair the footman had placed and sat down, "What is your view of the notion, Grace?"

"Why, that it seems to be considered so bold and daring that I had better take part or reconcile my reputation to becoming tame and dull."

"Never," Boothe said fervently.

Wenning did not even glance at him.

"May we rely on your escort, my lord?" Mrs. Fitzwalter asked brightly.

"Alas, no," Wenning replied, apparently regretful. He kept his gaze on Grace. "But if you need an escort, I believe Phineas will oblige."

Although she refused to do so in company, Grace wanted to stare at him, search his face for the elusive connection that had troubled her as soon as he had come into the room, some association of her husband and Maida Gardens.

Surely there was not one? She had never been to the gardens with Oliver, and the only association was the fact that she had lost the bracelet, his gift, there. Could he have found out?

Only Henley, her maid, knew about that. And Bridget. And Rollo. None of whom would betray her? Except by accident. And, of course, there was Rudolf...

Her gaze flew involuntarily to the Prince di Ripoli. No, he could not be Rudolf. He did not have the imposing, half-familiar, half-intriguing presence. Oliver, on the other hand...

Her breath caught as the buzz of voices around her seemed to recede. All she could hear was the singing of her own ears.

No. No, it is not possible. I would have known... He was not even in the country when I met Rudolf first.

Of course, he was not.

The voices of her visitors drifted back as relief flooded her. What a silly idea to have taken into her head! Just because he was of something the same height and build as Rudolf. Even now, with the opportunity of dallying with Mrs. Fitzwalter, he would not lower himself to attend Maida Gardens, although, like an indulgent parent, he was allowing Grace.

That didn't make sense either. She was too confused to worry about it.

Wenning stayed only half an hour among her guests before excusing himself and strolling off. By that time, of course, Sir Nash and Curtis had both left, according to the prescribed length of such calls. Had he made his appearance merely to remind them that he was home? To warn them off sniffing around his wife?

Or had he just lost interest because Mrs. Fitzwalter had left?

She wasn't sure that made much sense either.

Somehow, she got through to the end of the afternoon, although she thought she might have talked too much and laughed too brittlely.

When the servants came to clear away trays and teacups, she left them to it and, on impulse, went to the library where, stupidly, she had once felt closest to the man who had betrayed and abandoned her. Half of her hoped to find him there so that she could look at him and realize once and for all that he was not Rudolf.

No, she had realized that already. A man could not be two places at once. And since Wenning had not yet been in the country when she first met Rudolf, they could not possibly be the same person. But she had been churned up since he had come home, focusing on revenge, on inflicting on him even just a tiny fraction of what she had suffered. She had barely looked at him, and when she had, she had concentrated more on her own necessary strength than on his appearance.

The library was empty, although as she crossed to the shelf she wanted, she caught a hint of his scent. That, too, was a little like Rudolf's, a little of the woods, a little lemon, a hint of spice, although the balance was different.

Plucking the book of Elizabethan poetry from the shelf, she sank into her favorite armchair and thumbed through the pages until she found the Michael Drayton poem. Not because she imagined Wenning had penned that note, but because it actually meant something to her, reminding her quite inconveniently that...

That she was not ready to let her husband go.

She had longed to feel something of those cheerful, careless lines at the beginning of the poem—*let us kiss and part* and *I am glad, yea glad with all my heart, That thus so cleanly I myself can free.* And she still had confused hopes that when he suffered just a little, she *would* be free. But the truth was, that like the poet, she still hoped for a last-moment reprieve, for him to speak the words that would keep them together.

Because she loved him still.

"I don't," she whispered, wiping her suddenly wet face with the back of her hand. "I don't love you." How could she after what he did? He was never the man she had thought him. And now, after two years, they were both changed again. *This was not love*, she assured herself, *this was regret for* lost *love*. If she truly still loved her husband, she would never have felt the raw physical desire she had for Rudolf when he had kissed her.

And yet, what, if not love for her husband, had prevented her giving in to that desire? Had she not felt the treacherous flame of lust when Oliver had touched her last night?

She jumped to her feet, taking the book with her, and after wiping her eyes on her sleeve in case she met any of the servants, she retreated to her sitting room to win back some peace and some strength.

>>><<<

DINNER WITH FRIENDS that evening followed by a card party, kept her out of the house and away from her husband. She had not inquired about the earl's plans and didn't know if she was glad or not that she did see him among the other guests.

She did, however, see his friend, Sir Ernest Leyton, who made a point of joining her as she left one of her games to exchange a few words with her.

"What is this mad notion of Phineas Harlaw's to remove half the ton to Maida Gardens tomorrow evening?" he asked.

Grace laughed. "Oh, I don't believe the notion was Phineas's, but certainly he seems to have embraced it. Do you join us, sir?"

"I?" He seemed startled.

"Did Phineas not invite you?"

"Well, yes, but I felt no obligation to accept. I can't imagine Wenning is in favor of the idea."

"He has no objection, though he will not come, either." Too late, she remembered seeing Sir Ernest at Maida the first time she went. He had been dancing, always with the same unknown lady. "But you should come. The more respectable gentlemen who do, the happier, I suspect, will be the outing. And, of course, we will be incognito."

He searched her face, as though looking for hidden meaning. "Perhaps I will."

Grace sensed intrigue, but despite her curiosity, she did not pry. Instead, she changed the subject. "Tell me, Sir Ernest, do you find Wenning much changed by his long absence?"

"Not really. He is a little more assured, perhaps. Why do you both ask me questions about each other? Do you not live in the same house?"

"He asks you about me?" she said quickly.

"There, you are doing it again. My best advice? Talk to each other." He bowed and excused himself.

It was, Grace reflected, sound advice. She almost followed it too when she returned home and saw the light on in the library. She actually paused on the stairs, her hand quite still on the polished banister, while her heart seemed to beat its way into her mouth.

"One day, when you are ready, we will talk."

But she had come too far to slide down that slope into weakness again. At this moment, she was strong and had to stay that way to survive. And if she could not bring him to his knees—he would have to actually *care* for that to happen—she could at least cut him down to size. And she would do so in full knowledge of his character, the good, as well as the bad.

With sudden decision, she took hold of the handle and walked in.

She didn't know if she was relieved or annoyed not to see him at his desk. The lamps were still lit at this end of the room although the back lay in shadowy darkness. A faint smell of brandy lingered in the air. She could not have missed him by much.

A sudden movement from the far corner preceded a clatter that made her jump. A figure stepped from the shadows into semi-gloom, and her stomach lurched.

The earl was not in formal dress. He wore no cravat, coat or waistcoat, and his shirt was rumpled, his face half-concealed in darkness.

He waved a brandy glass in her direction. "My lady. Bring a glass and join me."

He thought she wouldn't. He believed she would not face his drunkenness and merely leave without a word.

But a Darblay was far too used to drunks to be deterred by one slightly too expansive gesture. His words did not slur, and his tone betrayed quite clearly his self-mockery.

Wordlessly, she walked to the silver tray, picked up a glass, and approached the dark half of the library. He watched her, a faint, appreciative smile lurking on his sinful lips. Why should elegance and decadence look so wretchedly attractive on a husband she hated?

As she came closer, she saw that he had been on the window seat when she entered. The clatter had been a book landing on the floor, no doubt when he had stood up. He set down his glass on the nearby bookshelf, retrieved the book, and replaced it on the shelf, before picking up the bottle. She halted in front of him and held out her glass. He sloshed some liquid into it—accurately.

His gaze lifted to hers, wary, almost unsure. Unless that was a trick of the poor light.

She turned away, leaving him to the window seat once more, and took the winged armchair by the fire.

He inclined his head, still with that hint of self-mockery, and raised his glass to her before sinking back onto the window seat like a sleek, comfortable cat, leaning against the shutter with foot up on the cushion.

"You said you risked your life on the journey because you didn't have me," she said abruptly. "What did you mean?"

"I was brought low, blue-devilled by your absence."

"You are a glib drunk."

"*In vino veritas.*"

She sipped her brandy.

"Why did you never redecorate this room?" he asked.

She shrugged. "You were far from home. No one else sees it."

"You did."

Her gaze flew to his once more. The servants must have told him that. Which meant he must have asked. Why?

"You are not drunk at all are you?" she guessed suddenly.

He considered. "No." He lifted his glass once more. "But I have been drinking. Don't ask me why."

"Why?" she asked at once.

A breath of laughter escaped him. "I was hoping it would quell my other desires."

This conversation was not going at all the way she wanted it to. They were both skirting around the huge question lying between them: why he had left her.

And she could not ask it. Not while he sat there like a large, graceful animal, with his face half concealed in shadows and his sensual lips just parted and curved. As the silence stretched between them, her mouth went dry. All she had to do was rise and walk the few steps between them, sit in his lap and his strong arms would close around her, those seductive lips would take hers and from there…

He set down his glass. "We should talk in daylight."

"Afraid of too much *veritas* with your *vino*?" she retorted, watching him rise.

He laughed and stretched his whole, long, lean body, temptation made flesh. Wicked lust flamed through her, both need and memory. But she did not move, afraid of giving in, of a surrender that would surely ruin such self-respect as she had left.

And yet, as he walked past her to the door, murmuring goodnight, nothing had ever been so difficult as maintaining her position, quietly, calmly, sipping her brandy in the darkness.

She did not watch him leave, but she heard the door click shut behind him.

THE MORE GRACE thought about the expedition to Maida Gardens, the more she wished she hadn't given in to impulse. Even if Rudolf were there, and she could begin a few rumors that might wend their way back to Wenning, it would do her confused heart no good to see him again before her own ball. He was temptation. Married temptation. And at the moment, it seemed she could not even deal with desire for her own, perfidious husband.

Oh yes, she was depraved in spirit. But she need give in to neither lust. She was a lady of strength and character, not an animal in heat.

Moreover, the oddest idea came to her as the carriage containing her and Bridget, Phineas and Sir Ernest, rumbled north toward the pleasure gardens: that everything would be more comfortable if Wenning were with her.

Which was clearly nonsense. There may have been a certain perverse enjoyment in sparring with her husband, but it was never exactly *comfortable*. And she did not really wish to risk confrontation in the gardens, where the rules of polite society were not necessarily observed.

Maybe, I am not cut out for intrigue and revenge, she thought ruefully. But then, she was clearly not cut out to pretend the last two years had not happened either. Under no circumstances could she be the accepting wife, happy to be lied to and treated as of no account. He would understand she *was* of account to someone. And that he, too, could be a figure of society's cruel fun.

"Is everything well with you?" Bridget murmured as they stood together for an instant at the pleasure garden gates.

"Of course."

Bridget leaned closer. "You have not arranged to meet *him*, have you?"

Grace didn't pretend to misunderstand. But since the gentlemen were offering their arms to walk up the path, she could only shake her head.

As she trod the now-familiar lantern-strewn path to the pavilion, she glanced up at Phineas, who, cloaked and masked, had acquired a serious, much more enigmatic appearance. "I wonder," she mused, "if I did not know you were Phineas, would I recognize you?"

He glanced down at her. "Is that not the point of masked balls?"

She considered. "Maybe, the real point is to get to know someone without being misled by that person's looks or status."

"Which we of the ton rely on. I believe you have discovered the true reason Society now frowns on public balls of this nature. The masks we wear every day are much more effective than a mere strip of silk and a gaudy cloak."

"How very cynical of you, Phineas. Or do I mean perceptive? In any case, you look much more serious in a strip of silk and a gaudy cloak."

"I am a serious fellow. And for what it is worth, I believe I would always recognize you, masked or not."

She sighed. "So much for my desire to appear mysterious and interesting. What gives me away?"

He considered. "I think it's the way you move and talk—restless and yet graceful, like quicksilver."

She laughed. "Which is a polite way of saying I'm a chattering jack-in-the-box!"

"You misquote me," Phineas protested. "Leyton, support me here! Is her ladyship's beauty not instantly recognizable, masked or otherwise?"

Sir Ernest, just ahead with Bridget on his arm, turned back and smiled, convincing her all over again that it *had* been him she had seen here the first night she had come. Unlike Phineas, he did not seem much changed by a mere mask.

"Why, yes, I would have to agree," he said.

Not for the first time, Grace wondered if *he* had seen *her* at the ball that first night. If he had told Wenning. At the time, it had worried her. Now, she wished he had. And if Rudolf was here tonight, then no doubt she could arrange for a hint of intrigue to reach her husband via any number of people.

In truth, she both dreaded and wished for Rudolf's presence and, for a tangle of conflicting reasons, that churned her up. Not least of those reasons being the suspicion that he knew her, that they had met before the first masked ball. And using him in this way, without knowing his identity, was downright dangerous. It could yet bring about her own fall rather than her husband's.

The ballroom was more crowded than on her previous visits. All the doors were thrown wide, and the curtains tied back, presumably to allow people to see something of the fireworks without leaving the pavilion.

Clearly some of their party had already arrived, for two tables joined together were surrounded by people with white roses adorning their dominos—the sign they had arranged in advance. As she and Phineas made their way to those tables, she gazed about her, looking in vain for a tall, graceful figure in black and silver, lounging against a pillar.

Which was silly. Whoever he was and whatever he did, he could not spend *all* his evenings at Maida Gardens.

The growing party of the ton greeted each other with great good humor. In the spirit of the event, they used no names or titles, instead addressing each other by the color of their domino cloaks. In this way, Grace was the only Madam Rose, though it became more complicated with the gentlemen who mostly shared staider colors like black and grey and dark blue. Champagne was already flowing, and more was ordered. To Grace, it felt like a secret outing of children who had given their governesses the slip, and as such, she began to enjoy it.

She had not taken more than a sip of champagne before someone stood and invited her to dance. She knew at once from his voice that it was Prince di Ripoli. He did not sound at all like Rudolf, and he wore a scarlet mask and domino, not black and silver. Yet still, her heartbeat quickened as she took his arm, and they walked onto the floor. Perhaps his voice was softer, huskier in the intimacy of the waltz.

But as soon as they took up their dancing positions, she knew this was not Rudolf. He might have been of similar height and build, but he did not *fit*. His grip was wrong. He moved differently, he smiled differently. Which at least meant she could relax and enjoy the dance.

And afterward, when, as was the custom at these masked balls, a stranger from another party came over and asked her to dance, she waltzed with him, too. Hopefully, that would get back to her husband, via Sir Ernest, Phineas, Mrs. Fitzwalter, or just general gossip.

The interesting stranger, who by his speech and conversation, was an up-and-coming merchant, behaved with perfect decorum, even reverence, and Grace was genuinely sorry to part from him.

Sir Nash, it seemed, had not given up his ambitions to be her chief escort if not her lover, for after this second dance, he appeared at her shoulder, murmuring, "Shall we walk in the gardens? Discover, perhaps, where the fireworks will be?"

"Excellent idea," she approved rather more loudly, turning to the group as a whole. "Shall we walk and choose our spot to observe?"

Sir Nash, resplendent in a domino cloak of midnight blue and a plain black mask, was clearly not best pleased, but he kept the smile plastered to his lips as they were joined by Phineas, Sir Ernest, Bridget, and Mrs. Fitzwalter.

They all trooped out together to enjoy the fresher air and the almost magical atmosphere created by the clever use of lanterns and torches. Following the path, they discovered that the fireworks would be lit on top of a small hill on the other side of a picturesque bridge. An odd folly had been constructed on the same hill, a cross between a castle and a Grecian temple. An ornamental waterfall tumbled down this hill and into the boating pond below. The whole scene was peculiarly magical, like a child's fairy tale come to life.

"How pretty it will look," Grace exclaimed. "The setting is rather beautiful, is it not? And I suppose everyone will see from this stretch of garden."

"We could keep these benches for our party," Sir Nash suggested, indicating the nearest three or four benches scattered around the area.

"But the fireworks will not begin for another hour," Bridget objected.

"When there will be a mad crush of people all pushing their way out of the pavilion to come here," Sir Nash replied. "But if Madam Rose and I fend off all comers, then the rest of you may take your time and know you may still watch in comfort."

"How selfless," Phineas observed sardonically. "What a sacrifice."

"It is impressive," Grace agreed. "I, however, am much too selfish to agree! I would rather use my time to dance and take my chances in the crush."

The whole idea was turned off with a laugh, but to Grace, it was an alarmingly blatant effort to be alone with her. What did he hope to achieve by that? Scandal? Revenge in the form of Wenning's anger with her? He *could* truly care for her, of course, but inviting scandal was hardly the work of a man who cared.

It was Grace who, without waiting for a male arm to lean on, led the way back to the pavilion.

"I suppose this must happen to you frequently," Mrs. Fitzwalter said, falling into step beside her.

"What is that?" Grace asked lightly.

"Gentlemen pursuing you to the edge of your ruin."

"On the contrary, I have found most gentlemen to have a little more respect."

"You are fortunate," Mrs. Fitzwalter drawled, apparently amused. "But one can over-do the self-righteousness. I don't believe anyone here is a tattle-tale."

Grace stared at her. "If you really believe that, you are frankly naïve. But in this case, as in most, I am moved by personal inclination rather than fear of tale-bearing."

"Truly?" The woman seemed both surprised and curious. "Yet the world knows Sir Nash has been at your feet for months. I don't believe Lord Wenning would mind, you know."

Outraged that another woman, *this* woman, would speak to her in such a way, let alone try to urge her into an affair she didn't want, Grace nevertheless managed an amused laugh.

"Blatant indiscretion, ma'am, is as repulsive to his lordship as to the next man." It might have been depressing that her infidelity would not break her husband's heart, but he would certainly not care for the humiliation—a truth she was certainly relying on.

CHAPTER ELEVEN

THE EVENING PASSED in somewhat hectic enjoyment. Grace drank champagne, she laughed and bantered, and danced with strangers as well as with members of her own party. And as midnight grew closer, everyone made their way to the garden by the waterfall to see the firework display.

It was indeed a bit of a crush, but they moved around the outskirts of the crowd for the best view. And just as the gentlemen began to force a passage through to a no doubt better vantage, Grace felt a light touch on her shoulder.

Glancing around with a suitably haughty expression, she felt the breath rush from her body. A tall man in a black and silver cloak and mask stepped back and vanished toward the trees behind.

She only had to stand still, and the space between her and Bridget was filled. Prince di Ripoli, who had been bringing up the rear, was distracted by a loud, barging man on his right, and without further thought, Grace slipped free of the crowd and hurried after Rudolf.

Straight ahead was a pretty, wooded area, to the left an ornamental maze that joined with the more enclosed garden she had walked in with Rudolf on her last visit. A line of lanterns had been threaded through the tree branches and across the front hedges of the maze. Grace had no intention of venturing into either wood or maze, but, thinking she might find him in the enclosed garden, she veered from the large oak at the edge of the wood to hurry in that direction.

Without warning, a hand shot out from behind the oak, closed around her arm, and yanked her behind it. Before she could cry out, she imagined a whisper of "Hush, it's me," although that might have been the breeze rustling among the leaves, and her mouth was covered by another.

The kiss was instantly devouring, passionate, and might well have scared her witless had she not worked out her captor was Rudolf. More than that, her heart, her whole body recognized him with a fierce surge of joy. And that *did* frighten her.

"Stop," she gasped into his mouth, pushing against his shoulders. Her feeble shove was no match for his strength, but at once, he released her lips, and if he didn't free her body entirely, at least his hold slackened.

"Why?" he murmured, his breathing not quite steady. "Are you afraid your husband will find out?"

Hysterical laughter tried to fight its way up her throat. "Oh, I *mean* him to find out," she said shakily. "But I will not—*you* will not..." She scrubbed her knuckles against her forehead, trying to think. "I will be faithful, but he will think me *unfaithful*."

There was a baffled pause. Then, "Why?"

"Because it might hurt him. It doesn't matter. But that is what I want your help with, at my masked ball. But you must understand, it will only ever be pretense."

"Why?" he asked again. He had a knack of shading available light with his head, so she could not read his expression, could barely even see his face. "Why deny yourself a little pleasure?"

"I will have all the pleasure I need if you agree to help me."

"I already agreed," he said slowly. "But still, I do not understand."

"You don't need to," she said with sudden bitterness. "Suffice it to say, he is the heart and core of all my hate. And, it seems, all my love. I will not betray my vows."

"But you *will* humiliate him?"

She had herself under better control now. "I am allowed some recompense," she drawled. "And if you want to reconcile with your wife, you should thank me."

Whatever he would have replied was lost in a sudden row of explosions from the hill. As one, they swung around to see the dazzling display of light and color against the blackness of the sky and the silvery reflection of the waterfall. It was stunningly beautiful.

There seemed no need for further talk, although his arm remained loosely around her waist. After a few moments, she realized she was leaning lightly against him, that the combination of the wonder before her and his nearness was producing a strange happiness, a comfort, and peace that was strangely familiar.

Familiar. That word again. If he knew her, then she must know him.

She glanced up at him as a fresh burst of pyrotechnics lit the sky. He met her gaze, and his lips quirked, and with that movement, in the glow from the sky, her world exploded, too.

Recognition, knowledge, fury, understanding, dread. Everything fell into place.

She had been attracted to *him* all over again. The same man, tricking her, testing her. Testing *her*. She should have known at once. Had Oliver not always been a wickedly clever mimic, able to change accents and voices like an actor?

Oh, but she *should* have known him... Only two years had blunted her memory of his appearance, and she had been afraid to look, *really* look at her husband since his return, in case she weakened.

And from the beginning, she had been fooled simply because meeting Rudolf had happened several days before the special embassy had returned to London. But she had not been paying enough attention to Mrs. Fitzwalter, who had told her in so many words that Wenning had not come home all the way home in company with his colleagues. Mrs. Fitzwalter had met him in Paris and returned with him. The rest of the embassy had not come via Paris but enjoyed a few days of rest in Lisbon before changing ship for the last leg of their voyage. Luck and the weather must have brought the earl home quicker, despite his extra mission. Early enough to have been here at Maida Gardens to steal the bracelet he must have recognized.

And now, *now* she would be sure beyond any doubt.

She reached up to his mask, to pluck it from his face. But something beyond him, in the nearby, thicker branches, caught her eye. A small round, dark hole protruding at the end of a barrel and pointing, it seemed, at *him*.

Without thought, she hurled herself against him, but abruptly, while fresh fireworks exploded, he fell to the ground, dragging her with him. The pistol barrel in the branches vanished.

His hands clutched her face. "Are you hit, are you hurt?"

She shook her head, unable to speak, terror for him uppermost in her mind. But before she could properly look or even ask, he was jumping to his feet, hauling her to hers. He shifted, letting the lantern light play on a hole in the bark of the tree as he probed it with his fingers.

"My God," she whispered. Someone really had shot at them.

"Go back to your friends," he commanded, already bolting into the wood. "Now!"

Even then, he used the voice of "Rudolf." She didn't know whether that was more funny or infuriating, and at this moment, it didn't really matter, for she simply picked up her skirts and flew after him into the wood.

"How did I come to suspect," he murmured as she joined him in his swift pursuit, "that you would not obey my wishes?"

"I suppose you must know me better than you think."

He spared her a quick glance, perhaps trying to work out if he was finally recognized. But in truth, there were more urgent matters at stake right now, and she saw that he was chasing a light winking through the trees.

He paused, holding her back, and for a moment, they waited in silence, listening. The fireworks and the awed cries of the crowd had stopped. Behind them was only the much lower murmur of talk and laughter. Closer, nothing stirred.

Her companion—her *husband*—parted the leaves and sighed, stepping back to show her the lantern standing all by itself at the center of the little clearing.

"He fooled us," the earl said in disgust. "I suspect as we blundered after him, he simply sauntered out of the trees to mingle with the crowd. My tactics were wrong. I should have gone with you to see who was missing."

She stared at him. "*Missing?* You think someone you *know* shot at you?"

His gaze dropped to her face. "Or at you," he said more grimly. Taking her arm, he began to walk back the way they had come. "It was a careful aim, and a narrow escape for us, judging by the hole he made in the tree."

"But...but who on earth would do such a thing?" she demanded. "And why?"

"Why, I suspect, depends on the who."

"But... Surely it is more likely to be some scoundrel, thinking to rob you when you lay..." *dying.* She couldn't even say the word.

"With you still standing to make a fuss and identify him? Besides, who would murder for the amount of money someone has in his pocket halfway through a public ball? They would be better stealing your bracelet while they danced with you."

"That certainly seems to be the preferred method of theft at Maida," she agreed. "Though I doubt our friend wishes to see either of us again."

"There, I would agree with you." As they emerged near the oak tree, he paused, his gaze darting around the garden before he turned to walk past the maze. "Come, we'll go back in by the other door to avoid the crush."

Or to avoid the rest of her party? Did any of them know he was here? Was he here to dally with Maria Fitzwalter? She couldn't quite believe that. His focus, at Maida at least, had always been on Grace. But it seemed he didn't want any of them to recognize him. Would they be any quicker than she in spotting the Earl of Wenning? Phineas and Leyton both knew him very well or had done before he went away. Or were they in on this masquerade with him? And then, there was Maria Fitzwalter, whom she didn't even want to think about.

Something else hit her with all the jolt of a punch.

Dear God, what had she said to "Rudolf"? She had let him dance with her, kiss her, had come to meet him here more than once against all sense. She had admitted she hated—and loved—her husband. Devastatingly for her plan, she had revealed her fidelity and her desire to make him suffer by evidence proving otherwise.

Heat flooded her skin. She only hoped he couldn't see it in the lantern light.

"You are very quiet," he observed.

"I have a lot to think about. Someone deliberately tried to shoot you or me."

"Perhaps it was your husband."

"Perhaps it was your wife," she retorted, and suddenly she wanted to laugh. Hysteria, no doubt, caused by the sudden, unthinkable danger they had both come through. But she also felt a peculiar *lightness*, like a burden removed. Sheer relief because the man who had tempted her was the same man who always had, because her revenge was in ashes before it had begun.

And curiously, she no longer felt helpless. Revenge would not have made her strong. Exposing him to public ridicule would have helped neither his career nor her own happiness. But...if he were testing her, could she not test him?

They walked on through the masked throngs, and into the pavilion where the orchestra had again struck up, presumably for the last dance before the unmasking. Without a word, he took her hand and drew her into the waltz.

Some new excitement was pounding in her heart, churning her stomach. He did not know she knew. They had already learned things about each other that she had never known or spoken of before. Here at Maida, in disguise, they had been close and comfortable like old friends, as they had not been in the open since he came home.

Oh, don't go down that path again, she pleaded with herself.

But there is a chance. I have a chance to win him back.

After he abandoned you without a backward glance and ignored you for two years? You had never won him in the first place, clearly, and after that, why would you want to?

His nearness, his warmth flowed through her. His scent filled her—masculine, woodland and citrus and spice… Even that had been a clue. A little of Oliver's familiar soap and something more exotic from the east that he had brought back with him, something that had been fainter but still present when he was with her as the earl.

Why would I want to win him back?

Because he must have had a reason for what he did. Because he is not the scoundrel I told myself he was for my own sanity. Because I spoke the truth. I may win, I may lose and make a fool of myself all over again, but God help me, he is the center of everything. Heart and core…

"Grace, you must take care," he murmured, his eyes serious behind the mask. "Never go anywhere alone, but only with people you can trust to protect you. Preferably at least two of them at any one time."

"Then you must do the same."

"I shall certainly pay more attention."

"Rudolf?"

A tiny twitch at the corner of his mouth told her he had acknowl-

edged her use of the name as she had meant him to. Was he glad she
still appeared not to recognize him?

"Grace?"

"Do you really have enemies who would kill you?"

"Apparently. With some level of planning, too. I never thought of
anyone hiding a pistol beneath a domino cloak. But we mustn't
assume I was the target. It could have been either of us."

Or both.

"Promise me you will be careful, Grace," he said urgently.

"Of course." However stupid, the pistol shot disguised as fireworks
seemed distant from the ballroom, almost unreal. Dancing with him
was real and wonderful, and she was reluctant to think of anything
else, except for the glimmer of hope, pale yet intense, that if she
managed things well, reconciliation, even happiness, might yet be
possible.

If he was the man she still believed him to be, despite everything...

"Will you tell your husband?" he asked.

"Why would I do that?"

Something flashed in his eyes. "Because he might be able to protect you."

"My husband has done nothing to protect me, ever. Why would
he begin now?"

That sally seemed to deprive him of breath, for he took a moment
to respond. "Because you are in danger."

"I imagine he would be more comfortable with me dead. He could
then marry someone more suitable."

He did not blink. She wished she could see the expression behind
the mask, yet she imagined waves of feeling sweeping over him, none
of it pleasant.

"Forgive me," he said at last, "but he sounds a terrible fellow. And
yet you say he is the center of your world and hold me at arm's length
on his account."

"Part of me still expects nothing of him. Ever. But if, somewhere, he is still the man I once believed him to be—still *want* him to be—I cannot close the door on the possibility of reconciliation. There must be a reason for what he did. I just don't know what it is."

There was another pause. "I'm beginning to think that this husband of yours deserves the thrashing of a lifetime. Would you like a friend, Grace?"

"A friend?" she repeated. Whatever she had expected, it was not that.

"Perhaps we can help each other understand our estranged spouses and find out who shot at us at the same time."

The music was coming to an end, just at the wrong time. Or was it? Would he unmask? Would he tell her everything?

"You want us to meet again?" she said in a rush as the last note sounded, and the dancers stilled. "How? Where?"

He smiled beneath the mask.

From beneath the large wall clock at the back of the ballroom, a master of ceremonies cried. "Midnight! Ladies and gentlemen, it is time to face your partner unmasked!"

Amongst the buffeting, excited throng, her husband leaned forward and murmured in her ear, "Don't worry. I will always find you."

And then she was alone while he vanished through the crowd.

A man made a drunken lunge at her, apparently aiming to pluck off her mask. She dodged his lumbering person and flitted through the crowd in search of her own friends. But her heart was beating, her whole being smiling, almost like the first night she had met him.

For the first time in two years, she was happy.

CHAPTER TWELVE

S INCE COMING HOME, it had begun to weigh upon the Earl of Wenning's mind that not only had he behaved badly to his bride, but that he had got everything horribly wrong. Which meant, he suspected, someone malevolent had meant one or both of them ill. Tonight's shooting certainly bore that out. Someone had tried to *kill* him or Grace.

The chilling events spun through his head, along with possible culprits, things he needed to discover, things he needed to do to ensure Grace's safety. He began by lurking outside the gates of Maida Gardens to be sure she was traveling home with people who were safe. From behind the next carriage waiting in line, he stuffed his mask into his pocket, then rolled the domino cloak up and hid it inside his coat while he watched Leyton hand her and Bridget Arpington inside then climb in beside them. Phineas followed.

Safety, he thought with relief, in numbers. But he wouldn't take the chance. Moving swiftly out of the shadows, he leapt onto the footman's plate at the back of the carriage just as it began to roll forward. Having never traveled in this position before, it was something of a novelty.

It was also weirdly soothing, for he could hear the hum of voices from within. His wife did not say much, but more than once he heard her merry laughter, and that made him smile—a distraction in his scouring of the road for threats, for the area between the gardens and Mayfair was not all well populated.

However, if the attack at Maida had been deliberate, then the culprit knew who they were and where they lived. He remained watchful, skulking on the far side of the carriage as Bridget was deposited at her front door. After the carriage drew to a final halt in Mount Street, he stepped off his platform once more, scanning both sides of the street and the windows of surrounding houses.

Fortunately, the street was empty. The neighbors might have found the earl's behavior odd in the extreme.

He waited until his wife was safely inside the house, then began to walk in the other direction to the carriage making its way to the mews. Five minutes later, he had doubled back and entered the house with his key before he made his way up to his lonely bedchamber.

Once, preparing for his marriage, he had made plans to change the apartments around so that his were next to his wife's instead of at the other side of the house. That had been the only one of his intended improvements she had not carried out in his absence.

Instead, the rooms that had been his since he had inherited the title as a boy felt alien and cold because she was not in them. And because, it seemed, he had been thoroughly taken in by someone he thought of as a friend. The question was, who?

IN THE MORNING, he rose early and made a number of calls, beginning with the Bow Street magistrate's house, and moving on to St. James, where he found his cousin Phineas breakfasting in his rooms.

Phin wore a luxurious dressing gown and seemed none too pleased to be interrupted. "What do you mean making social calls at such an uncivilized hour?" he growled.

Wenning lounged in the chair on the other side of the table and helped himself to coffee, Phin's landlady having helpfully supplied a cup and saucer. "Hardly uncivilized for a martyr to insomnia. Or a man who was enjoying a ride—or at least a gossip—in Hyde Park only a couple of days ago."

Phin sighed. "A man may choose peace occasionally, may be not?"

"Thick head?" Wenning asked sympathetically, "You must have had quite a night at the Maida masquerade."

Phin shuddered. "My dear, the wine is positively third rate, and the vulgar were so thick on the ground, one couldn't have mown them down if one tried."

Wenning sipped his coffee. "Being mown down seems a harsh price for mere vulgarity. What did you expect? Almack's with fresh air?"

"Yes, yes, call me naïve, foolish, over-optimistic. But I shan't be going back, I promise you."

"Was none of it to your exacting standards? Not even the fireworks?"

"They were pretty enough," Phineas allowed grudgingly.

"And I imagine your company was pleasant."

"The best, of course, although the ladies—especially Grace—were plagued by insolent fellows from other parties having the temerity to expect dances with them."

"And did Grace accept?" Wenning asked.

"Mostly, I think. Apparently, it's considered bad form to refuse."

Wenning set down his cup and twirled it in its saucer. "Tell me about the fireworks."

Phineas blinked. "They made a lot of noise, filled the air with the smell of gunpowder, and made pretty patterns in the sky. What more is there to say?"

"Who did you watch them with?"

"The party I was attached to. Why are you asking about the fireworks at all? You could just have come."

"I'm asking," Wenning said carefully, "because of an incident that took place during the firework display. Someone shot at my wife."

Phineas paled. "Dear God. But we returned her to you safe and unharmed! Surely, she was mistaken?"

"She was not. I saw it with my own eyes."

"Ah. So you *were* there."

"As you say. So, tell me, Phin, did you leave the others at all for any reason during the display?"

Phin's mouth fell open. "Are you accusing *me* of—"

"Hardly," Wenning interrupted. "I'm trying to establish if you could have seen who remained in the party for the whole display. And who did not."

"Of course," Phin said. "But have a care, Ollie. You can't go around accusing gentlemen—or ladies, for that matter—of shooting your wife! Especially since the same charge could be leveled at you."

"I shall certainly be careful. So, did you notice that anyone disappeared?"

Phin put down his knife and fork and frowned with the effort to remember. "I did notice that Grace vanished. Wherever she watched the fireworks from, it wasn't with us. I wasn't going to tell you that, in case you got—er…the wrong end of the stick."

"I was never likely to, since *I* was with Grace at that time."

"Being shot at," Phin said grimly.

"Go on," Wenning urged.

Phineas sighed in a long-suffering kind of way. "Let me think—no easy matter after a night on such inferior wine, I can tell you. Boothe and Curtis both milled around, restless. I don't recall seeing either of them after we settled to watch. Leyton wandered off, too, at one point, though he was back before we returned to the pavilion. And I lost sight of di Ripoli, as well, though he claimed later he had gone in search of Grace."

"I'm glad someone thought to. Anyone else?"

"Perhaps Mrs. Fitzwalter, who, it must be said, does not care for your wife for obvious reasons."

"I'd be surprised if my wife cares for her. I certainly don't."

"Perhaps you should tell her, for if ever I saw a woman hunting for a discreet—or not so discreet—*affaire de coeur*, it is she whenever she looks at you."

Wenning waved that aside, although he did make a mental note to discover if the woman had any skill with firearms.

"Seriously, Ollie, why would anyone shoot Grace? Who would benefit from such an atrocity? Except robbers, I suppose."

"It wasn't robbers," Wenning said flatly. "And it is possible the shot was not aimed at her but at me."

"But you are everyone's hero, dear boy. Who would do such a thing to you? To either of you?" He put another forkful of ham in his mouth and chewed thoughtfully. "A jealous colleague? A would-be or cast-off lover?"

Wenning regarded him for a moment, then finished his coffee and stood up. "Thank you, Phin. You have been most helpful."

Apparently mollified by such praise, Phineas called after him, "Game of cards this evening?"

"Alas, I must refuse. I am escorting my wife to the opera." Which would, he reflected as he cast an airy wave over his shoulder at his cousin, be news to his wife.

Since he was in the area, he called round to Leyton's rooms. Discovering his friend was out, he walked home to Mount Street, where he found his wife absent and the Marquess of Tamar painting the largest wall of the ballroom with a huge image of a turreted castle with a wild sea behind it.

"Based on your ancestral pile?" Wenning guessed. He did not know Tamar well—the man had enjoyed an unconventional upbringing, to say the least—but he had always found him engaging, good-natured, and formidably talented.

"Actually, it's my brother-in-law's Braithwaite Castle, up in Cumberland, though I've stylized it a bit."

"It does look very medieval."

Tamar, his smock and nose daubed with paint, grinned. "Well, I hope it inspires you to a particularly silly costume."

Wenning laughed and left him to it, returning to his own bedchamber, where he opened a drawer in his private desk and took out a packet of letters. From the middle, he took one crumpled, abused piece of paper that he had hidden there and spread it out on his desk.

He had read it only twice in his life. Once, on his wedding night when he had crushed it and thrown it across the room. He had almost left it there, but at the last moment, he had stuffed it in his pocket. And three days later, as his anger had died back and his guilt threatened, he had read it on board the ship and confirmed his justification in leaving his wife.

Each word had been like a nail hammered into his heart. Even now, reading it for the third time after two years, it wrenched at his guts.

What hurt most was not that she had not told him about this previous love, nor even that she had loved someone else when she married him. That was sad, heartbreaking in its way, for all of them. But young women were often pushed into marriages they did not want. Though disappointed, he would not have condemned her for that. He would instead have done his best to make her life happy, to win her until Anthony was a mere, faded memory of youth.

No, what had devastated him was the descriptions of *his* nauseating touch, her longing to know again the intimate pleasures she had known with Anthony. Her promise to return to Anthony as soon as the excruciating trial of her wedding journey was over. She even asked him to find a way to join her in Italy.

If he had loved her less, it would have hurt less. His reactions would have been less extreme. But the idea that her eager reception of his advances had been false, that her sighs of pleasure had merely hidden revulsion while she pined for the loving of another man whom she already planned to meet...

He could not even look at her, let alone speak to her. And so he had gone, letting anger win because it was more bearable than the agony of betrayal.

The words still hurt, but he read them now with fresh, critical eyes. Eyes that had witnessed the integrity of his wife under temptation. Eyes that had seen her pain, her anger at what he had done to her. He could almost swear she had no idea why he had gone. Either way, he would not let her destroy her reputation—only her reputation, he thought with awe, not her integrity—simply for revenge against him. It would not bring her peace or happiness. Only the truth had a chance of that.

And the truth, surely, lay in this letter. Several things about it bothered him. Why had she not sent it? Why carry it in a bag that would be opened by her maid and seen by any number of servants and porters, to say nothing of himself? And why had only that one piece of paper fallen out of the bag?

And then, the letter itself. It did not actually *sound* like Grace. He had always known that but put it down to the fact that he had never known her, that she had never written to him. In this letter, wild, florid flights of love had alternated with almost crude references to physical intimacies. But even now, beneath her veneer of languid sophistication, surrounded by a court of admirers—whom he could swear never got closer to her than a waltz—he could not imagine her even *knowing* such language, let alone committing it to paper for the delectation of a lover.

It sounds like a man.

The revelation took him by surprise, so he read it again. It did. It sounded like a man who used women and imagined females all regarded their lovers in a similar light.

The possibility that someone had forged this letter for the sole purpose of destroying his marriage did not hit him like a blow. It seeped in, almost like something he had always known and yet refused to admit.

Was he clutching at straws? Because after two years apart, two years of anger and torment, she still charmed him? Everything he had admired in the young girl had matured and strengthened in the woman who was still his wife. And God help him, he was falling deeper in love every moment. And deeper in shame for the suffering he must have inflicted upon her. That made his heart ache.

But if he was right, someone *really* wanted to part them. It had worked for two years, and now that he was home and reconciliation was possible, had this same person decided more drastic action was required?

Why? Who? Someone who had loved her before? Someone who would benefit from his death financially? Grace would, so perhaps her father or scapegrace brother, though the former seemed unlikely in the extreme.

Wenning's heir, should he have no sons, was Phineas. And Phineas had certainly been at Maida Gardens last night. However, Oliver balked at that idea, too. Phineas had always stood his friend and was one of the two people he had trusted to look after Grace in his absence.

The other was Leyton, his best friend ever since school. He of the deadpan humor and absolute honesty. And yet, Phineas kept hinting that Leyton had more than friendly feelings for Grace. And certainly, he had told Wenning off for his neglect of her. But surely that didn't fit with shooting him!

Then there were Grace's admirers: Sir Nash Boothe, and young Curtis, who actually had the Christian name Anthony. He preferred them as culprits, though, only because he didn't know them. Shooting a man with the intention of marrying his widow seemed extreme, even for a loose screw like Boothe, who, in any case, would be better concentrating on a wealthier bride. Grace's fortune, should Wenning die, was all tied up in trusts, largely to protect it from her father's depredations, but it would work for fortune hunters, too.

With an irritated shake of the head, he placed the letter among the others and put the packet back in his drawer. Then he drew a blank piece of paper toward him and dipped his pen in the waiting ink.

He wrote a short civil note to his wife informing her that he had taken a notion to go to the opera and, since he understood from Henley she also planned to attend, he would do himself the honor of escorting her to their box.

He wondered if it would annoy her. He wondered afresh how angry she would be to discover that he was Rudolf. In fact, he had meant to reveal himself several times, but something had always got in the way. Last night, just before the shot, he was sure he had seen some kind of shocked suspicion in her eyes, but that seemed to vanish during the rest of the tumultuous evening. And there was an undeniable challenge to winning her as a stranger, a man without the baggage of her own husband—although he had admitted to a wife, which might well continue to scare her off.

It didn't matter. If they could be friends, if they could find the truth in whatever guise, surely, they would both benefit. With that determination, he rose and strolled along the passage to her dressing room, where he left his note in the care of Henley, and again departed, this time for White's. There, one could usually find Ernest Leyton at this time of day.

Leyton, whom he discovered writing letters in the club, seemed pleased to see him and agreed to a constitutional in St. James's Park to walk off a late breakfast.

"You have a thick head, too?" Wenning inquired. "Phineas blames the inferior wine."

"Phineas would."

"Was the event as awful as he claimed? Or was he influenced by morning-after grumps?"

"He seemed to enjoy it well enough at the time," Leyton said wryly. He cast a veiled glance at Wenning. "You were there, were you not?"

"You spotted me?"

"Just before the unmasking, dancing with Grace. Did she know you, too?"

Wenning shook his head. "No, but then she has barely looked at me since I came home, and I did take some pains to be different to his lordship."

"Why?" Leyton asked flatly. "To spy on her?"

"To talk to her," Wenning said ruefully. "It seems to be the only way. But the thing is, Ern, a rather odd incident occurred while I was with her during the fireworks…"

Leyton looked genuinely shocked by his story about the shot, and for several moments, it was difficult to make him answer Wenning's questions.

"Who of our party wasn't there?" he replied at last. "Grace, for one, though now I know why. Di Ripoli went to look for her, and I let him."

"You didn't go yourself?"

"I didn't want all of us chasing after her, drawing attention to her, as though you had put us all up to it."

"Phineas said you went somewhere during the fireworks."

Leyton scowled. "How would he know if I did? He fled as soon as we left the pavilion, and I didn't see him again until we returned there."

"Is that a fact?" Wenning said thoughtfully. "And Boothe and Curtis?"

"I couldn't swear they never left, but I did see them from time to time. I was just glad neither of them was with Grace."

"Why?"

Leyton blinked. "Because I knew you wouldn't like it. Because I didn't think *she* would. And because I don't trust Nash Boothe farther than I could throw him."

"That's fair," Wenning acknowledged. "Tell me, Ern, between ourselves... You don't harbor a tiny *tendre* for Grace, do you? I could hardly blame you if you did."

Whatever reaction he expected from such a direct question, it wasn't Leyton's bitter smile or his sudden exclamation. "I wish to hell I did. Impossible as the situation would be, it would still be better than the one I'm in!"

"And what is that?" Wenning asked, intrigued.

"None of your damned business."

Wenning regarded him. "You were at Maida Gardens before, last week when Grace was there."

Leyton flushed, then paled in rapid succession. "Did Grace see me?"

"If she did, she didn't mention it to me. Phineas had it from someone or other. Who is she?"

Leyton sniffed haughtily, then sighed and gave in. "Frances Caldwell. She's quite a well-known actress, and God help me, I love her to distraction. But I can't marry her, can I? So we meet discreetly, including at occasional masked balls at Maida. It's about as public as we can risk."

"Sorry," Wenning said sincerely. "I'll try and think of a way to help."

A smile of affection flickered over the serious face. "I know you will, and I'm grateful. But your own problem is rather more urgent. Marital suspicions are one thing. Attempted murder is quite another. Have you approached the authorities?"

"I've persuaded Bow Street to set a couple of Runners to watch over Grace. But my thought is, it has to be someone who was part of your party."

"And who knew you were there," Leyton pointed out. "Did you come across anyone with a white rose in their domino who might have recognized you?"

Wenning shook his head slowly. He didn't want to believe the suspicion forming in his head. But discovering the truth would inevitably have a price.

CHAPTER THIRTEEN

FINDING HER HUSBAND'S note made Grace smile. Which was odd. Only two days ago, she would have immediately set about avoiding him. Today, she asked the servants if his lordship would be home for dinner, and learning that he would, she set about bathing and dressing for the evening, while a knot of excitement formed in her stomach.

She felt like the girl she had been the night after she had first met him and knew she would see him again at the ball. A whole new world of hope and the beginnings of love had seemed to be opening up for her. Well, she was no longer that naïve, but love might still be possible.

She was just regarding herself in the glass when an abrupt knock sounded at the door. Her heartbeat quickened, but when the door swung open, it was her graceless brother, Rollo, who strolled in.

"Oh, good, glad I caught you," he said by way of greeting. "Where are you off to?"

"The opera. I don't imagine I shall see you there."

Rollo shuddered. "Not likely." He threw himself into a chair and regarded her. "Everything well?" he asked.

"I believe so," she replied steadily. "To what do I owe the honor? Apart from brotherly concern, of course."

He grinned. "Of course. Thing is, pockets to let, debts to pay, and

I—" He broke off as the earl strolled into the room.

Oliver's gaze seemed to caress her, catching at her breath. But he paused to bow and turned, smiling faintly toward her brother.

"Rollo," he said, holding out his hand. "I don't believe we've met since I returned."

Rollo regarded the hand for a moment, then rose reluctantly to his feet and shook it briefly. "Been avoiding you," he said bluntly.

Oliver's lips twitched. "I'm glad the matter is rectified. Have you come for dinner?"

"Lord, no." He frowned. "Though I suppose it would be cheaper. But, no, I'm promised to friends."

"What a gracious refusal," Grace murmured.

Rollo ignored her. "Just came to ask Grace something."

"Don't let me hold you back." Oliver strolled to the window, and Rollo scowled after him, for he was hardly out of earshot.

"I've forgotten the question," he said lamely. "Must be the brandy."

"I believe dinner is ready to be served," Grace said. "So either join us or shove off, Rollo."

"Suppose I'll shove off," Rollo said without offense.

His eyes twinkling, Oliver bowed them out ahead of him. Rollo, very uncharacteristically, almost seized Grace's hand into the crook of his arm and all but galloped ahead to the stairs.

"Thing is, I find myself short," he muttered. "Any objections if I sell that damned pin you won from Boothe?"

"None. I gave it to you."

"Excellent," Rollo said, slowing up and releasing her. "Then I wish you joy of your caterwauling! Your servant, Wenning!" With that, he ran off downstairs, leaving the others slightly bemused.

"By caterwauling, he means opera?" Oliver hazarded.

"Sadly, yes. My brother is a philistine."

Oliver followed her into the dining room, which had been refurbished and lightened in his absence. "My compliments on the redecoration. I hope Rollo is not in trouble?"

"Lord, no. Well, no more than usual. He has run out of money—again—and wanted my permission to sell a trinket I gave him."

"What does he do with himself these days?" Oliver held her chair for her, and she sat.

"Rackets about town in the best family tradition. Papa won't let him near the management of the estates."

"Do you blame him?"

"Actually, yes. Papa's stewards haven't exactly excelled at it, and at least Rollo is interested. Besides, if he were in the country, he couldn't be going to the devil here, could he?"

"I suppose not." He waited while the soup was placed in front of them, and their wine poured out before he added, "I understand you are quite a dab hand at estate management yourself."

She shrugged. "That was easy. Your land thrives and makes a profit, and you have good people in place to manage it. I had little cause to intervene."

"But when you did, it was with purpose."

"I insisted on a few repairs and looked after a tenant in trouble. The cost did not require me to sell your silver or even curtail my dress allowance."

"I wasn't criticizing," he said mildly. "It was, in fact, a compliment. You cannot be unused to those."

"I am unused to *you*."

He met her gaze. "I am glad we begin to remedy that."

"As am I."

"Then tell me about this tenant in trouble."

The conversation, at first stilted by the past, by unfamiliarity, and by the presence of servants, grew gradually easier and more interesting. She told him about the estates, what she had done and why, mingled with a few amusing anecdotes. He told her a little about his journey, about the fascinating culture and beauty of China. So, by the time dinner was over and the carriage awaited, Grace was much more comfortable. And eager to know more.

Unwilling to upset this fragile truce, she did not ask the awkward questions to which she was desperate to know the answers. She did not mention last night's shooting, and neither did he. Instead, on the journey to Covent Garden, they discussed singers and operas.

"Tell me," he said in the carriage, "have you ever seen an actress called Frances Caldwell?"

"Why, yes. Never in the leading role so far, but she undoubtedly has talent. I look out for her name when deciding what I want to see. Why?"

"Between ourselves, Leyton just confessed to me he has a *tendre* for her. I'm not talking about the more common relationship between a gentleman and a lady of the stage. He wants to marry her."

"Ah!" she exclaimed, remembering. "I wonder... I saw him with someone once. At Maida Gardens. But surely, he will not marry her?"

"He is aware of all the reasons he shouldn't. Not least that if he does, her life will be miserable, for his own society will never accept her."

"It is unfair." She frowned, remembering Leyton's unfailing if distant kindness to her, and glanced at her husband. "He has looked out for me, you know. Sir Ernest."

Oliver seemed to hesitate. Then, "He would have, in any case, because that is his nature. But I confess I asked him to."

"Why?"

"Because I could not."

"*Did* not," she corrected.

His lips quirked in rueful acknowledgment, but before he could respond, the carriage came to a halt before the theatre, and the door was opened for them to alight.

When he spoke again, they were in the theatre foyer. "I'm afraid you will be the center of attention again. Our first public outing together."

She shrugged. "I thrive on the attention, my lord. Ask anyone."

"I would rather ask you."

Despite the light, bantering tone they both employed, she sensed a seriousness behind it. He didn't want merely to be reassured that she coped. He wanted to know what she felt.

"It takes a little courage at first," she murmured. "And then it becomes a game of pretend. I have grown into my pretend character so that I can no longer tell the difference. In short, let them look."

He settled her hand on his arm with a brief squeeze, and together they made their stately way up the staircase, nodding amiably to acquaintances and along the passage to the Wenning box, where there was more bowing to do to those in other boxes.

"I fell in love with you at the opera," he recalled unexpectedly. "Or at least that was when I acknowledged it to myself."

"What a pity."

He blinked. "Pity? Why?"

She was saved from answering by the arrival of her invited guests, who included her mother and Sir Ernest Leyton. Private speech with her husband was over for the time being, and while that was frustrating, she was also relieved. She did not wish to quarrel, to break the frail truce they had begun, with all its possibilities. And yet, she could not pretend that his sudden departure on their wedding night was pleasant, excusable, or right.

But if she could not ask Oliver such blunt questions, she could speak to Sir Ernest. During the first interval, when her mother moved seats, she found an opportunity to be relatively private. A little space formed around them, and the chatter in the box served to drown out their own conversation from all but each other.

"Wenning told me," she murmured, "that when he left for China, he asked you to watch over me."

Sir Ernest looked slightly hunted. "He asked me to have a care for you, not to spy on you."

She smiled. "Oh, I understand that and am grateful. You saved me from many a Town pitfall just waiting to swallow an unwary bride."

"You learned quickly," he said uncomfortably.

"Fortunately for both of us," she observed. "Tell me, sir, did he request this of you after he left or before?"

"After," he admitted. "He wrote from Southampton, just before the ship sailed."

She drew in her breath. "Tell me, did he give you a reason, then or later, for changing his mind about China?"

He met her gaze with reluctance, but his eyes were as open and honest as ever. "In two years, you never asked me that."

Her lips twisted. "One has to pretend one does not care."

"You should be having this conversation with Wenning."

"How can I when I do not know—" She broke off. "Before I can even begin to make this right, I need to know if there's a point. Was he somehow forced into marriage with me?"

"Of course not!" Sir Ernest looked shocked at the very idea.

"Then why did he change toward me?"

Sir Ernest shifted in his seat. "I don't believe he ever did, not in his heart. He discovered something that shocked him. A letter you had written to another man that seemed to convince him you had married him for nothing more than money. Please, don't ask me any more."

At that moment, Grace was incapable of saying anything at all.

She had never, to the best of her recollections, written to any man. Unless one counted Rollo or her father. Or all the letters she had begun to Oliver and torn up without sending. She had certainly never written a love letter. In fact, unless she counted the second footman when she was thirteen, or one of Rollo's friends who had stayed during the school holiday when she was fourteen, she had never even imagined herself in love with anyone. Until Oliver.

Then their separation had been caused by nothing but a lie. A lie Oliver had believed. Because the letter must have been convincing, but where on earth could such a letter have come from? There could have been no misunderstanding there of something she *had* written. So, who in the world would have played such a cruel trick?

A chill began to creep through her blood. *The same person who tried to shoot us?*

The second act had begun before she was again aware of her surroundings. And Sir Ernest was still beside her.

"Thank you," she whispered beneath her breath.

He cast her a distracted smile.

"I would return the favor," she murmured. "Would it help if I called on Mrs. Caldwell?"

His eyes widened in panic. "He told you!"

"I saw you together at Maida Gardens."

"The Countess of Wenning cannot call on an actress," he said bluntly.

"But I would like to meet her. If she is agreeable." She became aware that her mother and several other people were glancing toward them and lapsed into silence.

><<

THE HONORABLE ROLLO Darblay, impatient with the staid nature of the established clubs in St. James and bored with most of the entertainments offered by the ton, had discovered a pleasant home from home in the back streets of St. Giles.

Here, he had honored the Orange Tree Club with his membership. It had a lot to recommend it. Congenial, if rough company, cheap food and drink, women, gaming. Here, you were more likely to run into prize fighters and lowly born entrepreneurs than aristocrats, although there were a few of those, too. And the female company was not the kind one introduced to one's mother or sister. It also held a permanent hint of danger that appealed to Rollo's jaded heart.

The Orange Tree—named for the incongruous stained glass window in the main room—was not troubled by constricting rules of behavior, but the play was fair. And although Rollo was pretty sure to be rubbing shoulders with known criminals, thieving on the premises was dealt with very harshly by the two amiable brutes who guarded the doors.

One could also take care of small matters of business, such as selling or pawning valuables. The motive for providing such services was clearly so that patrons would then spend their newly acquired money on play at the club, and Rollo was certainly willing to oblige on that score. Once he had paid off his debts of honor, of course.

"There's no need to be in such a hurry, Rolls," his friend Mr. Meade said uneasily. "I can wait for my money, you know. Not going to dun a friend!"

"Not the point," Rollo said, taking the sapphire pin from his pocket. "Besides, we should have a damned good evening on the proceeds, too."

Having been there less frequently, Meade was a lot less comfortable at the Orange Tree than Rollo. "They're bound to cheat you, Rolls," he murmured warningly.

"Nonsense. Got a pretty decent price for my watch last month. And I won enough to get it out of pawn again the next night." Rollo dropped the pin in front of the man known as the Pawnbroker, although Rollo was fairly sure he doubled as a fence. This discreet but somewhat shifty individual sat casually at the table near the door, chatting with friends and drinking from a glass of gin at his elbow.

He broke off his conversation to glance at Rollo's pin and picked it up. "Pretty," he observed. "You pawning or selling?"

"Selling."

"Rolled up again, Darblay?" said a superior, drawling voice close by.

Phineas Harlaw sat with Nash Boothe at the next table, in company with a pair of young women who smiled winningly at Rollo. Rollo would have smiled back, except he was annoyed to find any connection to his sister here, and Harlaw and Boothe were among his least favorite connections to her, though for different reasons. Harlaw, he just didn't like. Boothe, he didn't trust to be a gentleman either—an odd objection in surroundings like this, but Rollo couldn't abide pretense.

"Temporary embarrassment," Rollo said, as the pawnbroker put a glass to his eyes and held up the sapphire pin to the light.

"Wait a moment," Harlaw exclaimed. "I know that trinket, don't I? Where have I...? Ha! It's Boothe's! How did *you* get your hands on it?"

"It isn't Boothe's, it's mine," Rollo said impatiently. "And you needn't make me sound like a damned thief!"

"Wouldn't dream of it, dear boy," Harlaw assured him with a quizzical glance at Boothe. "It is yours, isn't it? Did you *give* it to Darblay?"

Rollo, suddenly uneasy, scowled at Boothe, daring him to bring Grace's name into this.

Boothe, who seemed more affronted by the idea that he would make such a personal gift to a man, snapped, "Of course I did not."

"Well, now," Harlaw observed, looking about him.

Annoyingly, they seemed to have attracted a little too much attention. A couple of drunken young bucks untangled themselves from their female companions to see better. One of the large individuals known as the Thief-Catcher—although Thief-Ejector might have been more accurate—ambled closer.

"Not directly," Meade said unexpectedly to Boothe. "But the pin was given away by you and ended up with Darblay. I know because I was there."

"Were you? I don't recall you," Boothe said nastily. "But I do recall giving the pin not to you, Darblay, but to your lovely sister, Lady Wenning."

Fury rose in Rollo's blood. His hand clenched, and he longed to crash it into Boothe's disrespectful mouth. And yet he couldn't call Boothe out over Grace's name; that would only make everything worse.

"You lost a wager," Meade said. "Recall it very well."

"We all do," Rollo said savagely. "But the problem is, this piece of excrescence just called me a thief."

Boothe flushed, half rising from his chair until Harlaw closed a hand over his arm.

"Steady on, Rolls," Meade said uneasily. "In any case, fairly sure that was Harlaw. Come on, it's all cleared up now. Let's play."

"Damned if I will while that primped-up ape sits there calling me a liar and a thief to my face!" Rollo didn't much care now whether he caused a duel or not. His main aim was to move the quarrel away from Grace.

His insults had clearly riled Boothe, who flung off Harlaw's restraining hand. "Be damned to you," he snarled. "And as for you, Darblay, you needn't think your connection to L—"

The weasel was about to say Grace's name *again*. Rollo didn't hesitate, just picked up the nearest glass and hurled the contents in Boothe's red face.

Silence fell on the room, save for Boothe's spluttering, swiftly followed by a roar. "Damn it, Darblay, you shall meet me for that! Harlaw will act for me."

"And Meade will act for me." Rollo swung back to the Pawnbroker. "Well? How much?"

CHAPTER FOURTEEN

G RACE'S HEAD WAS still spinning the following morning. The shock of Sir Ernest's revelation that a letter she had apparently written to a lover had driven her husband away from her gradually gave way to a weird sort of dazed happiness.

He hadn't been lying to her about love. He hadn't found her wanting in matters of the bedchamber... Or at least, he might have, but that wasn't what had caused him to bolt from her arms on their wedding night. Her foolish mind had a tendency to dwell on this rather than on what she needed to do to find out more about the letter and make things right.

The simplest method would, of course, be to ask Oliver. Not his friends, not even his alter ego, Rudolf. But dare she risk bringing up the subject quite so soon? Last night they had at least grown a little comfortable with each other, but they circled still like prize fighters looking for a weakness, an opening. Not that she had ever been near a prize fight, naturally, but she had heard her brother discussing them at length when he had forgotten her presence.

Henley had finished dressing her hair for the morning, but instead of bustling off to collect Hope for an outing to various flower shops and silk warehouses, she remained at her dressing table, gazing sightlessly into the mirror.

"My lady," Henley interrupted. "Sir Ernest Leyton has called."

Grace blinked. "For me? Or his lordship?"

"He asked for you."

Grace stood. "Where is he?"

She owed Sir Ernest for much, not least for finally revealing something of Oliver's reason for abandoning her. But she didn't actually expect him to say what he did.

"Good morning." He bowed as perfectly as always but continued to speak almost at once. "If you still wish it, I will take you to call on Mrs. Caldwell now."

Grace didn't hesitate. She sent a footman to her parents' house with a message for Hope that she would be later than planned, then fetched her shawl and bonnet, and sallied forth with Sir Ernest.

"What changed your mind?" she asked when they were in the carriage. "I had just acknowledged to myself that I would have to work around you to do anything at all."

Sir Ernest cast her a crooked smile. "The knowledge that you would undoubtedly do so changed my mind. At least partially. For the rest... Mrs. Caldwell is lonely and needs a friend."

"Why is she lonely? Does she not have friends in the theatre?"

"Of course. And I can join her among them. But she cannot join me with my friends. She is too proud to wish to be only acknowledged as my mistress."

Grace merely nodded, although her heart sank a little as she steeled herself to meet a manipulative woman. Not that she blamed her. A woman's place in her society was always difficult. A woman moving between different societies found herself in an impossible situation, and surely everyone had a right to try for happiness.

She expected to be taken to a discreet house, probably in Kensington and quite clearly paid for by Sir Ernest. But instead, the carriage was traveling in the opposite direction, and stopped, eventually, in King Street.

"She has rooms here, with a private entrance," Sir Ernest murmured as he handed her down. And when Grace looked about her somewhat doubtfully, a smile flickered across his face. "I told you she was proud."

"Does she know I am coming?"

"I sent word ahead that you might accompany me."

Mrs. Caldwell opened the door herself. Modestly dressed, she curtseyed gracefully, cast a baffled look at Sir Ernest, and conducted them up a staircase to her parlor, where Sir Ernest made the introductions.

"Grace, allow me to present Mrs. Frances Caldwell. Fran, Lady Wenning."

Mrs. Caldwell curtseyed again, but she seemed more bewildered than awed by a countess's presence in her parlor. In fact, it was hard to recognize in this quiet woman the actress Grace had seen so often on stage. The strong bone structure of her face was the same, but beyond that, there was little similarity. Mrs. Caldwell had a powerful stage presence, but in real life, she seemed a much less certain figure.

"I'll bring tea," she said calmly and departed.

Grace sat on one of the three chairs and gazed about her. The room was adequately, even comfortably furnished, but beyond a couple of cushions, there was nothing that was not necessary, apart from a porcelain vase of flowers on the table before the window.

"The vase is one of the only two gifts she has accepted from me," Sir Ernest said quietly. "I do not pay for these rooms. She will not let me. Nor will she allow me to arrange something better."

Mrs. Caldwell returned a moment later, implying everything had been prepared in advance, and Sir Ernest rose at once to take the tray from her. She sat in the other chair to pour the tea. Sir Ernest passed a cup to Grace.

"Lady Wenning," Sir Ernest told the actress, "was moved by our predicament."

"And came, I think, to see the Jezebel for herself?" Mrs. Caldwell said calmly. She might have been quiet, but she was certainly prepared to stand up for herself.

"Of course I did," Grace replied in similar tones and sipped her tea. "What friend would not? You do not seem very much like a Jezebel."

A flicker of humor showed in the actress's profound and rather beautiful grey eyes. "Indeed, I am very boring. Middle-aged before my time, according to the young people of my company."

"How old—" Grace began impulsively, then broke off with an apologetic smile.

"I am one and thirty," Mrs. Caldwell said calmly. "Three years older than Ernest."

"I have seen you on the stage," Grace said. "You have a tendency to outshine other actresses."

"And yet leading roles are rare. I will never reach the top of my profession."

"Is that a grief to you?"

"No. I earn enough to keep myself and save a little for when I am no longer offered any roles at all."

"Have you always had a love of the stage?" Grace asked.

"Yes. And so that's where I looked for work when I left home."

"Were your parents happy with that?" Grace asked doubtfully. For Mrs. Caldwell's accent did not sound mimicked. She had at least been educated as a lady.

"They were happy that I left," Mrs. Caldwell replied honestly. "In fact, they insisted upon it. I was, you see, a fallen woman."

"At the age of seventeen," Sir Ernest said grimly. "Some scoundrel took advantage of her innocence."

"I had to make a life for myself, and so I did. I make no apologies for the one I chose."

"And why should you?" Grace agreed. "Do you enjoy it?"

"Yes, most of the time."

"Sir Ernest tells me he wants to marry you."

"He cannot marry an actress."

"Forgive me," Grace said, "but you were not always an actress. The world is censorious, especially for females, but I suspect your birth is not so different from his,"

Mrs. Caldwell smiled faintly. "Sadly, that no longer matters."

"So," Grace said thoughtfully. "Am I right in thinking you both want to marry but both refuse to do so because of the shame or distress it would cause the other? You would be scorned by his friends, and he would be demeaned by marrying an actress."

"As would our children."

Grace sighed. "The world is not always as we would wish it." She thought for a while, drinking her tea. "You cannot change the world, sadly, or, at least, not at once. So, you have to change what you can. Would you give up the theatre to marry him?"

"Of course, but—"

"Then do so. I gather Sir Ernest has been extraordinarily discreet about your relationship. Go abroad, use your own name, not Frances Caldwell, which I suppose is a stage name. Meet and marry in another country, far from society's prying eyes, and become the Lady Leyton you wish to be. And when you come home, live in the country for a while. You are so clearly a lady that no one will question it. Sir Ernest is well-liked, and you will be, too. Wenning and I will both call on you and vouch for you in face of any gossip. And voila, you are respectable again."

They both gaped at her.

"You make it sound so simple," Sir Ernest said at last.

Grace shrugged. "I don't see why it shouldn't be. Especially if there is nothing to connect Frances Caldwell with whomever she once was. I doubt anyone will care by now about the scandal of your youth. You might even try reconciliation with your parents after you are married." She set down her cup and stood. "Forgive me, I have promised to collect my sister for a shopping expedition."

Looking dazed, Mrs. Caldwell rose and took her outstretched hand.

"Thank you for the tea," Grace said.

"Thank you for the advice," Mrs. Caldwell returned, "which I shall consider carefully—though I have to say it sounds astonishingly clear-headed and sensible."

Grace gave a deprecating smile. "Ah, well, it is easy to be clear-headed and sensible about other people's problems. If you need anything—including more advice, sensible or otherwise—just send me a note."

"Do you always make decisions about people so quickly?" Mrs. Caldwell asked, smiling back.

"Yes."

"And are you always correct?"

Grace felt her smile fade and immediately pinned it back on her lips. "No. But I usually am. Goodbye!"

Leaving the rather stunned lovers alone, she took the hackney to her parents' house, collected Hope, and spent several hours choosing flowers and silks to decorate the ballroom in colors that matched Lord Tamar's mural, and finally returned to Mount Street for tea.

"I wish I could come to your ball," Hope said wistfully as they alighted from the carriage. "It sounds such fun."

Grace glanced at her thoughtfully. "Perhaps you could, just for an hour. You would be in costume, after all. Let me think about it!"

They swept into the house and across the hall toward the staircase. Some movement in one of the reception rooms caught her eye, and a familiar figure all but leapt out of sight. Amused, Grace turned aside and walked into the room.

"Mr. Meade," she said cordially. "How do you do? Are you acquainted with my sister? Hope, this is Mr. Meade, one of Rollo's friends. Sir, my sister, Miss Darblay."

Mr. Meade bowed, looking unaccountably nervous. "Delighted.

Absolutely delighted."

"Does your presence mean Rollo is scouring the house in search of me?" Grace asked lightly.

"Alas, no, my lady. I'm here on my own account."

Grace blinked. "How fascinating. Have a seat, sir, and tell me what I may do for you. Rollo is not in trouble, is he?"

"Rollo? Goodness, no, of course not. He's absolutely fine and dandy." Mr. Meade tugged at his neckcloth. "Truth is, I'm hoping to see Lord Wenning."

"Ah. I did not know you were friends."

"We're not," Mr. Meade assured her. "Hoping to remedy that!"

Wenning sauntered into the room at that point. "Grace, Hope, what a pleasure." He turned his amiable gaze on Mr. Meade, who now resembled a startled rabbit.

"Allow me to introduce Mr. Meade," Grace said obligingly. "He is a friend of Rollo's. Sir, my husband, the Earl of Wenning."

"Ring for tea, my dear," Wenning said, "and join us if you will."

"My lord, I was hoping for a private word," Mr. Meade blurted in an agony of embarrassment.

Grace took pity on him. "Then we shall leave you to your important matters and have our tea and cakes upstairs."

"What was that all about?" Hope murmured as they climbed the stairs.

"I have no idea." For some reason, that worried Grace. She doubted Meade would have come to the earl on some errand of his own, so she suspected his business concerned Rollo. In which case, it would make more sense for him to speak to Grace, would it not?

⟫⟫⟩⟨⟨⟨

"AND THAT," MEADE said gloomily, "is the matter in a nutshell."

"I see. So...do I have this right? Darblay forced a quarrel on Boothe to stop him talking about my wife?"

"More or less. And the truth is, Boothe did seem ready to blab her name again. Spur of the moment decision, and he made it impossible for Boothe to ignore him. But the quarrel is over Boothe calling Darblay a thief and a liar."

"Because Darblay was in possession of the pin my wife won in a wager from Boothe?"

"She did," Meade said earnestly. "I was there when he handed it over, and she gave it immediately to Rolls—I mean Darblay. All perfectly innocent. Even Harlaw recognizing the pin wouldn't have mattered a hang if Boothe hadn't blabbed he'd given it to Lady Wenning."

"Mr. Phineas Harlaw?" Wenning asked, just to be sure.

"Yes. He's Boothe's second. He didn't have a lot of choice in the matter, and I have to say he's as keen as I am to stop the fight. But the thing is, neither Boothe nor Rollo will apologize."

"And coming to me," Wenning said slowly, "was your idea?"

"Well, my original idea was that Mr. Harlaw come to you, but he declined, being as he is in a somewhat invidious position, as both your cousin and Boothe's second."

"Then, they are good friends, my cousin and Sir Nash Boothe?"

"Don't really move in their circles, to be frank," Meade said apologetically. "So I couldn't say. But they were certainly together at the Orange Tree."

"Hmm… And would you say anyone else overheard the quarrel that led to the challenge?"

"You mean was your wife's name bandied about the Orange Tree?" Meade said bluntly. "No, I don't think so. But it will be all over London if they fight. And yet, if Rollo backs down now, it will look as if Boothe is right. Either way, it seems to me, Lady Wenning loses, which is why I've come to you, sir."

"Thank you," Wenning said, gazing past him out of the window.

"That does you credit. You may safely leave the matter in my hands."

"Thing is, I'm fond of Darblay," Meade said apologetically. "Wouldn't like him to get killed either. Or have to leave the country for murder."

"It is a fate likely to befall someone before this is done," Wenning said with a hint of grimness. He held out his hand to Meade. "Good day! I appreciate your bringing this to me."

When Meade was gone, Wenning spent a long time gazing at the window, forming and discarding schemes in his head. It was annoying, for he had other, more enjoyable plans for the evening, and he wasn't sure he could fit everything in.

His relationship with his wife was too complicated. During one encounter in the library, he had found it so damnably difficult to keep his hands off her, that he had left her there drinking brandy alone. Just so that he did not ruin everything by lunging at her when he was hardly at his best or most sensitive. So much for brandy taking the edge off lust.

Rudolf, he thought, sighing, was complicating things. It had been a useful, though hardly honorable, way to get close to Grace, to understand her when she would not spend five minutes in her husband's company if she could help it. But perhaps it was time for Rudolf to bow out. He had become just one more thing she would have to forgive Oliver.

But as he walked out of the room and across the hall, excitement surged through him, just because he would see his wife tonight, learn some of her thoughts, perhaps, just be with her.

However, before that, he had better see what could be done about Rollo's quarrel with Boothe. Wenning picked up his hat and left the house in search of his adventurous friend, Campbell.

CHAPTER FIFTEEN

ALTHOUGH THE SEASON'S social whirl had lost much of its luster even before her husband's return, it was lowering how flat parties now seemed when he was not present. Phineas escorted her to Lady Barton's rout one evening, and the following evening, she accompanied her parents to the theatre. And on both occasions, she found herself looking in vain for her husband. She had barely glimpsed him over the last two days.

Nor had she seen any sign of his alter ego, so her bright optimism following the firework evening at Maida Gardens had faded somewhat.

Staring at the stage—she had long ago lost track of the plot—she came to the conclusion that she was going to have to *make* things happen. Request her husband's escort, visit him in his library again, which she had been avoiding since he had left her there the other evening. She could even seduce him…

Her whole body flushed, and she fanned herself vigorously. She was not ready for such intimacy. Was she? Not until they understood each other a little better.

On the other hand, two years ago, he had introduced her to true arousal and bodily delight. Ever since, desire had hummed beneath her skin, sometimes unbearably, and the idea of assuaging her lust with the only man she had ever wanted melted her bones.

"Where's that fellow who's always hanging around you?" her father said unexpectedly as the final curtain came down.

"Which fellow, Papa?" she asked distractedly. Not Oliver, that was sure.

"Weaselly fellow who thinks so much of himself. Boothe?"

"I have no idea. To be frank, I am happier without his presence."

"Good," Papa said, dropping a shawl around his wife's shoulders. "Are we taking you home first?"

"No, thank you, Papa. I have ordered my own carriage to pick me up here. I'm going on to Lady Hilsborough's."

"Will Wenning be there?" her mother asked.

"I really have no idea," Grace replied carelessly. Though she hoped so, she doubted it.

There followed the usual crush to get out of the theatre and then the greeting of more acquaintances as everyone awaited their carriages, but finally, the Wenning-crested vehicle pulled up just in front of the Darblay coach.

As Grace kissed her parents, her mother chose that moment to ask, "Is everything well with you and Wenning?"

"As well as one might expect," Grace replied lightly, although suddenly she wanted to cry. She might have replaced her revenge plan with a reconciliation plan—at least as a possibility—but she still felt *empty*.

Hastily, she accepted her father's hand into the carriage. She waved, smiling until the carriage began to move forward, then collapsed back against the luxurious cushions.

"Dull night?" inquired a soft male voice from the opposite corner.

Grace jumped an inch off the bench, her hand flying to her throat in startled alarm as a figure leaned forward. The lamplight from the outside of the carriage played over his masked face.

An unladylike snort escaped her, for she didn't know whether to laugh or hit him.

"Idiot," she uttered. "What are you doing here?"

"I came to see you, of course."

There were lots of questions she should have asked "Rudolf," such as how he'd got in without her coachman seeing him or how he had known where to find her. But she was too annoyed to play the game.

"Why?" she demanded.

"I said I would. What has upset you?"

The lamplight flickering over his masked face revealed his steady, concerned eyes. She looked away. "Nothing. I am merely tired."

"Then why go to Lady Hilsborough's?"

Something else "Rudolf" should not have known. "I might change my mind and go home."

"You could," he agreed. "Or we could talk."

"About what?"

"Your problems and mine. It might help."

"In a very limited way, given the few minutes it will take us to get to South Audley Street! Or Mount Street."

"I'm afraid I bribed your coachman to take a rather more circuitous route. Via the river and the park."

If he had really done such a thing, would she have been afraid or impressed? In reality, he had given his own coachman orders, though he may have slipped him an extra coin for his trouble.

"You take much upon yourself," she said haughtily.

"I do, but you haven't yet stopped the carriage to have me ejected."

"There is still time."

His teeth gleamed briefly, then he shifted across the carriage to sit beside her. "Are you unhappy, Grace?"

She thought about her answer for a moment before she replied, "Yes."

"Because of your husband?"

Habit thrust denial to the tip of her tongue, but she bit it back. If they did not talk, they would never resolve anything. "Yes," she admitted, then added with foolish difficulty, "he courted me with words of love that were clearly lies."

She felt his gaze burn into her cheek, but she could not look at him, even in the poor light.

"Why clearly?"

"Because he left me on our wedding night with a note so curt as to be insulting. And went off for two years during which I heard not one word from him." She did not mean to let emotion into her voice, but even to her, the pain and the anger were evident. She wondered if he would notice. Certainly, he did not rush into speech.

"Why?" he asked at last. "Why would he do such a thing?"

"He never told me that either. My only conclusion is that for some reason, he had decided I would do as a bride and discovered on our wedding night that I would not. He suggested I go on our wedding journey alone if I wished or take up residence in whichever of his houses appealed to me."

"Did he really say that?" There was an odd hoarseness in his voice, and Grace was fiercely glad.

"He wrote it."

Beside her, her husband stirred. "Before he did so, did you love him?"

Her hands clenched in her lap. "With all my heart. My naïve, gullible heart."

"Gullible?" he pounced. "Because you think he never loved you?"

"How could he have and still behaved as he did?"

"Perhaps something upset him. Convinced him otherwise."

"Like the letter?" she said, her heart beating even faster than before. She turned at last to look at him and found his glittering eyes staring at her.

"What letter?" he asked, and the soft, disguised voice sounded almost hoarse again, as if even he could not hide this emotion.

"I don't know," she replied. "I finally prised it out of a mutual friend that he had found some letter that convinced him I had already played him false."

"And had you?"

"Of course not! As he would have known if he had even spoken to me on the subject. If he even *thought* for a moment. For one thing, it must have been glaringly obvious that I had no experience in matters of love! But no, in one sudden moment, I was cut off from affection, respect, consideration. Tried and convicted in absentia, as it were. Is such a man worth my love, Rudolf?"

He tore his gaze free. She hated that the mask hid his expressions from her.

"No," he said. "He is not." Unexpectedly, his hand closed over hers on her lap and gripped. Even through her gloves, his fingers were warm, secure. He turned back to her. "And yet you let no other would-be lover near you, do you? Do you love him still?"

Her hand jumped in his, but when he relaxed his grip, she clung, threading her fingers between his.

"It seems to be my nature," she said carefully. "But I still have my pride."

"Meaning you will never tell him?"

"I told him once before."

"*Why* in God's name do you still love him?" he demanded with unexpected ferocity.

"I try not to. Then I hear things, see things, that show me he is still the man I believed him to be. And yet I cannot change the fact that he left me, and for what must have been a lie."

"His, or another's," her husband murmured.

The carriage was bowling along Park Lane, giving the momentary illusion of peaceful countryside.

"What of your wife?" she asked. "Why are you here with me instead of at home with her?"

"I believe...we had a misunderstanding. I did not trust her."

"She hurt your feelings?"

"Profoundly. Unbearably. Irreparably, I thought."

"You should speak to her honestly."

"And you should speak to your husband."

"Should *he* not speak to *me*?"

Perhaps he heard the indignation in her voice, for he smiled. "He certainly owes you that and a great deal more." He lifted her hand to his lips and kissed her fingers. "Do you know what I think, Grace?"

His eyes, profound and curiously enthralling, held her gaze. Wordlessly, she shook her head.

"Since there's no help, come let us kiss and part. I think we must end our little adventure and devote ourselves in honesty to our spouses."

In panic, she pushed her hand onto his shoulder and clung. She could not talk to Oliver yet, not the way she could to his alter ego. It was too soon to leave this masquerade, one-sided as it now was. How could she...?

"Why did you send me that poem?" she whispered.

"Because it seemed the saddest and yet most hopeful words I had ever read. I thought they might help your marriage and mine. How many lovers part because one is simply too proud to say the words that might save them?"

"Now if thou wouldst, when all have given him over," she murmured, staring at him in the darkness. *"From death to life, thou mightst him yet recover.* You believe it is not too late to prevent the death of love in our marriages?"

His breath caught. Something indefinable changed in his posture. He muttered something unintelligible under his breath, and quite suddenly, she was clutched against his chest, his arms wrapped hard around her as his mouth came down on hers. A definite if passionate farewell.

At least, she thought that was what he intended, for it felt like a parting kiss. Only, when she threw her arm around his neck and slid her other hand up to his mask-covered cheek, he groaned, and she opened wide to him. And suddenly, everything changed.

The kiss was no longer hard but openly sensual, tender, devouring, and his hands were under her cloak, caressing her back, her side, the softness of her breast. Desire surged through her, hot and searing and urgent. She was thrust back against the cushions with him half-lying upon her, his distinctive hardness pressing at the junction of her thighs, driving her wild.

He will take me here, she thought with joyous wonder. *He really will, and it will be so, so…*

Stupid.

He would think she had given in knowingly to a lover, not to her husband. Or it would all be over. Nothing in the world had ever been as difficult as this, but somehow, with an inarticulate sound alarmingly like a sob, she pushed him away, slid free, and threw herself onto the opposite bench.

She had time to see the bewilderment in his eyes, to know with triumph that this had not been yet another test. It had been instinctive, impulsive, and he was at least as frustrated as she. With hands that shook, she drew the hood of her cloak over her disordered hair.

A rueful smile flickered over his lips. His breath was still ragged as he reached up and knocked on the roof. And then the carriage drew to a halt, and she realized they were in Mount Street.

Neither of them said a word as the carriage stopped outside Wenning House, but neither did eye contact break between them.

"Goodbye, Rudolf," she said and slipped down without waiting for the steps to be lowered. She all but ran up to the front door, which, fortunately, opened to receive her at the last moment, and then she was home and safe.

But as she ran upstairs to her own apartments, she was smiling again from ear to ear.

APPALLED BY HOW difficult it was not to follow her into the house and confess all before persuading her into his bed—*please, God!*—Wenning swallowed, bumped his head back against the frustratingly soft cushions, and rapped once more on the ceiling.

The carriage rumbled on around to the mews, from where Wenning made his way through his own back garden, tearing off the silly mask as he went. He entered by the back door, but without going into the kitchen, he turned immediately right and through the door to the wine cellar.

Here, he inspected the recent adjustments, which included two sturdy locks on the two smaller rooms, two stools, and two blankets.

Satisfied that all was prepared, he grabbed a few bottles of brandy and a couple more of wine and moved into the house through the dark, empty kitchen. He made directly for the large ground floor salon where he, and his father before him, had been in the habit of holding gentlemen's only parties, consisting largely of cards and drunkenness.

Setting down his bottles, Wenning began shoving the furniture into a more haphazard arrangement, found several packs of cards, which he distributed about the tables, some in untidy heaps, some set out as though still in the middle of the game. He threw some coins and pre-prepared, illegible vowels around the tables, too. Then, he quietly collected glasses from various places and prepared to waste his best brandy and some inferior wine, splashing various amounts into each glass and swirling it around. The glasses themselves, he plonked down in all sorts of places—teetering on the edge of tables, on the mantelpiece, and the floor and the windowsill, on top of a picture frame, on chair arms, and one upside down on an alabaster statuette he had never liked. The bottles he left open, scattered across various tables.

Offering up a silent apology to his staff, he spilled brandy on the cushions and the carpets. He paused a moment at the doorway to admire his handiwork. In a couple of hours, it should smell even worse.

It was going to be a long night, he thought ruefully, as he closed the door on the mess. As he crossed the now-dark hall, with only one candle for light, he noticed a note on the silver tray addressed to him. In the handwriting of his cousin Phineas.

Intrigued, he took it up to the library, where he lit the lamps and opened Phin's note.

Cousin,

I scarcely know what to do for the best and have finally come to the conclusion that I must lay the matter at your feet, in the hope you might be able somehow to stop tomorrow's foolishness.

The matter, simply, is this. Your brother-in-law, young Darblay, forced a quarrel on Sir Nash Boothe, who happened to be in my company at the time. I was therefore roped into standing as Boothe's second in the duel that takes place at dawn tomorrow at Putney Heath. Obviously, I cannot be happy about such an event, where your brother-in-law might kill or be killed, and besides, whatever the outcome, the danger remains that your wife's name may well be dragged into the scandal. But despite my best efforts at reconciliation, both parties remain determined to fight.

Though I was hoping to keep you out of it, my final play is your last-minute intervention to make young Darblay see sense.

Your cousin and friend as always,
Phineas Harlaw.

Wenning read the letter through twice, then slowly, thoughtfully, closed it into his desk drawer. His emotions were bleak. But more than that, he felt profound anger.

Well before first light, he left the house once more via the cellar and crossed the back garden to the mews stables. Here he found the men he expected: his old China colleague, Gordon Campbell; Campbell's valet, John Coachman; the undercoachman; two of Wenning's large footmen; and two burly clerks who had accompanied them to China.]

"The hired carriages are waiting," John reported. "And their drivers sent home with their pockets well lined."

"In that case, let us be on our way," Wenning said cheerfully. "Everyone knows what to do."

They piled into the two hired coaches and made off toward the district of St. James, where both Rollo and Boothe had rooms. Here, the carriages parted, and Wenning's drew up outside Boothe's lodgings.

"Watch out for the seconds," Wenning murmured. "They should have received messages to tell them the duel is off, but it's still possible we'll have to deal with them, too. Remember, it's Boothe we need. Ignore any others as best you can."

The footman, Graham, and the clerk, Smithers, both in plain, black coats, nodded their understanding and got down from the carriage to loiter on either side of Boothe's front door. Wenning waited in the carriage so as not to give their quarry advanced warning.

The front door opened, and Wenning and his helpers all straightened, poised for action. But it was only a servant who took off at a run, perhaps to fetch a hackney for his master to take to Putney. Wenning hoped Boothe wouldn't wait for it before he emerged from the building.

But five minutes later, the door opened once more, and Boothe himself stepped out, impeccably dressed in black, with a smart beaver hat on his head, and a warm cloak wrapped around him against the early morning chill. As he closed the front door behind him, Wenning pushed open the carriage door, and Boothe actually walked toward it, as though he thought it was his hackney.

Graham and Smithers closed in from either side. Boothe glanced idly into the carriage. By the expression of horror on his face, he recognized the shape within. But before he could back off, Wenning seized him by the lapels, the others grabbed his arms, and he was tossed into the coach. Graham and Smithers leapt in after him, and the coachman set off at a spanking pace.

"What in the name of...?" Booth began blustering. "My lord, I must protest!"

"My dear, Boothe, you are in no position, moral or physical, to complain about anything at all. I hear you have been bandying my wife's name around one of the more deplorable clubs."

"Then you hear wrong. I am currently on my way to an affair of honor that has nothing to do with your wife."

"It has nothing to do with my wife only because Darblay threw a glass of wine in your face. Even he would not begin a quarrel with his sister's name as the prime cause. I take exception in either case."

"Then your fight with Darblay—who was eavesdropping on a private conversation—must wait upon my own."

"On the contrary, you will not be fighting Darblay at all."

Boothe, who seemed to have recovered his confidence, sat back in his seat and dusted off his coat front and sleeves. "I am to go straight to the husband?" he mocked. "That should stop all the talk about your wife and me. And I shall be delighted to shoot you."

"I'm sure you would, but I'm afraid you won't get the chance this morning."

Boothe glanced out of the carriage windows and frowned. "We are going in the wrong direction for Putney."

"Of course we are. You are coming to a party at my house."

At once, Boothe looked alarmed again. "I can't! I have to be at Putney Heath, or I will be accused of cowardice!"

"But you are a coward. The word is you are a crack shot, famous at Manton's, and yet you picked a fight with a twenty-two-year-old boy."

Even in the gloom, Boothe's flush was obvious. "That *boy* has fought duels before. And it was he who picked a quarrel with me!"

"After you uttered his sister's name. What did you expect him to do? Shake your hand and invite you to dinner?"

"None of this is any of your business," Boothe exploded. "Now—"

"You made it my business as soon as you uttered my wife's name."

"Stop the vehicle this instant, or I shall have you arrested for abduction!"

"My dear Boothe," Wenning said amiably, "you must know you can't have me arrested for anything. Peer of the realm and all that. Anyone would think I was taking you away to torture you or kill you!"

Boothe didn't look convinced that he wasn't. "What are you up to?"

"I'm going to show you my wine cellar."

Graham, the footman, snickered.

⟫⟩⟨⟨

WENNING COULD HEAR Rollo's voice as soon as he opened the cellar door, swiftly followed by the softer tones of Campbell and John Coachman as they tried to calm him.

"*Him!*" Boothe exclaimed. "Darblay put you up to this, the filthy coward!"

"Actually, if you listen, you'll hear he is as furious as you."

Rollo, through the half-open door of his "cell," was remonstrating loudly with his jailers, but catching sight of Boothe, he lunged at the door with a cry of fury. It took Campbell, John, and Lance, the clerk, to hold him back.

Boothe was duly wrestled into his own cell but didn't waste his time screaming obscenities at Rollo. Instead, he turned to Wenning with some desperation.

"Come, my lord, there is no need for this strong-arming. Your point is made, and I shall be good if you let me out now. No harm has been done."

"Let you out?" Wenning said, amused. "So that you can spread lies about Darblay's cowardice?"

"No," Boothe retorted. "So that I don't spread the word about your wife's spread legs—*ouff!*"

No thought went into it. Wenning simply swung his arm and punched Boothe in the stomach. It shut the weasel's foul mouth for, doubled up, he could only clutch his stomach and gasp for breath. But more than that, it gave Wenning a fierce satisfaction. He strode out of the door and locked it, shaking his stinging knuckles, which had struck some of Boothe's buttons.

He walked straight across the cellar and into Rollo's cell.

"Enough, Rollo," he said without raising his voice. It was a trick he had learned at university—cutting through a rammy by using just the right pitch and imposing his own utter confidence on his fellows. He had refined it in later social situations, dangerous ones and diplomatic ones, and it now seemed to be second nature.

Rollo and those struggling with him fell silent immediately, staring at Wenning.

"Here's the problem, Rollo," Oliver said curtly. "I understand you couldn't let it go, and I commend you for doing your best to keep Grace's name out of it. But if you and he fight, her name will *inevitably* be shouted as the true cause of it all. And there's no way we'll keep such a delicious scandal quiet. To say nothing of you dying or being taken up for murder.

"So, *this* is what we're going to do."

Rollo listened, his mouth falling open, then snapping into a mulish line before a snort of laughter seemed to take him by surprise, and he thought about it, gazing all the while at Wenning.

"Very well," he said with a curt nod. "I'll do it."

"Good man. Give Campbell and the others a hand if you would. I'm off to Putney."

"Why?" Rollo asked, baffled.

"Oh, just in case the odd second turns up," Wenning said vaguely. "I don't plan to be long, and the room is set up, all but the bodies..."

CHAPTER SIXTEEN

WENNING TOOK THE hired coach to Putney but stopped it at the local inn before it reached the heath. He walked the rest of the way in order to give anyone watching and waiting less warning of his arrival.

Dawn was breaking at last, casting a pale grey light across the heath. Wenning kept off the paths and the open grassland, striding instead among the trees. Even so, the hairs at the back of his neck stood to attention, and the moment of the shot at Maida Gardens kept repeating in his memory. He kept his eyes peeled, scanning all the surrounding area until at last, he saw two carriages.

An unknown man leaned against one as though chatting idly with the occupant through the window.

Wenning walked on, keeping, still, to the trees. Before he reached the carriages, the fellow standing by the coach took a drink from his flask, pocketed it, and waved a hand in farewell. He looked, Wenning thought, like a doctor, for he carried a small bag as he strode across to the other coach and got in.

As it drove off, Wenning increased his speed, but it seemed whoever was in the other carriage was in no hurry to leave.

Wenning strolled out from behind the tree nearest to the waiting carriage. Inside, he could clearly see his cousin, Phineas, gazing up the heath toward the inn.

"Morning, Phin," Wenning said cheerfully.

Phineas's head snapped around in understandable startlement. "Wenning! Good God, what a fright you gave me!" He clutched his heart and wheezed out a laugh. "Have I you to thank for neither duelist turning up?"

"Yes," Wenning said modestly. "I appreciated the warning and took the matter in hand."

"How? I could not get a civil word out of Darblay!"

"One has to know how to handle him," Wenning said. "Come back to Wenning House with me for breakfast, and I'll tell you all about it."

"Jump in," Phineas invited. "Where is your carriage? Or did you ride?"

"I left it at the inn. They can return from there."

"Mount Street, if you please," Wenning said to the driver and joined Phineas inside. On the seat beside his cousin sat a beautifully inlaid case that contained, no doubt, the dueling pistols.

"A very bizarre affair of honor," Phineas remarked during the journey. He shifted restlessly, causing the folds of his cloak to part and draw Wenning's gaze. "Nobody turned up at all, except the doctor and me. Not the principles, not Boothe's other second, nor either of Darblay's."

"Bizarre, as you say," Wenning agreed, lifting his eyes from his cousin's half-open cloak to his face. Even more bizarre was the fact that his cousin seemed to have found it necessary to bring his own pistol to someone else's duel.

⟫⟫⟩⟨⟨⟪

GRACE WAS NOT sure what woke her. She was not used to early rising in London, but there seemed to some kind of commotion in the house, reaching her as a sort of low hum.

Daylight seeped through the bed curtains, so she didn't bother trying to go back to sleep. Instead, she rang for Henley, who duly arrived with a tray of coffee, toast, and letters.

"What's going on, Henley?" she asked, yawning after her first sip of coffee. "Is there some kind of disturbance downstairs?"

"Oh no, I don't think so, my lady. His lordship has a few visitors, according to Mr. Herries."

"Ah." Grace, her mind still very much on her last encounter with his lordship, flipped through the usual array of invitation cards and bills to get to the more interesting letters from friends. Among those, she came upon one in her brother's scrawling hand and frowned, dropping the others to open Rollo's first.

She almost choked on her coffee. "Oh dear God! What o'clock is it, Henley? Am I too late?"

Too late to stop a duel? Of course she was. They were fought at dawn, were they not? Rollo could already be dead or taken up for murder.

What an imbecile!" she raged. "My clothes, Henley, anything that comes to hand!"

She scanned the scrawled note again to make sure she had not misunderstood.

Dear Grace,

You should get this in the morning, by which time all should be right and tight. But just in case it isn't, I want you to know I'm sorry, but that Boothe deserves to die. You really need a more gentlemanly court, for I'm dashed if I can fight them all. Drop Boothe like a hot coal, and pretend you know nothing about this. Which, of course, you don't. But look after the old parents if anything happens to me. Wenning should help, for despite everything, he doesn't seem such a bad fellow.

Rollo.

Throwing down this epistle, she thrust the tray aside and leapt out of bed for the speediest wash and dress she had undertaken in years.

She barely waited for the bewildered Henley to pin up her hair before she bolted out of her rooms and ran downstairs.

"James, I need the carriage!" she called to the nearest footman. "Immediately!"

"Hold one moment there, James," said her husband's mild voice, just as she became aware of an unpleasant stale-alcohol smell drifting up the stairs, along with a sudden surge of male voices and laughter. As Oliver shut the door of the blue salon behind him, the noise was instantly muffled to some degree, although the stench lingered. "Where are you off to so early, my lady?"

"To see Rollo," she blurted. "I'm afraid he is in trouble, and it's all my fault."

"Rollo is here," Oliver said, holding out his hand to her. "I'll give you a peek if you like, though I doubt you will wish to join us."

The smell and the noise and her husband's somewhat rumpled state—which was not unattractive, she realized inconveniently—came together in her mind for the first time. As she gave him her hand, she exclaimed, "You've been holding a party in there! All night!"

His smile contained more mischief than anything, like a schoolboy discovered breaking rules and regretting nothing. Drawing her with him by the hand, he opened the salon door. A new waft of alcohol and masculinity crashed into her as she entered hand-in-hand with Oliver.

The room was full of men and cards, bottles and glasses. The first person she saw was Rollo, sprawled on a sofa, looking disheveled and handsome as he often did, though not usually with the companionship of Sir Nash Boothe, who slumped beside him, his head on Rollo's shoulder, clearly sound asleep while Rollo finished a card game with Lord Effers.

"Tell you what, old fellow, you have a very heavy head," he informed Boothe. "We should take him home, put him to bed." He nudged Boothe amiably, causing the man to humph in his sleep. "Five minutes, Boothe, and we're off."

Rollo, in perfect friendliness, looking after the man who deserved to die, according to the letter he had written to Grace. She let her gaze wander around the rest of the room, finding a rather pale Phineas, Rollo's friends Meade and Montague, Mr. Campbell, Sir Ernest, and the rakish new Duke of Dearham—previously the Marquis of Fishguard, and therefore still known to his intimates as Fish. Judging by the number of glasses and the disordered state of the room, there had, at one time, been several more attendees who had by now heeded the call of their beds and gone home.

Rollo glanced up. "Evening Grace!" he said cheerfully. "We'll be gone in two minutes!"

"Not evening, Rolls," Effers informed him, rising to bow to his hostess. "Been light for hours. So sorry for the intrusion, my lady."

The Duke of Dearham unfolded himself from an armchair to bow with surprising elegance. "We should go *now*, thanking you profusely for your hospitality."

"No, no, finish your games, gentlemen," she said faintly. "I only wanted a word with my husband."

"Who is happy to oblige," Wenning said with the faintest slur. He bowed her out with the exaggeratedly polite gesture of the inebriated, though as he closed the door and they walked across the hall, the slur in his speech seemed to vanish. "Shall we go and have breakfast? In your sitting room, perhaps? We'll leave the breakfast room for my ravenous guests."

"Shouldn't you join your own ravenous guests? Or are they too drunk to notice the absence of their host?" Even as she spoke, she realized that *he* did not smell of brandy. Nor were his feet on the stairs remotely unsteady.

"Oh, most of them are less drunk than you might think," he murmured.

"Including you."

"Including me," he admitted.

"And Rollo?"

"I'll tell you about Rollo over breakfast," he promised, though she picked up the unspoken order, *Don't talk of Rollo where anyone can hear.*

When they reached her sitting room, she sent Henley to acquire more coffee and breakfast for his lordship. Then, she brought the remains of her own breakfast through from the bedchamber and set it on the table.

"Sit. Speak," she commanded her husband. "And I want to know about the duel Rollo carefully didn't mention in his farewell letter!"

A spark of laughter lit his eyes. "He is far too amiable to go to the devil, you know." Lifting the coffee cup, he drank the remains and poured more from the pot, which he offered to Grace.

She took it impatiently. "Well?"

"Rollo, being Rollo, frequents a rather low club in St. Giles. A few other more adventurous gentlemen also go there, for the general atmosphere of danger, I suspect. In any case, Rollo tried to sell a cravat pin there. The one you gave him."

She met his gaze and tilted her chin. "I won it from Sir Nash Boothe in a wager that I would not dare meet him at Maida Gardens."

"So I understand." He did not seem angry, but then he already knew this because he had been there. Sometimes it was hard to sort out who knew what and how and whether or not she was supposed to be aware of it.

I hate this, she thought suddenly and thrust it aside for later contemplation. "Go on."

"Boothe was in the club that night, along with Phineas. I wouldn't have thought it the kind of place to attract either of them, but then I don't really know Boothe. At any rate, Phineas seems to have recognized the pin Rollo was trying to sell and remarked upon it. Boothe, apparently without thinking, blabbed that he'd given it to you. Which, naturally, infuriated Rollo."

Grace groaned and gulped her lukewarm coffee. "God preserve me from protective men!"

"It was not well done," Oliver agreed. "He should have taken Boothe outside for a friendly word. But at least he knew he couldn't fight him over you, so he accused Boothe of calling him a thief and a liar and then threw wine in his face so that Boothe had to challenge him."

"The idiot!"

"Well, it was only ever half a disguise, for the true cause was bound to come out, especially considering who was involved. But one has to allow that Rollo tried."

"Risking his life!" she fumed, appalled all over again by the tragedy that might have occurred. "And the duel was actually for this morning? What happened? How did you find out?" For somehow, she knew Oliver was responsible for the lack of duel.

"Meade," he said. "He recognized the disaster the whole thing could turn into and asked for my help."

She gazed at him. "So now, Rollo and Boothe are bosom friends, cuddling up on our sofa, drunk as lords?"

"Well, Rollo might have had a celebratory glass of brandy, but he isn't really that drunk. Boothe, on the other hand, imbibed a bit more than he had intended."

Her eyes widened. "How long have they been here, Oliver?"

"Since around dawn," he admitted. "We rounded up a few all-night carousers and gossips and brought them here, along with a few good friends, who will all spread the word that not only was there no duel but that Rollo and Boothe are fast friends, playing cards with me, in our house—which proves there was no reason for a duel in the first place."

"But when Boothe sobers up, surely he won't play that game anymore!"

"He might gnash his teeth a little, but he's unlikely to admit being kidnapped by the husband he had hoped to cuckold, had brandy poured down his throat, and been set up like a puppet show. Besides, no one would believe him. Am I not the height of amiability and respectable heroism?"

Her lips twitched. "And you have Phineas and Rollo's friends and even Fish—I beg your pardon, His Grace of Dearham—to back up your play. I believe I am in awe."

"I hoped you would be."

Henley and Oliver's valet arrived then with fresh coffee, toast, and a large, covered plate, which was set before his lordship. Oliver set to with a will, while Grace poured fresh coffee. In spite of everything, this mundane domestic scene felt comfortable, homely, and curiously right.

And, once the servants were dismissed, it became excitingly intimate. Trying to ignore that, she said, "Thank you for what you did."

"There is no need of thanks. For better or worse, our families, like our names, are inextricably linked."

Her heart beat hard, but somehow, she found the courage. "I think you regret that link. And did so almost from the moment it was formed."

He paused, then laid down his cutlery. "No. There was anger, grief, self-pity, and hurt pride, but never regret. Tell me, if you would, did you *ever* love a man called Anthony?"

"No," she replied. She didn't need to think because she had never loved anyone but Oliver. She frowned. "But I have heard the name before… For the record, I never loved Nash Boothe either. If you want the truth, I have been sailing close to the wind, scandal-wise, and knew it was time to freeze him out. But he held me to the wretched Maida wager, and since then, I have seen a different side of him. I prefer my admirers unentitled and at a distance, although I don't suppose you believe that."

"Why would I not?"

"Because I have taught the world I am just a little fast and care for nothing but my own pleasure."

"A way to survive after I left you with little pride and a great deal of gossip."

"Something like that. I suppose it is no use asking you why or who *you* loved?"

"It would only be fair," he allowed, sitting back in his chair. "Who I loved is easy—only you. The why is a little harder to explain."

She sipped her coffee and regarded him over the rim. She would not let him off the hook, and yet she was ready for the blows to fall. At least he had loved her, and that would give her strength for whatever came next.

"Try," she urged.

"The catalyst was a letter," he said steadily. "I think Leyton already told you that. A letter you had apparently written to a man called Anthony, a love letter longing for him and reviling me."

"I never wrote it," she whispered helplessly, though the impossibility of making him accept the truth overwhelmed her.

"No, I don't believe you did," he said, causing her mouth to drop open. His lips twisted. "But I accepted it at the time. I don't know why. Some knowledge nagging at the back of my mind that I did not deserve you, that you were too good to be true. If I had loved you less, I would, perhaps, have thought more clearly, behaved less badly. But those are excuses. Perhaps, somewhere, I still yearned to prove myself in China. But I never wanted that more than I wanted you."

Distractedly, he reached for his cup and drank. "I should have talked to you, not condemned you, unheard. I should not have bolted and left you alone to face everything. I knew that by the time the ship sailed."

"You did not write," she pointed out, trying to keep her voice steady. "Not once."

He closed his eyes. "I know. That was more pride. And the sheer impossibility of writing chatty letters to a woman I had wrongfully abandoned."

"Was Maria Fitzwalter your lover?"

His eyes flew open again in shock. "God, no. Why would you think such a thing?"

She laughed, and he had the grace to blush.

"She was on the ship as far as Lisbon," he admitted. "Pandering to my male pride. She was not happy in her new marriage either, so it seemed we had something in common. Although I never told her about the letter, about Anthony, or the reasons I had chosen to sail, after all, she must have known some serious quarrel between us had to have taken place. She implied you were a flighty friend and had a past your parents were not proud of, hence the extent of their relief to receive my offer."

"That was all to do with money," Grace said cynically. "And birth, a little. You were certainly a better option than a wealthy cit."

"I don't seem to have been. But to answer your question: no. Mrs. Fitzwalter was never my lover. In fact, despite many and varied opportunities, I was boringly faithful to the wife I thought unfaithful."

"I gave you a disgust of all women?"

He smiled ruefully. "Hardly that. I think it was more self-righteousness, coupled with the simple fact that no one else measured up to you. I really was horribly in love with you."

"Horribly," she repeated, unreasonably hurt in the midst of the words that should have been balm for her soul.

"Well, it was horrible when I believed you loathed me in return." Slowly, he reached across the table, palm upward.

With butterflies soaring in her stomach, she laid her hand in his, watching his long, firm fingers close around it. There was a graze across his knuckles.

"Did you hate me?" he asked.

The heart and core of all my hate, and all my love. "I think you know the answer to that." Her fingers gripped his convulsively. "Phineas told me I should not regard your little adventures abroad, that it was bound to happen when a man was away from home for so many months, and that it meant nothing."

"*Did* you regard them?" he asked steadily.

She thought about it. "It was merely part of the whole, swirling pain." As soon as the words were out, she cringed at her own honesty, but his fingers tightened on her.

"Would it surprise you to know," he said, "that Phineas wrote to me that I should not regard the rumors concerning you either because you were young and flighty and meant no ill."

She frowned. "Phineas knows nothing happened. He was my chaperone often enough! Such implications amount to downright lies. Why would he tell you lies about me?"

"Why would he tell you lies about me? Things he could not have known at the time, even if they were true."

Her breath caught as she stared at him, thinking, going over old memories from the point of view that Phineas lied.

"To keep us apart," she said slowly. "Phineas is your heir only so long as you do not have a son. Could Phineas have forged the letter you saw?"

"He could—or paid for someone else to do it. And he must have paid to have it inserted into your luggage. Whatever happened to that abigail who came with us from London? For it wasn't Henley."

"No, she ran away to France. I had to travel home without a maid and engaged Henley when I returned to London."

"A suddenly wealthy maid, able to live abroad without a character from her last employer? The trick gave Phineas two years to live on his expectations of inheritance. He probably hoped I would be lost at sea or die of some foreign fever."

"And when you didn't, he tried to kill us at Maida."

"And then, I suspect, at this morning's duel. He wrote to me, informing me of the time and place, begging for my intervention, never guessing I had already begun to intervene. Yet, according to Meade, he was pretty half-hearted in his attempts at reconciliation, the first duty of a second. He meant me to turn up at the duel and get in the way of the bullets, and if I didn't, or the duelers were too careful of me, I suspect he meant to shoot me himself—he carried his own pistol—and blame either Rollo or Boothe, whosever's gun he could manage to fire in secret later."

"Phineas, your *cousin*… I trusted him because he was your cousin."

"I trusted him, too, though only in certain matters. I grew up with him and so never bothered to look beneath the surface. He was just amusing Phineas, who, out of the goodness of his heart, would look out for you while I was away. It makes my blood run cold just thinking about it. Thank God for Leyton."

"Phineas must hate you," Grace said. "*Really* hate you, for he is not so *very* poor, is he? He wants to inherit your wealth and title, but he must also be jealous and resentful, and…" She shuddered. "One never really knows anyone, does one?"

His thumb moved, idly caressing her wrist. "I think you have to look. With your eyes and heart open."

"Is that how you look at me?" She didn't mean to ask, but the words slipped out before she could stop them.

"I did once," he said softly. "And I am beginning to do so again."

"Do you see that I meant to punish you for hurting me? To humiliate you and make you a laughingstock?"

With his free hand, he rubbed his eyes and jaw. "I see that I deserve it. I see that only total honesty will serve between us now. But I have been up all night, and I am suddenly too tired to think, let alone speak more right now. On top of which, I have an insane urge to fall asleep on your bed, surrounded by the scent of you."

Wordlessly, she rose, leading him by their joined hands across the room and into her bedchamber. Without releasing her, he sat on the bed and kicked off his boots. He loosened his cravat, unbuttoned his coat and waistcoat, and lay back against the pillows.

The movement tugged her closer.

"Lie beside me," he whispered. "I will not touch you."

Her heart beat a strong, quick rhythm, and her mouth went dry with fear as well as with hope and something perilously close to desire. She sat on the bed beside him, and he bumped himself farther over to make space.

As she lay down at his side, their hands still joined between them, he closed his eyes. He inhaled and smiled, as though the scent of her pillow, her person, pleased him. And his scent, woodland and cinnamon, Oliver and "Rudolf," filled her senses, too. With wonder and a knot of delight in her belly, she watched his face relax into sleep.

Even when his fingers loosened on hers, she did not move, just lay beside him and *felt*.

She only rose when Henley came into the room, and that was largely to shoo the maid out.

CHAPTER SEVENTEEN

F OR ONCE, GRACE had no desire to leave the house. While her
husband slept on her bed, she crept downstairs to the ballroom at
the back of the house to find Lord Tamar putting his finishing touches
on the mural. Footmen were busy lugging large potted plants to place
around the floor and the terrace according to her instructions.

"This is marvelous, my lord!" she said, standing back to admire the
painting. "I could actually believe it is real and try to go inside."

"I don't advise it. Apart from the bruises, the paint is still wet."

She laughed. "I cannot thank you enough for this. I hope we'll see
you and Lady Tamar at the ball, duly disguised."

"Serena loves a masked ball. We're looking forward to it. I shall be
off now. Don't let your servants brush against it until the day after
tomorrow."

"I shall threaten them with direst retribution."

Once she had bade farewell to the marquess, she issued a few
more orders concerning the preparation of the ballroom and then
made her way back to her sitting room in order to write a few letters.

She could not resist tiptoeing across to the bedroom door, which
was not quite shut, and peeping through the crack. In her heart, she
really didn't expect him to still be there. She expected him to have
wakened with the discomfort of his clothing and taken himself off to
his own chamber.

But he lay where she had left him. Except he had somehow got under the covers and was sleeping like a baby. She couldn't help smiling, though she didn't know what to do with the surge of emotion in her breast.

She closed the door over once more and returned to her desk, where she wrote a quick note to her sister. And then, more thoughtfully, set about an invitation to Frances Caldwell, and wrote to Sir Ernest Leyton, too, to tell him what she had done.

Leave before the unmasking if you both wish it. But I am also happy to receive Mrs. Caldwell under whichever name she chooses.

That done, she took the letters downstairs to be delivered by hand and consulted with Cook about a few outstanding details to do with the ball supper. And then, because it seemed she couldn't stay away, she returned to her sitting room to sit down on the harp stool and think.

While she softly plucked the harp strings, she let her mind wander over what Oliver had told her, about the duel and about Phineas Harlaw. And about the letter and his reasons for abandoning her.

So much anguish could have been saved if only they had spoken to each other two years ago. Instead, they had each endured two years of supposed betrayal, been constantly fed with drips of Phineas's subtle poison, all spilled while claiming the opposite of what he was implying.

Oliver would not stray from you, not in any way that matters.

He is putting a good face on things. According to his colleagues, no one would know he is in pain. He is the life and soul of every gathering, and the ladies adore him...

You must be patient with him if he seems reluctant to come home. The reluctance cannot be real with you here waiting for him.

She thought of their distant wedding night, of more recent kisses with "Rudolf." Of her ruined plans for revenge and her sudden, thrilling hopes...

Some movement made her turn her head toward the bedchamber

door. All the air left her lungs. Her fingers stilled in delicious shock.

Her husband leaned in the doorway, clad in nothing but a tangled sheet held loosely about his hips. Tall, lean, muscled, and rumpled from sleep, he was stunning. More than that, the hunger in his eyes devoured her, melted her in their heat.

"Don't stop," he said huskily. "I love to hear you play."

She swallowed and forced a breath. As if the harp burned her now, she leapt to her feet, backing away from the instrument—which took her closer to him.

"I was not playing so much as thinking," she blurted.

"About me?" he asked steadily.

Little flames seemed to dance in his eyes. Like the fires of hell or of domestic bliss. At this moment, she didn't care which, didn't know what to do or what to say.

"Yes," she managed.

He straightened, took a step nearer her, to the imminent danger of the sheet falling off him altogether. He didn't seem to notice. "*Do* you forgive me? *Can* you?"

When she said nothing, he laid one hand on her shoulder and used the other to tip up her chin for his urgent scrutiny. His fingers were warm and caressing, shooting little shards of pleasure and desire through her whole body.

"I don't think it matters," she whispered achingly. "You are the center of everything. All my emotion and all my desire." She didn't mean to cry, but the tear trickled down her cheek unbidden. She tried to dash it away with the back of her hand, but she was too late. His head bent, and it was his lips that caught the tear, softly kissing her cheek and then her lips.

Her hand had found the back of his head and clung to his hair. Helpless, almost fearful, she gazed at him without making any effort to move away. His bent closer again, and his lips sank into hers.

Oliver's kisses... This one was everything she had dreamed of in her loneliest moments, her hottest lust, even her bitterest tempers. Firm and sensual, exploring her mouth like a long-lost friend, passionately missed and fiercely welcome. And with the passion came a new tenderness, a new awareness. And then there was only raging desire.

He swept her up against him, and the sheet fell around their ankles. Her eager fingers remembered the warm, velvet skin of his shoulders and back, the hard muscle beneath, and the delightfully rough stubble of his jaw. The hard column pressing against her hip.

She kissed him back with an urgency that matched his own and almost sobbed with joy when he lifted her right off the floor and carried her into the bedchamber, kicking the door shut behind him.

Even the sheet was warm where her back landed on it, and then there was his weight, hard and wonderful between her legs. She wished the gown gone and her petticoats with it, but she could not bear to move and miss a moment of his wonderful embrace, his bone-quaking kisses.

His hands smoothed up her legs, rucking her skirts with it, and then his mouth opened wide and he groaned. "Damn it, Grace, forgive me something else. I am that scoundrel Rudolf as well."

"I know." She took back his mouth, wriggling beneath him to find a better position. Between her legs was fire and need, but he paused, breaking the kiss.

"You know? Since when?"

"Since the night of the fireworks. I should have known before, but it seems I had forgotten so much. When did you know me?"

"From the beginning," he admitted, his fingers caressing her inner thigh now and moving upward. "I overheard a conversation and, instead of coming home, curiosity drew me to Maida."

"To spy on me?" she gasped as his fingers caressed her most secret places.

"Yes. At first. And then to know you." His fingers slid aside, and at last, she felt again the wonder of him inside her.

She moaned.

"Honesty," he whispered. "No more pretense, no more hiding, or keeping things to ourselves. I never stopped loving you, Grace, even believing the worst."

She tried to answer, but words seemed to be impossible, so she spoke with her body's movements, with her kisses and caresses, sighs and gasps of bliss that led all too quickly to wild, explosive joy.

⟫⟫⟩⟨⟨⟨

WENNING LAY IN his wife's bed, still at last. Grace curled languorously against him, her arm flung across his chest. Although she was still half-dressed, there was enough naked skin to content him.

He had not really had enough sleep, and the strains of harp music that had filtered into his semi-consciousness a bare half-hour ago, had been too quiet and too pleasant and should not have disturbed him for long. But finally, after two years, he had been again surrounded by Grace's perfume. And the combination of that scent with his waking desire was powerful. Then he had worked out that Grace must also be responsible for the harp music, and any notion to sleep on had fled.

He had meant only to watch her before returning to his own chamber and giving her back the privacy she was used to. But he had seen how he affected her and was suddenly flooded with desperation not to lose this chance. Aching tenderness had kept his ravenous hunger in check—mostly—but even so, he could not hold out for the long, sweet loving he had once planned so optimistically. Urgency and passion had taken over, driven by Grace's blissful moans and bold caresses.

Somehow, he had made sure of her pleasure before giving in to his own massive release. But it had been a near thing, a mere shadow, he feared, of gentlemanly care.

Lethargically, Grace's fingers twined among his chest hair. A beam

189

of sunlight shone through the bed curtains onto her tangled curls which fell across his shoulder.

"I'm glad it is daytime," she said. "I won't fall asleep and wake to find you gone."

His arm beneath her, lightly holding her against him, tightened. "I'm so sorry, Grace. I must have hurt you very much."

"Yes," she admitted.

"If it's any consolation, I hurt myself at least as badly."

She considered that. "I think it is consolation of a sort, because at least it means you loved me. Even if you behaved like a bigger idiot than even Rollo has ever been."

"I did, didn't I?" he said ruefully. "I wonder about that sometimes. If we had not married so quickly, if I had known you just a little more, would I also have known better than to believe such tripe? If I had been a year or two older and wiser, would I have been so quick to condemn you unheard?"

"It doesn't matter. We can't undo the past."

"But we can make the future. And delight in the present. I delight in you, Grace Wenning." He pushed a lock of hair off her face and kissed her brow. She smiled and kissed his shoulder. But his smile was twisted, "And then I worry that I, who trusted you so little, can never win your trust again. Even now, you think I will vanish if you close your eyes."

Her hand slid up his chest to his cheek, and she propped her chin up on his shoulder. "I think it will take time for both of us. To get to know each other again, to understand who we have become. Because we must have changed in those two years."

She kissed his lips, a voluntary gesture that moved him far more than mere submission to his demands.

"I will enjoy that journey," he whispered and kissed her back.

With the edge of his hunger assuaged, his arousal was deliciously slow and languorous, fed by her kisses and caresses, by her softness in his arms and her scented, responsive skin beneath his lips. He undressed her properly, little by little, removing the remaining pins from her hair.

"If you have no objection," he murmured huskily, "I propose to lock the door and spend the rest of the day here with you."

"I believe I have no engagements," she replied, only a little unevenly.

He rose from the bed, padded across the floor, and turned the key in the lock. When he swung back to face her, she was watching him avidly, and he felt like swaggering across to bed, proud of her desire for him, and excited by it in a way that felt new and wonderful.

"I think," he said, moving over her and beginning to kiss her all over, "I should simply worship my countess." For she had only known the intrusive physical intimacy of love twice in her life, with two years between. Now, more than ever, she deserved his care, his tenderness, and all the selfless joy he could bring her.

Which, it turned out, was a great deal.

⋙✦⋘

IT WAS TEATIME before they finally donned clothes and emerged as far as Grace's sitting room for sustenance.

Her body was singing. She felt she would burst with happiness. And yet there was more pleasure in store, of the simple domestic kind—sitting in his company, pouring tea, talking about the ball, and costumes, and, eventually, reluctant to leave the bubble of wellbeing, what to do about Phineas.

"The trouble is," Oliver said, "you and I have guessed what he's about, but we have no evidence, no proof. And even if we confronted him with what we know, we could not trust him to stop."

"If we did have evidence, what would we do with it? Give it to the magistrate, have Phineas tried and transported or hanged?"

"For putting you in danger—for putting us both through the past two year's misery—I could cheerfully hang him myself. Don't look so alarmed. I won't. I won't even challenge him, though the chances are my peers would acquit me if I killed him."

"There would still be a terrible scandal," Grace pointed out. "I doubt that would be good for your career in the Foreign Office."

"Do I care?" he wondered.

"Yes, I think you do. And so do I. You have land and wealth. You don't need another career, but it seems to me you do a great deal of good for the country, and will do more yet."

"Would you come with me on my next posting, Grace? Whether a special mission to some wild part of the world, or to a formal embassy?"

"Yes," she said at once. "If you wanted me there."

His gaze met hers. "There were times I wanted you with me so much that I could imagine you sitting on the other side of the table from me, walking beside me, waiting for me in bed. I even talked to you sometimes, said all the things I *should* have said before, discussed the new dilemmas of the day..."

"We have wasted much time."

"*I* have. But to the matter of Phineas. I shall probably have to pay him to go away, though it goes against the grain to reward him for betrayal."

"It's less reward than dying and letting him inherit."

"Which makes me wonder if he would even accept it." Oliver rubbed his chin. "Perhaps we need a stick as well as a carrot."

"Take the lesser reward or languish in prison?" Grace guessed.

"Something like that. Though he might suspect I don't want the scandal and simply call my bluff."

Grace paused with her teacup halfway to her lips. "Then perhaps we need to introduce him to a scandal of his own, distant enough not to affect us, but public enough for him to know that even if he inherited the title, he would never be accepted into polite society again."

Oliver finished his sandwich, a gleam growing in his eyes. "That would appall him. I think...I really do think that he would rather be toadied by some other society than ignored by the ton. I believe, my love, that we have the germ of a plan..."

CHAPTER EIGHTEEN

I T WAS AN odd time to visit Maida Gardens. The gardens were empty, and since dusk was still hours away, the many lanterns lining the paths and dangling among the trees were not yet lit. The place was eerily quiet, without the magic of its nighttime brilliance, or even the sunny serenity of morning. And yet for Grace, walking up this familiar path on her husband's arm carried its own enchantment.

He did not go up to the central pavilion but led her around to the right and through a gate to a private path that led to a white-washed cottage.

A young woman was sweeping the front steps. When she glanced up, Grace recognized her as the girl from whom she had bought a ticket on her first daytime visit.

The girl smiled with what seemed genuine pleasure. "Good day, sir! How wonderful to see you back," she said cheerfully and curt-seyed. "Ma'am."

"This is Miss Kitty," Oliver said. "She is the proprietor's niece, and was kind enough to make my accommodation comfortable when I first came home."

"Accommodation?" Grace repeated, gazing at the cottage. "This is where you stayed before you came home?"

"Oh, no, ma'am, he slept in the barn with Old Betsy," the girl assured her.

Grace blinked.

Kitty let out a breath of laughter. "The pony," she assured her. "She misses him terribly since he left us."

"Miss Kitty," Oliver said firmly without raising his voice, "this is my wife. Is there somewhere we might talk?"

Without hesitation, Kitty led them inside the house and into a small, cozy parlor. "Can I bring you tea? Wine?"

"No, thank you," Oliver said, sitting down beside Grace, while the girl hovered before them uncertainly. "We come to pick your brains and possibly ask a favor. When I stayed here, there was one afternoon I came upon a game of cards in the garden. I believe your uncle was playing."

"You don't want to play with my uncle," Kitty said uneasily.

"I wouldn't dream of it," Oliver assured her. "I'm fairly sure I would lose badly—the cards being marked, as well as hidden in some unlikely places."

Her eyes fell. "I know nothing about such matters."

"That would be a pity," Oliver observed. "Because I would be happy to pay for this favor. Perhaps it is your uncle or cousin I need to speak to."

Kitty frowned. "You want someone to cheat you at cards?"

"Not exactly. Tell me, Miss Kitty, do you or your cousin have any skill at sleight-of-hand?"

⊰⊱⊰⊱

PHINEAS WAS UNEASY as well as frustrated. The duel between Boothe and Rollo Darblay had not gone according to plan, and Wenning, though he had eventually turned up, had crept far too close, unseen, for anything to be done. Phineas didn't *think* any harm had been done, but he disliked his cousin's luck as well as the further signs he had witnessed of rapprochement between the earl and countess.

Any closeness between them was bad for him. If they compared notes, they could quite easily work out that he had not been strictly accurate in the reports he had passed to each during Wenning's absence. And if they got *too* friendly, then the possibility of an heir reared its ugly head once more.

Nothing had ever gone exactly right with his schemes, even at the beginning. Grace's erstwhile maid, whom he had paid extremely well, had been supposed to *give* the damned letter to Wenning and *before* the wedding night. But from what he had gathered since, she had simply taken Phineas's money and bolted, leaving the discovery of the letter up to the fates. But at least it had been just one night, and Wenning had still made it to the ship and to China. Phineas had *known* he would seize that opportunity if his bride no longer commanded his loyalty. And fortunately, Grace had not conceived from their one night together.

But neither had Oliver had the consideration to drown or die at the hands of bandits or sickness. Instead, the entire embassy had returned triumphant, with Wenning the hero of the hour.

And now Phineas was running out of time. Once his perfidy was suspected, he would be unable to get near his cousin, and in any accident or attack, suspicion would inevitably fall first on him. He had to diffuse suspicion and act quickly.

But infuriatingly, neither the earl nor the countess were present at the parties which expected them on the evening of the abortive duel. Nor did he come upon them at church or in the park on Sunday. He had no idea if his cousin blamed him for the quarrel between Boothe and Darblay, and so he slept badly that night and rose unrefreshed but determined.

Accordingly, he dressed with exquisite care and took a hackney round to Mount Street. Here, he discovered the earl at breakfast and was relieved to be greeted with apparent delight.

"Ah, Phin! Just the man. Help yourself and sit down. Coffee?"

"Thank you, Ollie! Glad to see you in such fine fettle. I was quite worried not to meet you at White's or at Lady Wheelan's on Saturday night."

"Oh, we just stayed home for once."

Phineas's stomach tightened, but he beamed with what he hoped looked like approval. "Both you and Grace? I'm sure it did you the world of good."

"Up to a point," Wenning said with a quick grin. "Trouble is, I now find myself committed to the morning—morning!—concert at the thrice damned Maida Gardens. I swear between us, we are in danger of making the place fashionable again. But Grace swears she has heard something wonderful about one of the singers and wonders if she might engage her for her next musical soiree. In a moment of weakness, I agreed to escort her, but frankly, Phin, it's a long way to go for an inedible luncheon among the vulgar. Especially if the singer is as commonplace as I suspect."

"Are you asking me to escort Grace instead?" It would certainly show trust and, hopefully, insert a fresh wedge of resentment between the couple.

Wenning cast him a sardonic glance. "Wouldn't that be the height of insolence? No, I could hardly do that to you. But I *am* begging your company. I'll ask another few choice spirits, and perhaps we can get up a game of cards while the ladies enjoy what my estimable brother-in-law refers to as the caterwauling."

"Sounds an ideal solution," Phineas allowed, while his brain hummed with possibilities, and he calmly drank his coffee.

"Excellent. The concert will be in the rose garden, apparently. I'll have them set up a table at the back and serve us wine and luncheon among the warbling. I'll bring the cards since I imagine anything at Maida is marked."

"Good idea." Phineas stood. "Then I'll go now and take care of the day's business before I join you at Maida." He paused, raising one quizzical eyebrow. "Will there be female company for Grace? Or doesn't she want anyone else to spot the next musical triumph?"

Oliver smiled benignly. "I imagine Lady Arpington will join us."

Phineas bowed and departed. His next call was on Mrs. Fitzwalter, who had just returned from her morning ride in the park and seemed out of sorts. His offer of an escort to the morning concert at Maida was greeted with derision.

"My good sir, I have had more than my fill of that place. The novelty has decidedly worn off!"

"That is a pity." Phineas regarded his fingernails. "My cousin Wenning will be there. And her ladyship will, no doubt, be much distracted by the music."

She returned her gaze to his face and, fortunately, came up with the wrong answer to his unspoken question. "You covet the countess for yourself," she said admiringly. "Now Wenning is back, you must feel your wings severely clipped."

Phineas let it stand and kept smiling. It wasn't that he had never considered such an idea, but he had seen early on that it would never answer. Such trivia no longer mattered to him. Maria Fitzwalter's help in removing Oliver into a secluded part of the garden was all he needed of her.

Next, he walked to the hackney stand and took a carriage into the less salubrious environs of St. Giles, where he strolled into the Orange Tree.

At this time of day, there were no aristocrats to be found gracing the rough tables. Instead, it was more openly the den of thieves it had always been, and the few patrons glanced at him with suspicion and dislike. He sat down by a man he recognized slightly—hardly a gentleman, but he dressed well enough and betrayed the odd glimmering of intelligence. The man, whose name he could not remember, had been enjoying a solitary pint of ale over a closely written ledger, which he closed when Phineas sat down.

"Tell me," Phineas said, once the pleasantries were out of the way. "A friend of mine needs an urgent favor, with no questions asked. My friend will pay well. Who should he speak to?"

※※※

UNTIL THE MOMENT Henley left her tastefully dressed and coifed for the occasion of a daytime concert, Grace had found it difficult to concentrate on the task of besting Phineas. Instead, she could not help dwelling on the wonder of sleeping all night in her husband's arms.

She had smiled to find him still with her when she woke. "I thought you might be gone."

The words had been blurted. She had not meant to cause the flash of pain and shame in his eyes, and she had reached to comfort him at the same time as he had reached to comfort her. And somehow, comfort had been forgotten in something much more intense and pleasurable.

After which, he had risen to go to breakfast as normal. "If Phineas doesn't drop in as he often does, I will go in search of him. I want to make him think you and I are growing toward an understanding without him worrying he is too late."

He had kissed her forehead and departed, leaving her to delicious reminiscences, which had lingered until the door closed behind Henley, and they were ready to begin.

"If he thought he was too late to prevent our reconciliation—and even an heir—would he not just give up?" she said suddenly.

"He might," Oliver allowed. He sat in the armchair close by, meeting her gaze in the glass.

"But you would never be safe, would you?" She stood abruptly. "Very well, let us go and ruin him."

But once focused on the matter in hand, anxiety intruded, so that she kept firing questions at him in the carriage.

"What if he does not come?"

"Then we have lost no more than a few hours at an indifferent concert."

She smiled, holding his hand in her lap. "And in each other's company."

"Exactly."

She frowned. "What if he catches Kitty in the act?"

"Then we must protect her. Not that I imagine her uncle is incapable of protecting his own."

"Will he not object to us using his niece in such a way?"

"Not if she is paid for it," Oliver said cynically.

"But he *is* protective if he does not let her work after dark."

"She is not working for us after dark."

She swallowed and spoke the most important worry on her mind. "What if he uses this opportunity to try to kill you once more?"

"That is why we mustn't let him out of our sight. And we have friends and allies." His hand turned in hers, clasping her fingers. "Would you rather go home? I can plead you have a sudden headache."

"Oh, no," she said with sudden determination. "I will see him punished for what he did."

"That's my girl."

"Do you know, I'm not sure I ever did actually *trust* him," she said thoughtfully. "I clung to him because he was your family and less openly hostile than your sisters. And he often had news of you. Mostly made-up news, as I now know."

"Then your instincts were better than mine. For years now, I have been flattering myself on my ability to read accurately people's character and level of threat. I misjudged Phineas utterly until I came home. And I misjudged you."

"Family and emotions get in the way of sensible judgment," she replied. "That doesn't mean we should give them up."

He smiled and kissed her wrist.

Phineas was already in the rose garden when they arrived, holding a chair for Mrs. Fitzwalter to sit.

"Did you…?" Grace began.

"No," Oliver muttered. "But he brought her for a reason. Don't trust her."

Maria Fitzwalter had never been high on Grace's list of people to trust, for obvious reasons, but she rather liked the warning on Oliver's lips.

The large table had been set up at the back of the garden, beneath a canopy. At the front was more of a platform than a stage. A few musicians already sat around it, unpacking their instruments and chatting with each other. Several other people strolled about the garden, as though undecided whether or not to stay.

Through the gate on the other side of the garden stepped Lord and Lady Arpington, with the Duke of Dearham lounging along behind.

Mrs. Fitzwalter laughed. "Good grief, has everyone but me brought their husband to the party?"

"No, I haven't," the duke drawled, taking the tray from Kitty, who was coming up behind Mrs. Fitzwalter, and plonking it onto the table before bowing. "Lady Wenning. Ma'am. Hat off to you, Wennings! Never been to a morning concert combined with cards before!"

Mrs. Fitzwalter laughed. "Your Grace is so droll."

Kitty was hovering, serving tea and wine. No one paid her any attention, including Grace.

"The concert will begin in about ten minutes, ma'am," she murmured to Grace. "Do you want luncheon served now or wait until after?"

"Oh, after, I think. It is still early!" Further movement at the garden gate caught her eye, and her jaw dropped. "Good grief, is that Rollo?"

"He likes a game of cards," Oliver said blandly.

"Morning all," Rollo said with his surprisingly graceful bow. "You know, I might have to give this place up, now all you respectable people have discovered it. You all know Effers, don't you?"

As Rollo and Effers slouched into chairs, Grace was surprised to see her brother eschew the brandy in favor of tea. The orchestra began to tune-up.

"I suppose it's a novelty, Wenning," Rollo observed. "Never played cards to an orchestra before."

"Or while drinking tea," Effers added.

"The day is young," Oliver remarked. "Who plays and who listens? For the first hand, at least."

Grace's chair had already been placed to face the stage while still allowing a view of the table. Bridget sat beside her, while Mrs. Fitzwalter joined all the gentlemen in a game of cards. People settled in a few of the smaller tables around the edges of the rose garden, while the rows of chairs in the middle filled sparsely. The orchestra played something pleasant that Grace did not recognize, and then a woman walked onto the stage to polite applause and began to sing.

Rollo clapped his hands over his ears. "For the love of...! Wenning, you might have warned us about the dashed caterwauling!"

Oliver smiled and took a card. "Don't be such a barbarian. Grace has heard good things about both the singers."

"Both?" Rollo repeated with undisguised horror.

"Concentrate on the game," Phineas said impatiently. "Play, Darblay."

⤜⤜⤜⤛⤛⤛

As KITTY RETURNED to the second kitchen, located halfway between the rose garden and the ice garden, she found her uncle at the door, frowning toward the table where her special guests had settled down to play cards and listen to the concert.

"*That* is your party?" Uncle Renwick said.

"Yes, hosted by the gentleman who stayed with us. I knew you would like me to help him. Oh, and it turns out he's an earl!"

Renwick, who, she suspected, had known the identity of his unusual guest for some time, regarded her, brooding. "And all you have to do is plant a card on one of the party? Which one?"

"The one in the lavender waistcoat."

"I was afraid you were going to say that," her uncle growled.

She paused on her way to the fire for more boiling water, turning back to him. "Afraid? Why?"

"Because I just pointed the gentleman in the lavender waistcoat to a cutthroat for hire. No close families among the nobs, are there?" He transferred his scowling gaze to Kitty. "You be careful, girl. Do what you have to, and otherwise stay away from them."

Kitty stared at him. "You'll let him kill *our* gentleman?"

Her uncle lips twisted into a smile. "Somehow, I don't think it's *our* gentleman we need to worry about."

"I hope you're right," Kitty said worriedly and set about making more tea.

⫸⫷

WHILE THE CARD games were underway and the singer performed, Bridget cast occasional inquiring looks at Grace. There had been no time to explain what was going on. On stage, the soprano gave way to a tenor. Around the table, the players agreed to move from vingt-et-un to a form of whist.

The sun came out from behind its clouds, and Grace decided the young tenor's voice was better than the soprano's. She almost considered hiring him before she remembered the true reason they were here. At the card table, the stakes had gone up. Rollo had developed a serious frown of concentration—and a decent pile of coins at his elbow. Oliver, too, seemed to be winning. Phineas was scrawling promissory notes on scraps of paper.

A few curious patrons wandered over from elsewhere in the garden to watch the play. One fellow, in yellow pantaloons that did not flatter his stocky, muscular frame, lounged against the hedge behind the table, watching the play with unusual closeness.

"What is *he* looking for?" Grace murmured to Bridget.

"Cheating? Or perhaps he has a side bet."

Neither of those possibilities appealed to Grace. She didn't want anyone paying too close attention.

The soprano returned, joining the tenor in a duet of such perfect harmony that Grace almost forgot the game. Then, feeling someone's gaze upon her, she glanced around to find Oliver watching her. Her stomach performed a pleasant little dive, and her lips began to curve in response.

He seemed to be sitting out this hand, for he sat back, one hand in his pocket, smiling at her. Abruptly, Mrs. Fitzwalter got in the way of her view. She had flitted from the other end of the table and murmured something to Oliver, who rose at once, civilly, inclining his head to hear her. Then he bowed and offered her his arm.

Grace's stomach clenched. Wildly, she wondered if it was jealousy or simple fear because he was walking away from the safety of friends. At least Phineas remained seated, apparently unaware of his cousin's departure.

But the stocky man in the yellow pantaloons was moving, too, strolling along the back of the table and out of the same gate.

Alarm bells screamed in Grace's head. Of course, Phineas would not act himself in such company. He had tried that at the firework evening, and it hadn't worked. Now, in daylight, had he sent an assassin, the man in yellow pantaloons, to kill Oliver?

"I FIND IT just a bit overwhelming," Maria Fitzwalter said, all but hugging Oliver's arm. "Such a powerful scent of roses among that of the unwashed—for the place is undeniably vulgar!—the loudness of the music with chatter over the top, and then the intensity of play..."

"I'm sorry you are not enjoying the event," Oliver said politely. "I thought it would be amusing."

"Oh, it is," she assured him at once, managing a happy smile while turning up the narrower path among thicker bushes. "I shall enjoy it all again directly. I just needed a few moments to ensure I do not faint. And you being such an old friend..."

"And my cousin, your escort, so engrossed in the game," Oliver offered.

"Precisely. And you were sitting out the hand, so I'm afraid I picked on you. Your wife will not mind, will she?"

"My wife knows there is no need to," he said. "Since we are such old friends."

It won him a sharp glance which the lady immediately turned into another smile. "You must find it strange to be back to the constraints of your home life after the freedom of being abroad."

"I find the freedoms and constraints rather the other way around. How is Mr. Fitzwalter enjoying his new position?"

"Well enough. At any rate, he does not prose on about it. I often think of our time together onboard ship. Don't you?"

"I think how boring I must have been. And how kind you were to a morose and grumpy fellow passenger."

He kept his tone light and civil, for he was not blind to her maneuvers. She should have picked up on his distance and left it there, but she either couldn't or wouldn't.

"You were always far more than that. At one time, I almost regarded myself as engaged to you."

He raised both eyebrows in astonishment. "Now you are teasing me! I assure you, I never made an offer for anyone except the wife I cherish."

Her hand tightened on his arm. "Enough, Oliver. Don't play any more games. If you had cherished her, you would not have left her on your wedding night to bolt to China."

"That was not well done of me," he admitted. "It is, in fact, the shame of my life that I will never scrub clean."

This seemed to surprise her, for she stopped dead, and Oliver, who had kept his eyes sensibly peeled throughout their stroll, took the opportunity for a closer look around him. They had come to one of the many artful little spaces between paths and bushes, groves and streams. Here there was a wrought iron bench and some stones built up like a shrine at the edge of a stream. There seemed to be no path but the one they had come along. Otherwise, the clearing was surrounded by the stream and a lot of thick bushes.

A fine place for an ambush.

"The heart does not acknowledge shame," Mrs. Fitzwalter declared.

Oliver smiled, patted her hand, and turned back toward the path. "This one does. I hope your head is cleared, ma'am, for I must be dutiful and return to my gues—" Before the last word was out, something—someone—flew out of the bushes, rushing straight at them.

Mrs. Fitzwalter let out a gasp that was almost a scream. He shoved her unceremoniously toward the path, snarling, "Go!" before spinning to face his attacker head-on.

Of course, it was not Phineas. And there was no gun this time, since the sound of a shot would hardly be covered by the slightly muffled music and song from the nearby rose garden. Instead, his attacker wielded a wicked-looking knife, and he was quick enough to dodge Oliver's initial lunge. Oliver had to leap back out of the sweeping path of the knife, although, immediately taking advantage of the attacker's momentary imbalance, he threw out his arm, trying to knock the knife aside.

Stumbling slightly, the attacker still managed to keep hold of the weapon, but Oliver managed to seize his wrist. With their free hands, the two aimed and parried punches, while Oliver inexorably squeezed and squeezed at his opponent's thick wrist.

He had a moment to realize that he did not know this man—some hired thug in a coat so small for him that it had probably never belonged to him. Through the distant sound of the music, he could hear Mrs. Fitzwalter whimpering. Why the devil hadn't she run for help? For by her sheer surprise, he doubted she was in on this attack, though Phineas may well have used her to lure him here.

His attacker drew back his head to butt, and Oliver threw up his elbow to fend him off. They both stumbled but held their balance, and then, suddenly, in a flash of yellow pantaloons, a third man seized the attacker around the throat, hauling him off. Oliver finally seized the knife, dropping it into his pocket.

But the would-be-assassin had not given up. He fought like a wild animal, and it took both Oliver and the man in yellow pantaloons to subdue him. Finally, they rolled him onto his stomach and fastened his hands behind his back with nifty handcuffs drawn from the pocket of Oliver's ally, who promptly sat on their victim's back.

"Lord Wenning, I presume," he said, panting. "The name's Smellie."

Oliver held out his hand. "Very pleased to meet you, Mr. Smellie. I trust you'll have no further trouble getting this individual to Bow Street?"

"None. Got a vehicle waiting, and a partner to help. This cove is only hired muscle, though, my lord. He's known to us, you might say. And even if we get him to give up who paid, I doubt he'll know any names."

"Give it your best shot, Mr. Smellie." Oliver brushed down his coat and pantaloons with brisk fingers. "I should have other means of dealing with the rest of the problem. My thanks for your assistance."

"What in God's name is going on?" Mrs. Fitzwalter demanded, joining them at a safe distance from the still growling attacker beneath Mr. Smellie.

Oliver turned to her politely. "Ah, allow me to make known to you, Mr. Smellie, one of the justly famous Bow Street Runners."

Smellie, who was engaged in hauling his captive to his feet, accorded the lady a nod, which she was too dazed or too superior to return.

"Did that man try to rob you?" she demanded, her eyes darting around the clearing in some horror.

"Something like that." Oliver brushed off his sleeve and offered the arm to Mrs. Fitzwalter. "I believe it's time we returned. And I would not be a friend," he added as they walked along the path together, "if I did not warn you about your escort."

She stared at him, tried to smile. "But you could not have known this man would leap out of nowhere to attack you!"

"I wasn't referring to myself, but to my cousin, who brought you here. He really is bad ton, you know, but I believe for your own sake and your husband's, you should keep this story to yourself."

CHAPTER NINETEEN

INSTINCTIVELY, GRACE ROSE to her feet just as the singers reached their crescendo, and the audience rose to applaud them. Bridget clutched her arm to drag her back into her chair, and suddenly the Duke of Dearham was on her other side.

"Don't," he murmured, clapping. "Wenning can take care of himself, and you can't have anyone noticing you in pursuit of him and the fair Mrs. F."

"You don't understand. Someone might—"

"Trust me, he's protected. Your place is here, with *him*." Dearham gave the faintest jerk of his head toward Phineas's position.

Grace spared a quick glance at the table and the players and saw Kitty approaching with a tray of wine and fresh glasses. In an agony of indecision, she hissed at His Grace, "A man followed him. Rough fellow in yellow pantaloons."

Dearham winked. "Bow Street."

Grace's jaw dropped. Could no one have told her a Runner was here? But no, that was not fair. Oliver had told her ages ago that he had got the aid of Bow Street to protect her. Or at least to catch whoever had shot at them.

She closed her mouth and stared sightlessly at the stage. Giving in to the sparse but definite demand, the two singers began another duet, and Dearham sauntered back to his own place, smiling at Kitty to receive a refill.

Kitty flushed a fiery red—perhaps she knew his reputation or the fact that he was a duke—and poured his wine before turning to Arpington, and then Phineas, who was scowling hard over his cards, one forearm spread flat on the table.

Kitty flicked a cloth over a clean glass at Phineas's elbow. Grace blinked. For Kitty, with extraordinary quickness, used the moment to slide a card from her own sleeve, straight up Phineas's cuff. She then moved smoothly to pour his wine and stepped behind him to reach Rollo, who, this time, accepted a glass.

If Grace had not been looking so closely, she would never have seen the card planted. She still wasn't sure she had. Her heart thundering, she turned back to the stage. *If only Oliver is well ...*

It was the longest ten minutes of her life, but Oliver did eventually stroll back through the gate with a dazed-looking Mrs. Fitzwalter on his arm. While Grace tried to keep her anxious gaze away from them, Oliver escorted the lady politely to her place beside Phineas, and sat down next to Grace, but facing across the table as before instead of at the stage. His thigh brushed against hers, comfortingly warm and strong.

"Lovely voices," he observed, and only then did the relief seem to flood her. He was alive. He was whole. And he was still playing.

"Indeed," she managed. "I am so glad we came. Are you winning?"

"I was. Thought I'd give the other fellows a chance, but I'm back in for this hand."

"Make it the last before luncheon," Grace suggested. "For I believe this will be the final song of the performance."

"Oh, I do hope so," he murmured and leaned forward to claim his cards.

The singers departed to a scattering of applause, for half the audience were already escaping in search of luncheon or fresh entertainment. Still, a harp was brought onto the platform, and the orchestra remained to accompany the young female harpist.

Oliver's return had sent Grace's spirits soaring. Now that he was safe and by her side, they would succeed. And even if they didn't today, they would tomorrow or the day after. The sheer enormity of his presence at her side, of his love, almost overwhelmed her.

"I'll tell you what, Grace," Bridget murmured. "I think the harpist is the best of the lot."

Grace blinked and realized the music had become part of the emotion surging within her. She listened in silence for a few moments. "I believe you are right…"

Phineas shifted irritably on his chair. By the pile of coins and vowels at his side, he was now doing better, but clearly, his current hand annoyed him. He reached for his glass, and quite suddenly, the Duke of Dearham jerked forward and seized him by the wrist.

Phineas's jaw dropped, his eyes widened as he stared at the other man. "Your Grace?"

Dearham raised Phineas's elbow and shook it. An ace of hearts dropped half out of his cuff and then, with another shake, fell onto the table.

Utter silence surrounded him. Phineas stared with horror at the ace from his sleeve. So did everyone else before their eyes lifted to his face.

"What is this, sir?" Grace had never heard the amiable Dearham speak with such icy contempt.

Phineas swallowed, his gaze darting desperately around the table. "I wish I knew! I have no idea how the card came to be resting there!"

"*Resting?*" Rollo exclaimed in disgust. "No wonder I could never get my hands on the dashed ace of hearts!" He threw down his hand. So did everyone else.

Dearham rose to his feet and bowed stiffly to Grace and to Oliver. "Forgive me. No one blames *you* for this, Wenning, but I cannot sit at the same table as a cheat. We'll wait for you by the Eros fountain."

And he stalked off, swiftly followed by Effers, Rollo, and the Arpingtons. At the last moment, Bridget swept up the bewildered Mrs. Fitzwalter, and they all left the garden to the plaintive strains of the harp.

Grace and Oliver were left alone with the stunned Phineas, who could clearly not quite grasp his sudden, irrevocable ruin. A man who cheated at cards had no honor, was beyond the pale, intolerable.

At last Phineas focused his gaze on Oliver. "I didn't," he said wildly. "I didn't hide that card!"

"Oh, I know," Oliver said softly. "My wife and I planted it there."

Phineas blinked several times as though to assure himself he was not dreaming. "Is this some kind of joke, Ollie? For I take leave to tell you that it is already out of hand! The damage—"

"Damage? You mean, like forging a letter purporting to come from my wife? Was that a joke, Phin? Or a cynical attempt to keep us apart until I, hopefully, died at sea or got killed by bandits?"

"I don't know what you are talking about," Phineas said with dignity. "*You* took yourself to China if you recall."

"Thus playing right into your hands. Did you laugh—it being such a great joke—while you continued to drip poison to me by letter? And into my wife's ears? Only, you were a little too sure of yourself to keep your stories straight. If Grace's true love was the mysterious Anthony, then why did he never reappear in the two years I was away? Why did Grace immediately take up with other rakes and scapegraces? And yet, when I came home, she was fending them off. And still no Anthony."

"I told you her flirtations were nothing but that," Phineas pointed out. Grace had never seen his eyes so serious, and although he seemed relaxed, even poised, his fingers on the stem of his wine glass looked white and rigid. As though the glass were about to break with the force of his grip.

Oliver, his gaze on those fingers, said, "And you told her mine were nothing important, mere peccadilloes to be expected in a man away from home for so long. I never told you that, Phin. I never told you anything about my private life. The funny thing is, while believing the worst of Grace, I lived those two years as celibate as a monk."

Phineas shrugged, impatient now. "Mere misunderstandings! For which you have ruined me?"

"No, I've ruined you for endangering my wife and trying to kill me."

"Oh, for the love of—"

"I know it was you," Oliver interrupted. "I asked questions. You told me a lot of nonsense about the firework party, who was where and for how long, but the thing is, Phin, I asked everyone else, too, and you were the one who was missing. You were the one who provoked Rollo to a duel with Boothe and then told me of it so that I would charge to the rescue and be shot in a tragic accident. And you just sent a man after me with a knife."

The glass didn't break. Phineas shoved it away from him. "Rot. Nasty stories made up to account for your own ill behavior! You have not a shred of probability, let alone proof."

"Actually, I have. The man you hired has been arrested by Bow Street Runners. I expect he's already implicating you. And I doubt Mrs. Fitzwalter appreciates being used in such a way, either. She was terrified, you know."

Phineas's eyes had narrowed. "I don't believe you."

"What, that a Runner has been protecting us since the night of fireworks?" Grace asked with contempt. "Actually, we don't care whether you believe us or not. It's true the evidence against you will come largely from a man of less than perfect character. But no matter. You are ruined and had best leave the country."

Phineas's gaping mouth shut with a snap. "You set all this up! Brought your tame duke and your righteous Arpingtons and your gossiping Effers... You lured me here to ruin me!"

"We do seem to have developed a taste for the theatrical," Oliver allowed. "I think it was abducting Boothe and Rollo Darblay and staging their so friendly card party that inspired us to greater feats. You can go where you like, of course." He took a scrap of paper from his pocket and passed it across the table. "But Europe might not be far enough, being full of British travelers since the end of the war. This ship is bound for Australia and sails tonight. Take it or not, but make no mistake, Phineas, there is nowhere in these islands for you to hide, and you can never come back."

Oliver rose and held out his hand to Grace. She took it and rose.

"Ollie," Phin said hoarsely. "I am your cousin. We are family, *friends!*"

Oliver stilled. Suddenly, a white line had formed around his lips. "*Now*, you remember that, Phin? Only now?"

Grace took his arm, urging him forward, and they left the garden together.

"I'm sorry," she whispered. "That can't have been easy."

His hand covered hers and squeezed convulsively. "No. Phineas has always been part of my life. And yet, it wasn't as difficult as losing you."

PHINEAS, HIS WORLD in tatters, eventually rose stiffly from his solitary seat at the empty table. At some point, the music had stopped, and now there was no one left in the rose garden. He picked up his hat and his winnings, which no one had troubled to relieve him of, and walked out of the garden.

He was a pariah now. He had known he needed to act speedily before the Wennings started comparing notes, but he had never expected them to be quite so quick or quite so ruthless. Or to be this clever about it. There was nothing he could do to come back from this. Criminal charges he could have fought, and he had somewhat relied on Wenning refusing to allow the family name to dragged through criminal courts. But they had got around that, too, by besting him at his own game—lying.

As he walked blindly toward the main path, he glimpsed them at another table in the outdoor eatery by the fountain of Eros. Everyone, from Dearham to Maria Fitzwalter, sat with them. They no longer played cards, though they were laughing and chatting as if nothing had happened. As if Phineas's life was not over.

Oliver had always had everything. More toys, ponies, clothes, money, the title, and the houses and lands that went with it. Women, sycophants, a beautiful, loving wife ready and willing to breed heirs and exclude him, Phineas, from the succession.

There would be no forgiveness now from the cousin he had once imagined to be so malleable. Perhaps he never had been. Or perhaps he had grown up.

Either way—damn him to hell—there had always been something about Oliver, some elusive charm, some velvet-covered steel, an instinct to strive despite all the advantages that had landed in his lap from birth. With Oliver's title and fortune, Phineas would have been content, not chasing after diplomatic or political glory. Phineas had sought to use that against his cousin, too. And now he had nothing.

While Oliver still had everything. Including, apparently, the beautiful, loving wife. For some reason, that added insult to injury.

No one looked at him as he walked alone down the path to the front gates. No one in his world would so much as speak to him again.

In this last belief, it turned out he was wrong. In fact, Sir Nash Boothe spoke to him some three hours later.

Boothe arrived in his rooms as he was throwing things randomly into a trunk. Sir Nash didn't trouble to knock, let alone have himself announced, merely sauntered in.

"What's this I hear about you cheating at cards?" Boothe asked without preamble.

"I did *not* cheat at cards," Phineas said between his teeth.

"You'd be a damned fool to do so in that company. One thing among a houseful of Captain Sharps at the Orange Tree. Quite another among gentlemen."

"Do not," Phineas snarled, "lecture me about gentlemen! My gentlemanly cousin set me up, staged the whole thing. Much as he did with you and your spectacular reconciliation with Rollo Darblay."

"People find that hilarious," Boothe observed. "Can't say I'm laughing, though there's nothing much I can do about it." He shrugged. "At least I didn't have to shoot the divine Grace's brother."

Phineas threw his hairbrushes and shaving set into the trunk and scowled. "Are you still pursuing that prey? She's thick as thieves with Wenning again. He'll never believe you touched her."

"I didn't," Boothe said morosely.

A gleam of light shone in Phineas's darkness. "No, but you might once she's ruined in public, and he repudiates her. What do you have to lose?"

<hr/>

"TWO NIGHTS IN a row," Oliver murmured as he held Grace's chair for her at the dining table. "People will talk."

Grace sat. "Two nights in a row that we have dined at home, alone?"

His finger trailed across her nape in a caress that made her shiver. "Exactly." He moved and took his place at the head of the table.

"We have an excellent excuse," Grace said as the footmen brought in two soup tureens, plates of new bread, and a jug of cream. "We are making last-minute preparations for tomorrow's ball. And, in fact, we have a dinner party before it, with my family and yours."

"But not Phineas," he said lightly.

"No, not Phineas. I have asked Mr. Meade instead, since he was so helpful about Rollo's silly duel." She waited until the footmen withdrew before she added, "I also invited Sir Ernest and Mrs. Caldwell—to dinner as well as to the ball. He has accepted the invitation to both. Mrs. Caldwell has said she'll come to the ball, though I expect she will leave before the unmasking."

She ladled a light, fragrant soup into his bowl. "I told them they should meet up abroad, and she should use her old name. She is a lady by birth, her name spoiled by youthful scandal—and by her subsequent career, but I doubt anyone would recognize the new Lady Leyton as Frances Caldwell."

"Probably not if they carry it off with enough panache. Not sure panache is Leyton's thing, however."

"He just needs to dote. She is an actress, who can play her role in public and be exactly who she is in private."

"Just like the rest of us, in fact."

She cast him a quick glance over her soup spoon. "Are you thinking of Rudolf?"

"Are you?" he countered.

"I'm glad to be rid of all pretense," she said. "Even before you came home, it was beginning to feel like an unbearable strain, as if I would snap. And then, when you came…"

"Old wagers, stolen bracelets, and masked men called Rudolf made it even worse."

She sighed and nodded. "I couldn't keep track of the deceits, even after I recognized Rudolf as you, and I had to work out what he could be assumed to know as distinct from what you would know. I wanted it all to stop."

"I wanted to win you as Rudolf," he admitted. "So that it would wipe away Oliver's crimes in your mind."

"I was sorely tempted," she confessed.

"But it was another pretense, and a stupid one. I'm not sure how I planned to work that into my new honesty with you."

Grace laid down her spoon. "The true dishonesty was Phineas's. The rest was merely hiding for survival. I think we can forgive ourselves and each other for that. But between *us*, Oliver, no more hiding?"

He took her hand and kissed it. "No more," he said fervently.

She smiled mischievously. "Apart from our masked ball, of course. More soup, my lord?"

"No, thank you." He sat back and regarded her, while the footmen removed the used dishes. "I doubt a mere costume can hide us from each other now," he said softly.

It would take time. They were still feeling their way toward each other inch by inch, but pleasure in his company, pride in his achievements, sheer love for him was seeping deeper into her bones with every passing hour.

"Are you needed in London over the next few weeks?" she asked.

"No, I am on extended leave for some months. Why?"

"I was wondering how you would feel about going into the country, to Harcourt? I was thinking about it before you came home, and now I feel more than ever that I would enjoy the peace."

A rather wicked smile lit his eyes, causing a flush to rise up her neck to her face. "So would I," he said softly. "Shall we make arrangements immediately after the ball?"

She nodded, smiling back with an odd, breathless shyness.

After dinner, they repaired together to the drawing room, still talking, although they sat close together on the sofa. This was what should have happened on their wedding journey, a gradual, growing knowledge of each other through talk and companionship. It was wonderful to be reminded of his humor, of his wide interest in the world, to learn his views on important matters and tell him of hers. To discuss large things and small, to discover more and more about China, and about his past.

As a result, the time flew by, and it was after midnight before they climbed the stairs together. Their voices had fallen silent at last. All Grace could hear was the beating of her own heart.

On the landing, he turned with her toward her own apartments. She had not imagined he would do otherwise, but it still made her smile and anticipate. But to her oversensitive nerves, the mood of his silence seemed to have changed from companionable to something else she couldn't quite grasp.

When they came to her door, she turned to him impulsively, just as he leaned across her and opened the door. He took her hand from his arm and softly kissed her fingers and then her lips.

"Good night, my love," he murmured. "Until tomorrow."

And he turned and walked away.

It felt like being drenched by a bucket of cold water. Grace walked into her room in something of a daze and rang for Henley.

Why did he not stay with me? Has he tired of me already?

She had grown too used to sharing her bed and her love. But there was a reason why married couples kept their own apartments. To maintain privacy when they wanted it.

It hurt, that, but she could not deny he was entitled to privacy. While Henley helped prepare her for bed, worry whirled around her mind. She wondered if he was ill, if he needed time alone to come to terms with the day's events. If he had simply had enough of Grace. If, now that he had got to know her better, his passion was already waning.

"That will be all, Henley," she said at last as the maid began to brush her hair. "Good night."

Obediently, Henley replaced the hairbrush on the dressing table. "Good night, my lady."

"Thank you," Grace said distractedly. She frowned at herself in the glass as Henley's footsteps retreated along the passage to the servants' stairs.

She and Oliver had promised each other honesty. No more hiding.

She would rather die than intrude, and yet she needed to know. Should he not say, *I need this time to myself?* Or was she expecting too much? Anxiety soared. Her new confidence in herself plummeted.

In the glass, her shoulders had slumped. For a moment, she stared at her reflection, then straightened. *No. I will not allow that distance again.*

With sudden decision, she rose and picked up the candle from the table by the door. She wore only her night rail as she hurried along the passage and crossed the landing, but by now, the servants were all in bed, and she had to act quickly before her courage failed.

She had been in her husband's bedchamber only twice in her life and never in his company. The first time when she had first arrived at Wenning House and inspected every room. The second, to make sure it was aired and ready to receive him when he came home from China. On neither occasion had she lingered. In fact, on the second occasion, she had barely stepped inside.

Now, she was relieved to see a light still shone beneath the door. Before her determination could wane, she rapped the door and stalked in without waiting for a reply. She strode across the empty sitting room and into his bedchamber where she found him sprawled, bare-chested against the pillows, a book open on the covers. His lips parted in astonishment as she came to an almost military halt beside the bed and set down her candle.

Part of her could not help acknowledging his sheer, male beauty as he gazed up at her in the pale light of a solitary lamp and one flickering candle. But she refused to be distracted from what she had to say.

"Excuse the intrusion," she began loudly, more like a declaration than a request. "I shall go in one moment, for I understand the importance of privacy. But please tell me the truth. Are you tired? Hurt? Or do you need time away from me? I need to know—"

He loomed out of the bed, depriving her of words and even breath. Stark naked, he wrapped her in his arms.

"I have *yearned* for you in this room with me," he whispered.

"Then why did you not say so?"

Even now, he held her loosely, his face buried in her hair. "I don't know. Awareness that I owe you consideration, that I should not pester you constantly."

Pester? She slid her arms around his waist, loving the feel of his warm, smooth skin over hard muscle. Anxiety began to drain away. "And?" she prompted, for she knew there was more.

He swallowed, and with something like awe, she realized that this big, confident man, her husband, whom she had imagined never at a loss, was struggling for words.

"Phineas," he said with difficulty. "We made fun of each other since we were boys. In some ways, I never took him seriously, but I… I looked on him as the brother I never had. And now I cannot even mourn him for he isn't dead, just not… He hated me."

"Not always." In compassion, she pressed closer. "He was just eaten up with envy."

"I took him for granted. I never want to do that with you, of all people."

Revelation washed over her. There was more here than Phineas's betrayal. She was not the only one who suffered anxieties and uncertainties. Her husband was, stunningly, unsure. Of himself, of his attraction. Of her lasting love, perhaps, and certainly of his worthiness of that love.

And somehow, in that vulnerability, she loved him all the more.

She swept one arm up his back, feeling the muscles undulate beneath her fingers, and extracted her head from under his chin. She brushed her lips across his, a soft butterfly caress. "May I lie beside you?"

For the space of a heartbeat, he stared down at her. "You may do anything you wish with me."

She let the smile curve her lips as she kissed him again, this time with long, aching tenderness. At the same time, she swept her hand down over his hips and buttocks and pressed closer to feel the wonder of his growing hardness. He let out a groan, and his mouth bore down on hers. She moved her body, rubbing against him from breasts to thigh in deliberate, wicked seduction that most certainly aroused her, whatever its effect on him.

But she was left in no doubt of that either. "You are a very naughty temptress," he murmured breathlessly against her lips and turned her so that her back was to the bed. She tugged him with her, falling backward, and when she landed on the bed, somehow her nightgown was gone, and they were skin to skin, the weight of him sweet and welcome.

"I love you," she whispered, gazing up at him.

"And I love you."

His hand caressed the length of her body, but she pushed, rolling him over beneath her, and because he needed it, and she wanted it, she made long, languorous love to him.

CHAPTER TWENTY

THE DAY OF the ball was a flurry of last-minute preparations.

"I take it we will achieve *shocking squeeze* status, and therefore the accolade of the Season?" Oliver said, discovering Grace in the ballroom around midday.

She turned from the silk awning created before Tamar's painted wall to look like a tent from which ladies might watch a joust. She was always still surprised and delighted to see her husband.

"No one has declined the invitation, so far as I can recall. So yes, I imagine it will be quite a squeeze! But I believe the weather is with us, and we can spill out onto the terrace. Both terraces if need be."

There was a large terrace accessed from French doors opposite the mural. And a smaller one through a single door to the right. Grace had held a ball here last Season and kept the single door open only for air, with a curtain over it, for the small terrace's view over an outbuilding was not inspiring. The bigger terrace looked over a pleasant patch of lawn and the kitchen garden to the left. It had not been well used on the last occasion, for the weather had been wet and cold—there had been precious little summer that year. This year was very different, and already Grace had lanterns placed around the terrace and two pitch-soaked torches in sconces to keep the medieval theme.

"For intrigue and cigarillo smoking," Oliver approved, looking around. "You have made it all very beautiful."

"Well, Tamar made the difference. I wonder how we will cover it up for our next theme?"

"A worry for the future. Phineas took that ship to Australia."

Her gaze, which had been critically surveying the ballroom, swung quickly back to him. "Really? Then you are safe?"

"Unless he left behind any little surprises—apart from the scandal, for which we will be commiserated rather than blamed. Do you have time to join me for a quick luncheon?"

She took his arm at once, though she warned him, "I ordered little more than a snack for luncheon, for we will dine early."

"Ah yes, and who are we entertaining for dinner?"

"Family, largely. We should have invited them to dine when you first came home, but I was too busy avoiding you."

He dropped a kiss on top of her head. "Then your parents and my sisters?"

"And Rollo and Hope. I know Hope is only fifteen, but she will be out in no time, and she might as well get used to society in safety. Don't mention it to my parents, but she will be at the ball, too, for a couple of hours. And I invited Sir Ernest and Rollo's friend Mr. Meade. Also, your cousin, Mrs. Dove, and her daughter, who made her debut this Season."

His brows flew up. "Elvira Dove? I thought her eldest was still in the schoolroom!"

"Viola is nineteen years old and quite fun. Her come-out was post-poned because of Mr. Dove's death. I presented her at court and made her a gift. I assumed you would want to."

But there was no accusation in his eyes, only a rueful awareness. "Of course, you were quite right. You have taken on my family responsibilities as well as everything else."

"Say what you will of my mother. She brought me up to be a good wife," Grace said lightly.

His arm slipped around her waist, hugging her quickly to his side.

"Perhaps. But I love your natural kindness."

Grace spent the rest of the day on costume adjustments and making sure there were enough well-appointed rooms for her dinner guests to change into their costumes for the ball. And then it was time to bathe and dress for dinner, a mundane matter that would have been achieved much more quickly had not Oliver arrived in his shirt sleeves—to wash her back, as he blandly put it, before shooing the scandalized Henley away.

There was a good deal of intimate washing. At one point, he ended in the bath with her, clothes and all, and the fun and laughter of that ended with a very different kind of pleasure once he lifted her bodily from the bath and carried her, dripping, to bed.

As a result, Grace was rather more rushed than she meant to be, and the first of her guests had already arrived by the time she descended the stairs to greet them.

She found her parents and Hope and the Trewthorpes ensconced in the drawing room with glasses of sherry and ratafia. Honoria Trewthorpe looked her up and down as she entered, watching like a hawk as Oliver stood to greet her. Eager, Grace thought, to spot any signs of disrespect.

By the time she had finished welcoming the first guests, Mrs. Dove and Viola had arrived, and Honoria looked inexplicably astonished to see her cousins, as though she had forgotten them. Or perhaps she just hadn't expected Grace to remember them.

Sir Ernest arrived then, on the heels of Lord and Lady Barnton, and the company became pleasantly diluted. Inevitably, Rollo was last, though not as late as he would have been, Grace suspected, had not Mr. Meade harried him there.

There was little opportunity for private speech with Oliver, although they did brush hands by the sherry decanter as she topped up her father's glass.

"Has Honoria been any help to you these two years?" he murmured unexpectedly. "Or did she leave you to sink or swim?"

"She wanted me to swim with her," Grace said humorously. "Which I wouldn't do, since she already disapproved of me. We are, you see, frigidly polite." Catching his expression, she smiled fleetingly and entwined her fingers with his. "It is past. Let us just enjoy the evening."

They separated again. Grace arranged her guests in pairs to go into dinner, Grace on Lord Trewthorpe's arm, Oliver escorting Lady Darblay. Rollo, inevitably took in Viola Dove, and Mr. Meade looked positively reverential to have Hope on his arm. In her first evening gown, Hope looked beautiful, if slightly awkward and heart-breakingly young. But Grace was glad to see Meade made her laugh and relax.

Rollo, inevitably, flirted with Viola Dove.

"What's this I hear about Phineas fleeing the country?" Lord Trewthorpe muttered to Grace. "Honoria's convinced you had something to do with it."

She and Oliver had already decided how to deal with such queries, so she replied calmly, "It was His Grace of Dearham who caught him. There were many witnesses and no way to cover it up."

Trewthorpe shook his head. "Bad business. I wouldn't have believed it of him. Though if rumor is correct and he had taken to playing at the Orange Tree... Is Maida Gardens any better? What on earth were you all doing there?"

"I heard a rumor of a talented soprano, which turned out to be exaggerated. However, there is a harpist I will chase up one day. Let's not talk of Phineas. It is not easy for Oliver."

"Nor Honoria."

There was no lingering over wine after dinner since everyone had to change into costume for the ball. Grace swept Hope up to her rooms.

"Mama thinks I will sit here dozing and reading until three in the morning," Hope said mischievously.

"And so you will. From half-past eleven! No supper dance. No leaving the ballroom unless I am with you. Or Oliver or Rollo escorts you. Do *not* be enticed onto the terrace with flattering words, and do *not* remove your mask under any circumstances. Or let anyone else try to do so!"

"There are a lot of rules," Hope said mutinously.

"There are when you are fifteen. The alternative is, you do as Mama says and wait here all evening. With Henley."

Hope wrinkled her nose. "It's very strange, this life you live. I am only curious."

"I know. But it is only fun, Hope. Too much, during the Season, perhaps. The rest of life still awaits you beyond balls and parties. One way or another, you will have at least one Season in London. Mama will insist upon it, so you might as well have an early glimpse to inspire you."

"Or not. *Is* it fun, Gracie?" Hope asked shrewdly. "Sometimes, I've thought you don't find it so, just go through the motions, albeit with a certain amount of enthusiasm."

Grace thought about that, and, curiously, honesty was easy now. "I enjoyed it before I was married. The novelty of new people and constant entertainment, theatre, dancing, talking of everything, all the admiration and genteel flirting. Afterward, it was different. I had more freedom as a married lady, but I was, largely, playing a role. Like an actor on a stage."

"For your pride? Because Wenning left?"

Grace nodded.

"And now?" Hope pursued. "Are you glad he is back?"

"Yes," Grace admitted. "Now I am glad."

"And the playacting?"

"That is a good question," Grace allowed. "I suppose there was always something of me in it. We all playact to some extent… Just not, perhaps, with those I love." She shook off her philosophical mood and reached for Hope's costume. "We're going down to the country next week."

"So am I. With Miss Fenchurch. I think Mama and Papa will stay in London until next month."

"You can come to us for a while, too."

Hope hugged her. "I think I will leave you alone for a little. This is your wedding trip, is it not?" And she laughed with delight when Grace blushed.

⋙✦⋘

OLIVER STROLLED EARLY into what he thought was the empty ballroom until he was greeted by a snort of laughter from the terrace. Rollo, glass in hand, stood on the terrace, gazing through the open French window at him. Apart from a mask dangling around his neck, he looked much as he always did. Though he was certainly amused by Oliver's portrayal of King Charles II.

"No costume, Rollo," Oliver observed. "Can it be you are not joining in the spirit of the event?"

"Oh, no, I'm here in flesh and spirit. Forgot about the costume, to be honest, so thought I'd just masquerade as a viscount's heir."

"You are a viscount's heir," Oliver observed, strolling over to join him. The servants would be out any moment to light the outside lanterns and torches. For now, it was quite pleasant in the dusk of a summer evening.

"Tell that to my father," Rollo said bitterly.

"I can't imagine he needs reminding."

"What's the point of being heir to something that won't exist by the time you inherit it? What's the point of being heir if you can't touch it or do anything with it?"

Oliver cast him an assessing look. "Am I right in thinking this is more than just a lament for a lost allowance?"

228

Rollo let out a reluctant laugh. "You inherited young, didn't you? You never had time to feel useless."

"Grace said you had ideas to bring the land back into profit, ideas that your father is reluctant to implement?"

Rollo shrugged impatiently. "He has no faith in me. Can't blame him. I'm a wastrel, and everyone tells me I'm going to the devil. Thing is, I know I'm expensive, but I've got nothing else to do."

"What would you do if you got the chance?"

Oliver was almost sorry he asked, for Rollo was still telling him when Grace came to find him.

Resplendent in an auburn wig and Elizabethan ruffles, with a tartan sash across her breast and matching mask over her upper face, she looked incredibly beautiful in a way that was entirely light-hearted. Mary, Queen of Scots, clearly, before tragedy broke her.

"There you are!" she exclaimed. "The guests are arriving."

Oliver rose obediently from the wall on which he had been sitting and dusted off his backside. Through her mask, Grace's eyes danced at Oliver's long, black curly wig and ornate coat of black and silver grey.

"Do you have an unlimited supply of that cloth?" she teased.

"It was a gift, and it seemed to suit the Merry Monarch."

Rollo followed him inside, so Oliver waited a moment to let him catch up.

"I'll tell you what, Rollo," he said casually. "You've clearly read up on the subject, so give me a few weeks, and then come down to Harcourt in time for harvest. Follow my stewards around and learn the practicalities. And then, perhaps, we can speak to Lord Darblay together."

Rollo's mouth fell open. "Really? You'd do that?"

"Of course. Unless I see you're not interested, in which case, I'll withdraw my offer."

Rollo stopped in his tracks and thrust out his hand. "Tell *you* what, Wenning, you're really not a bad fellow at all. I almost forgive you for what you did to Grace. In fact," he added with an engaging grin, "you can look on having me under your feet as penance."

⋙⋘

THE BALLROOM FILLED up with almost alarming speed. Queen Cleopatra and ladies of Greek, Roman, and medieval times, arrived in droves, escorted by Roman soldiers, knights in half-armor, pirates, and bygone kings, to be welcomed by the Queen of Scots and King Charles II.

Both Bridget Arpington—in a coned hat and gorgeously embroidered, flowing medieval gown—and her husband, a gallant knight, laughed when they saw her.

"Mary preexecution," Arpington mourned. "I am disappointed."

"I decided carrying my own head around was undignified," Grace told them, and they were still grinning as they bowed to His Majesty beside her.

Grace did not recognize everyone, though their voices usually gave her a hint. Sir Nash Boothe, she knew at once—in a piratical costume that didn't quite suit his Brutus hair style. However, as she did with all but closet friends and family, she merely smiled and welcomed him without any sign of recognition. Although she didn't want him there, it would probably have caused more talk if he hadn't come.

An obvious Queen Elizabeth sailed alone into the room, a crown topping a wig that almost matched Grace's own. Her ruffles were higher, her gown wider, and her mask more glittering. They curtseyed gravely to each other, and only when Queen Elizabeth's lips curved did Grace begin to suspect that she beheld one of London's most talented actresses.

"Your Majesty is most welcome," Grace assured her, and "Elizabeth" moved on to exchange "Majesties" with Oliver.

230

But at last, the bulk of the guests had arrived, and Grace nodded to the leader of the orchestra in the gallery. At once, they began to bring their pleasant background music to a halt and would pause to let everyone prepare for the first dance.

"You are good at this," Oliver murmured.

"My mother's training," she reminded him.

"No," he said simply. He was smiling beneath his mask, no doubt much as the merry monarch's when in pursuit of ladyloves. "Do you suppose we would shock the world if we opened the dancing together? At least we would be in disguise."

"Sadly, I am promised to a pirate."

Oliver laughed as she walked away. Already, she had never enjoyed a ball so much in two years. Immediately, she was accosted by Eleanor of Aquitaine—she knew, for she had already discussed costumes with Mrs. Dove.

"Might I ask one more favor?" Queen Eleanor murmured. "Not for the first dance, but at some point, if you can see through his disguise, could you possibly introduce Viola to the Duke of Dearham?"

"Dearham?" Grace repeated, startled. Mrs. Dove was aiming high and not necessarily wisely for her daughter. She took her arm, drawing her a little aside to avoid an approaching couple. "Ma'am, you do know His Grace is a confirmed rake? And every hostess knows that the only beauty he *never* pursues is the marriageable variety."

"Viola has already attracted a number of very eligible suitors," Mrs. Dove replied with dignity. "And his grace will eventually have to marry. I see no reason why Viola should not be the one to capture his heart. Someone has to."

"That is true," Grace allowed. "I would just hate him to break *her* heart. But yes, of course, I will introduce them if the moment allows."

And so the marriage mart moves on, she thought wryly. And with her faith in love restored, she allowed the possibility of genuine affection in a ducal marriage. Once, she had believed only love had led to her own marriage. And then, when Oliver abandoned her, that she had merely been sold for generous settlements to an aristocrat who just wanted a vessel for an heir of his body before he risked a dangerous journey. Now, her cynicism dampened, she could wish Viola and Dearham well, whether with each other or not.

A piratical gentleman, with an eyepatch over his mask and a scimitar clanking at his hip, materialized by her side. He made a much better pirate than Boothe, though she might have been influenced by the flashing smile.

"My promised dance?" said none other than His Grace of Dearham.

"I believe it is." As the orchestra struck up, she walked with him to the center of the dance floor, which she had worked hard to make look like a courtyard. As the waltz began, more couples joined them, and Grace was able to murmur, "Thank you for your help with Phineas."

"I hear he's flown." For a moment, his eyes were unusually serious. "Did he really cheat? Or did I ruin an innocent man?"

"He was not innocent. He tried to kill Oliver. Three times. And he was responsible for the estrangement between us that you will be too gentlemanly to mention. For that, Oliver and I, not you, ruined him."

"You are a sweet girl," Dearham said. "I wish now I'd cut Wenning out with you. Or at least tried to."

"No, you don't, Fish."

He laughed and spun her in the waltz. Her anxious gaze discovered Hope in her medieval costume, deep in conversation with a similarly dressed Viola Dove. Eleanor of Aquitaine hovered nearby. As did the not terribly piratical Sir Nash Boothe. Her stomach twinged in faint alarm. But there were, surely, enough people looking out for her.

When her dance with Dearham was over, she took his arm and led him toward Viola and her mother.

"Here is a wicked fellow in need of encouragement to reform. Mr. Pirate, allow me to present you to this most beautiful of our maidens."

The ducal pirate appeared delighted with the introduction and immediately asked Viola to dance.

Her duty done, Grace turned in search of Hope and found her walking onto the dance floor with the over-smart pirate, Sir Nash Boothe.

⟫⟫⟫⟪⟪⟪

HOPE HAD NO idea who her piratical cavalier was. And, in fact, it took some time for her to realize he was flirting with her. This both amused and flattered her, not least because he clearly had no idea that she was only fifteen years old, and so she was quite happy to dance with him.

"You remind me of someone," he told her as they came together in the country dance. "And yet, I am sure I would know you if we had met before."

"I assure you, we have not met before."

He smiled tantalizingly. "How can you know that? Do you know who I am?"

"Should I?"

"If you have been in London for most of the Season."

The dance parted them, but she picked up the conversation when they next joined hands. "I have been here for several weeks."

"Then how strange that we have never met."

"Not really."

Apparently intrigued, they danced together up the line, exchanging conversation when they could, between smiles for temporary partners.

"Then you are so far above me?" he suggested. "Like a royal princess?"

"Alas, I am kept in my solitary tower."

"Perhaps you are in need of rescuing?"

"Actually, I like my tower."

"Even though you have met me outside it? My lady, you wound

233

me."

"No, I don't. Besides, no one in their right mind would choose to be rescued by a corsair. Out of the frying pan…"

"Don't you read Lord Byron?" he asked, dancing her back to the end of the line.

"That is poetry, not real life."

He laughed.

Only as the dance ended did he say, "Grant me one more favor, my lady?"

Remembering Grace's warnings, Hope smiled noncommittally.

"Pass this message to our hostess, the Queen of Scots," he murmured, drawing her hand onto his arm. Beneath her fingers was a small, folded piece of paper. "And I'm sure we will be allowed to meet again."

She blinked at him in some surprise, but he only gave her a flashing smile, released her, and vanished into the milling throng.

Disconcerted, Hope retained the folded paper hidden in her hand. Someone using her to get to Grace seemed both rude and underhanded. Now she felt the opposite of flattered, for she did not believe for a moment that the note to Grace was a civil request to call upon Hope.

In all, she was glad Grace had warned her and thought she might retreat now to the gallery to watch rather than participate. Fortunately, Grace was bustling toward her, sweeping her up and into a silk-curtained alcove.

Unfortunately, the alcove was not empty. A togaed Roman sat there, holding the hand of Queen Elizabeth, who snatched her hand free as soon as they appeared. Grace didn't seem to notice they had company until she let the curtain fall back, saying urgently, "Hope, did that pirate—" She broke off. "Oh. Sorry." She peered at the Roman. "Sir Ernest?"

The Roman pushed up his mask and let it fall again.

As though relieved, Grace turned back to Hope. "They are friends.

Is everything well with you?"

"He—that pirate—gave me this for you." Hope handed over the paper, and definite anger flushed over Grace's face.

"Why, the absolute scoundrel! How *dare* he!" She tore open the note, scanning it furiously. Her lips thinned, and she read it aloud. *"I do not speak of debt but of love. If there is no other fate for me, at least allow me to say goodbye. On the small terrace, when the third dance has begun."*

"Send Oliver," Sir Ernest the Roman advised.

"But I don't want anyone eating their own teeth at my ball," Grace said. "Besides, what the devil is he about? He knows he is persona non grata. I could hardly *dis*invite him since it would cause talk. But he should know better than even to be here."

Sir Ernest scowled, causing his mask to twitch. "He'll have someone else bringing Oliver, and no doubt half the ballroom, to find you on the terrace in a compromising position. It wouldn't matter if you were forced. Your reputation would still be tarnished. But he is probably hoping for your estrangement from your husband."

"He is an absolute blackguard," Grace said shortly. "Why did I ever even tolerate him?"

"Boredom," Hope said, and Grace laughed and hugged her. "Exactly. Well, I hope he enjoys his solitary half-hour on the terrace."

"I don't see why he should be left there in peace," Queen Elizabeth said unexpectedly.

Grace cocked her head to one side, "What do you mean?"

"We could punish him a little…"

SIR NASH BOOTHE was not vindictive by nature. He had never regarded himself as a bad man. But he did have a right to pursue what he wanted, and Grace Wenning had become, with increasing obsession, exactly what he wanted. The trouble was, the more obsessed he grew, the cooler she became, and the time he had already devoted to the pursuit of her, surely, justified a little…manipulation.

Especially after her husband's brutal trick to stop his duel with young Darblay. Not that shooting Grace's brother would have put him in terribly good order with her, of course, but he had never heard that they were close. Despite his escorting her to Maida Gardens on the evening of their wager.

The truth was, he loved Grace in his own way. If she had been free, he would have married her, even though everyone knew the Darblays didn't have a feather to fly with. But her damned husband had the ill-manners to come home from the wilds, and Boothe's chances grew increasingly dim.

Phineas Harlaw had been right. Boothe really had invested so much time and effort on Grace that he was entitled to win her. And to use somewhat…underhand methods to do so.

And so, as he stepped through the single, open door onto a small, romantically dark terrace, he felt perfectly justified—and excited that he would win her at last. She might well be angry at his methods if she ever realized he had brought about her ruin, but by then, they would be lovers, and she would forgive him anything.

Lord Wenning, who had abandoned her on their wedding night, was clearly a slow top and a laggard in the bedchamber, too. No, he, Boothe, would give her what she had never had…

He leaned against the low wall, watching the shadows dance against the house. Like the gentle glow of light, the shadows came from the lanterns around the corner, on the larger terrace. His heart was beating fast because he didn't doubt that she would come. He had seen the girl talking to her, and he had struck just the right note with his message.

He wasn't sure who the girl was that he'd been dancing with. But he had seen the way Grace followed her with her eyes and knew it was someone she was responsible for. So he had used the girl as a messenger, even though it would have been easier to simply slip Grace the note.

As for the rest of his plan, that was masterful. A lesser man than Boothe would simply have used the embarrassingly obvious Maria Fitzwalter, who pursued Wenning like a lovelorn puppy. Boothe was wiser than that.

He had to acknowledge he had a talent for intrigue. In a romantic, devoted kind of way, of course. Grace would be his. Hewould be the one to finally win her, and in the full glare of...well, everyone. Especially the damned husband who had abducted him and poured brandy down his throat and set him up as Rollo Darblay's best friend.

Later, Boothe and Grace would probably laugh about that because it had actually been quite funny. But two could play those games, and Boothe would prove the ultimate master.

The curtain covering the open door swished, and he turned to see Mary, Queen of Scots enter the terrace in her rather fetching red wig and tartan sash. Her mask was made from the same cloth as the sash, which was a perfect touch. Grace had a certain style, a certain panache, whatever she did.

She stood before him, quite still and silent.

Boothe smiled. "I knew you would come." He strode the few steps between them and seized her in his arms.

OLIVER WAS ENJOYING himself. In the last two years, he had become a master of social events in many different countries and cultures, watching his smile and his words and actions, making sure they were all appropriate for the occasion and perfectly natural. He was good at such things, which was why he had been picked for the embassy to China in the first place. And in truth, he enjoyed them. He liked making friends, for himself and for his country.

But this, dressing up like a boy, among a whole ballroom full of other adult children, was exactly what he needed to relax. Of course, beneath his sense of fun lurked a much more mature hum of happiness, anticipation, contentment. Because Grace was here. Even when he strolled through the card room, exchanging jokes with an amusing array of historical figures all gaming and bantering, he was aware of her presence. He didn't need to see her *all* the time—although he wouldn't mind—to rejoice in her presence.

Because finally, amazingly, they were one. Had always been, if only they had known it.

And she was more, so much more than he remembered or deserved.

This masquerade was a delightful, public end to the beginning of their reconciliation. His whole body and soul looked forward to the next stages of knowing her, loving her, in the peace of the country, side-by-side. They would always be together now, and that brought its own fierce contentment.

"Oliver." A formidable Roman matron confronted him as soon as he stepped from the cardroom into the main ballroom.

"Honoria." It wasn't difficult to recognize his eldest sister. Her voice alone would have told him.

She drew him aside, leaning closer to speak quietly and urgently. "You have to stop your wife behaving with such public recklessness. Go at once to the small terrace and bring her back inside!"

Oliver blinked, half-amused, half-irritated—a common enough reaction to his sister. "Why?"

"Because someone told me quite blatantly that he had an assignation with Mary, Queen of Scots. I just saw her go out there less than five minutes after him. And dear God, the curtain is half-open! Everyone will see…"

Abruptly, Queen Elizabeth, crowned and ruffled, threaded her arm through his. "Come."

It was a regal command, issued with apparent seriousness but all the underlying fun he had always associated with her. He did not hesitate but smiled at Honoria and walked off with his wife. Why had she changed costumes?

Unexpectedly, Honoria followed them, brisk and determined. So did Sir Ernest Leyton, and, as they drew nearer the same terrace Honoria had been going on about, several other people who were not dancing seemed to be intrigued enough to follow the procession.

Through the half-open door, he glimpsed a woman clutched in a pirate's close embrace.

He slowed, frowning suddenly. "No. Take everyone back to—"

Grace resisted. "Trust me, Oliver."

Even as she spoke, he realized the embrace on the terrace was one-sided. The woman, in a flash of tartan, was boxing the ears of her supposed cavalier, shoving him away from her.

A scandal was hardly what they wished their ball to be remembered for, but he could not allow such a blatant assault on a lady. He strode onto the terrace, Leyton at his heels.

"Unwelcome attentions, sir, are not tolerated," Oliver snapped.

The assaulted Mary, Queen of Scots, clutched Leyton's arm and, Oliver, with unusual sluggishness, finally caught on.

The pirate, undisturbed by discovery, even triumphant, judging by his curving lips, bowed elaborately. And then, abruptly, his smile vanished.

For Grace stepped elegantly forward, removing her mask. The pirate—surely the unspeakable Boothe?—met her gaze with something like horror. For two heartbeats, there was total silence.

The pirate's Adam's apple wobbled as he swallowed convulsively. His gaze flickered to Oliver. "I assure you my attentions were quite welcome a moment ago. No one likes to be discovered."

"No one likes such ungentlemanly conduct. You are, sir, only *pretending* to piracy. I must bid you good evening." Grace turned, showing all the avid watchers exactly who she was.

Honoria's jaw dropped.

"Our apologies for the ill-mannered display." Grace put her arms around the unknown Mary, Queen of Scots. "Come with me, my dear."

A couple of footmen loomed around the corner from the larger terrace, advancing on Boothe, and Oliver almost laughed. He wanted to hug his wife in front of everyone, for she really was magnificent.

<hr/>

"Grace."

The voice stayed her in the hallway, beyond the ballroom as she hurried the alternative Queen Mary away. Grace turned and saw Honoria, Lady Trewthorpe, pulling off her mask as though it irritated her.

"Might I have a word?" Honoria said stiffly.

Since Oliver and Sir Ernest were following in her wake, Grace stepped aside. She raised one quick, humorous eyebrow to her husband as she walked back to Honoria.

"Do you wish to be more comfortable?" Grace asked, "We can go upstairs."

"There is no need. I won't keep you beyond a moment." Honoria swallowed uncomfortably. "I want to say, I am sorry. For doubting you."

"Thank you," Grace said in surprise.

"I always did, you know," Honoria said in a rush. "I thought the Darblays too volatile, and you too…lightweight for Oliver, or for the position of countess. And then, when you returned alone after the wedding, I knew that Oliver had discovered I was right, that there was some skeleton in your cupboard that even he, in all his gentlemanly infatuation, could not overlook. And my cousin Phineas told me…"

Perhaps she saw the flash in Grace's eye, for she broke off and swallowed again. She tilted her chin, though more as if seeking courage than looking down her nose at Grace.

"Oliver told me about Phineas," Honoria said, clearly mortified. "I have never been so astonished, so disgusted in my life. It is natural to believe family over... But that is an excuse. You are my family. I apologize, and if you love Oliver, I wish you well."

Honoria spun on her heels, taking Grace by surprise once more.

"I do love him," Grace called after her. Honoria's foot paused in midair. "I always did."

Honoria glanced back over her shoulder. "Then I'm doubly sorry for what Phineas did to you."

From Honoria, that was a handsome apology. This was, it seemed, an evening of surprises.

Grace walked on to the salon where, not so long ago, Oliver had held his apparent all-night card party. There, she swapped masks with Frances Caldwell once more, received back her tartan sash, and returned the crown to Frances.

Oliver was smiling as he stepped around to retie her sash for her. Sir Ernest was helping pin the crown to Frances's wig.

"That was rather well done," Oliver said admiringly. "Whose idea was it?"

"Frances," Sir Ernest said proudly. "She happened to be there when her ladyship received the note. And I have to say, once they swapped masks and so on, Frances almost *became* Lady Wenning. Her every movement, every gesture could have been your wife."

"I am an actress," Frances said dryly.

Sir Ernest smiled fondly. "And I have never been prouder of your talents. No wonder Boothe was fooled."

"Actually, there was an instant when *I* was fooled," Oliver confessed. "And I *knew* Grace was beside me! Although I was reprehensibly slow in working out what was going on."

"I didn't have time to tell you," Grace said, "But I could not let him ruin the trust we have only just won…" Aware she had said too much before Sir Ernest and Frances, she broke off with a glance of apology.

But to her surprise, Oliver caught her chin between his finger and thumb, forcing her gaze back to his. "That would never have happened," he said deliberately. "Never."

With something approaching wonder, she read the truth in his intense, serious eyes, and could not help smiling as he deliberately kissed her lips.

"What's more, our ball is not ruined," Oliver added, his voice a caress. "And I was about to ask my wife for the supper waltz."

"If nothing else," Sir Ernest murmured. "It will give the gossips something else to talk about."

Reluctantly, it seemed, Oliver released her and turned to Frances with a graceful bow. "Mrs. Caldwell, it is a pleasure to meet you at last. Thank you for your assistance."

The actress, suddenly diffident once more, gave an uncertain smile as she shyly laid her hand in his. "There is no need of thanks. Lady Wenning has been kind to me and given Sir Ernest and me sound advice."

"Which we mean to follow," Sir Ernest added.

"I am glad," Oliver said warmly, releasing her, "and wish you all the best. And now, my lady, shall we dance?"

⫸⧐⧐⤜⤛⧏⧏⫷

INSTEAD OF LEAVING a nasty taste behind, the contretemps on the small terrace seemed to vanish into the fun of the ball. Even dancing with her husband was only remarked because no one was quite sure anymore exactly who Mary, Queen of Scots was behind the mask. Grace did not really care. She had waltzed with "Rudolf," of course, but it was more than two years since she had waltzed with her husband as the earl. And it was both achingly familiar and intriguingly different.

A deep sense of comfort was growing beneath the pleasure and excitement of the ball. She knew she smiled a great deal during the dance, yet they spoke little.

When the dance ended, it was Herries, the butler, who gravely declared the unmasking. Grace and her earl gravely untied each other's masks.

"No more hiding," he murmured in her ear.

"No more," she agreed, smiling.

There was a moment when their eyes met in silent communication, and then they were parted by the laughing throng, who couldn't understand how or why she kept swapping from Queen Mary to Elizabeth and back but found it a great joke.

Laughing, she finally found her husband's arm once more, and they walked into supper and a new life without secrets and full of hope, excitement, and love.

EPILOGUE

Late September 1817

T HE HARVEST WAS in, and the days were turning cooler. But in a wink of late afternoon sunlight, Grace ordered tea set up on the terrace. There would only be herself and her husband, and possibly Rollo, although sometimes he stayed out in the fields all day. She would say this for her brother—he did everything with enthusiasm. He looked better for his stay at Harcourt, too. The outdoor life, with earlier nights and less drinking, was definitely good for him, although there was no guarantee he would stick to such a life when he left them.

Oliver slipped onto the chair beside her, and she smiled because she knew it was him without looking.

"Tea, my lord?"

"Thank you, my lady." Casually, he threw a letter on the table. She recognized it as the one that had come from London that morning.

"A summons?" she asked lightly, passing him his tea.

He helped himself to a sandwich. "The warning of one. Castlereagh wants me to lead a special mission to the Ottoman Empire. And if I succeed even partially, I should then have my pick of posts at home or abroad. Including a cabinet position if I want it."

She blinked. "Do you?"

"I don't know. Yet. If I take the Ottoman posting, it will mean setting off in the spring and being away for at least six months."

Her stomach twisted. They had grown so close, lived so happily here, but she had always known it could not last. And yet she found it ridiculously hard to ask the question: *Do you want me with you?*

"I thought," Oliver said, caressing the handle of his teacup, "that, if you were willing, we could, perhaps, depart ahead of time. Leave here in early November and enjoy a belated wedding trip through Europe before we end in Constantinople. Would you like that?"

Grace was speechless. Until, leaning forward with a quick grin, he kissed her on the lips. Which seemed to break the spell.

"More than anything!" she said fervently. Smiling with new excitement, she listened to the beats of her own heart, and almost didn't tell him, because it might interfere with what she wanted, what *he* wanted. He might put his foot down, and then they would quarrel.

But they had promised honesty, and she would not, *could* not, break that now.

She took his hand and held it in her lap while she drew in her breath. "I have something to tell you, too. It is early days yet, but I think I might be expecting our first child."

The flash of awe and happiness suffusing his face was unmistakable. "Oh, my dear…" He wrapped her gently in his arms, kissing her hair, her forehead, her mouth. "Aren't you clever?"

"I think you might have had something to do with it, too. And it was not so much cleverness as—"

"I know exactly what it was, minx, and I have a sudden desire to do a lot more of it. As long as you are well," he added hastily. "You must always send me away if you feel any—"

"Oliver. We have already promised honesty, and I feel very well indeed! A little strange, perhaps, as though I am someone else, but that is novelty. And I could still be wrong, because this is my first time, but I believe we should have a child in May."

He kissed her again. "Then to the devil with Constantinople! This is much more exciting!"

She touched her forehead to his. "It is. But we need not go down that road again of one or the other. I would love to travel with you. If I have difficulties, well, they have doctors and midwives abroad, too."

"Travel is tiring," he said doubtfully.

"Travel is interesting. And we have months! May we not set +off and see how we are?"

He pulled her face up to his, searching her eyes, and slowly, the anxiety in his face gave way to a smile, to the excitement she had longed to see there.

"I don't want to be apart from you," she whispered. "We will take care, and we will have fun. Together."

"Together," he repeated, almost like a vow, and kissed her.

About Mary Lancaster

Mary Lancaster lives in Scotland with her husband, three mostly grown-up kids and a small, crazy dog.

Her first literary love was historical fiction, a genre which she relishes mixing up with romance and adventure in her own writing. Her most recent books are light, fun Regency romances written for Dragonblade Publishing: *The Imperial Season* series set at the Congress of Vienna; and the popular *Blackhaven Brides* series, which is set in a fashionable English spa town frequented by the great and the bad of Regency society.

Connect with Mary on-line – she loves to hear from readers:

Email Mary:

Mary@MaryLancaster.com

Website:

www.MaryLancaster.com

Newsletter sign-up:

http://eepurl.com/b4Xoif

Facebook:

facebook.com/mary.lancaster.1656

Facebook Author Page:

facebook.com/MaryLancasterNovelist

Twitter:

@MaryLancNovels

Amazon Author Page:

amazon.com/Mary-Lancaster/e/B00DJ5IACI

Bookbub:

bookbub.com/profile/mary-lancaster